I0726818

When Angels Speak

The Awakening:
A Pleiadian Endeavor
Book I

Nakala Akasie

A Point of Light
Pleiadian Publishing

When Angels Speak: The Awakening A Pleiadian Endeavor
SECOND EDITION

Pleiadian Publishing
26905 Old Edgewood Rd., Sp. 26
Weed, CA 96094

PleiadianPublishing.com
WhenAngelsSpeak5@aol.com
PleiadianTraveler.com

Interior Design: Frances Buran
Proofreader: Raymond Fuller

ISBN: 978-1-942445-08-1 (sc)
ISBN: 978-1-942445-09-8 (e)

Library of Congress Control Number: 2016959903

Because of the dynamic nature of the Internet, web addresses or links contained in this book may have changed since publication and may no longer be valid. The views expressed in this work are solely those of the author and do not necessarily reflect the views of the publisher, and the publisher hereby disclaims any responsibility for them.

Printed in the United States of America
10 9 8 7 6 5 4 3 2

When Angels Speak is dedicated

to the ONE,

The inner voice of the Presence

that is shared

through the written works of the Akasie.

Contents

Contents

Contents

Introduction and Message by Quem Akasie

The ancient Akasie [Ä-kä-sē] gifted me long ago with my name, Quem [Kwŏm]. My name simply means "to venture forth and to begin anew." I am one of the many Akasie leaders, master teachers, and guides from Pleiades, who give forth the teachings through the written word.

Many years have passed since the time when I ventured forth with the thousands of other members from our star system. We become as One to give forth our services to all of those of your great planet. Our intention is clearly stated: we have pledged our lives to be of assistance to the many and diverse peoples of the Earth plane.

In addition to those from Pleiades, there are a great many other benevolent beings who represent numerous star nations and who have also chosen to join in this great cause. We have all traveled far from our homelands to forge beautiful and lasting friendships benefiting all of creation. Together, we have built a solid foundation pledging that we as a whole will always be of a people who are united in one cause, always giving of ourselves to all peoples in all places in all ways, who promote not only peace and harmony, but love.

We are a diverse group, and collectively we have joined as one nation serving God, our Creator. As we go forward into the new age of Aquarius, we strive to serve those of you who walk the Earth plane for your highest good. To you, we offer our alliance, allegiance, knowledge, and wisdom. To you, we offer what we hold most dear to our hearts, which is none other than our own selves. In full faith, we come to you as you remember your true essence of love.

Always, I, as with all others, wait until the time is nigh, when you on the Earth plane ask for guidance from those of us from the angelic realms—the Ones of the Most High. It is only then that we may work through you by giving you the universal teachings.

So you see, as you continue on your path, there are scores of masters and guides from untold nations who are readily available for you as you make your steps toward evolution, ever gaining a higher level of understanding. Always, we pray that you will welcome us and allow us to remain by your side as together we continue through the evolutionary process.

As one of the coauthors of this work, *When Angels Speak*, I wish to make it known that during the writing of this book, in addition to the ascended masters and archangels who came to work with Jackie, there were several groups of guides. It was always our intention that those personal interactions and teachings would be included in this book. I thank all of those who worked on this project to bring it into the physical reality.

This book is the compilation of Jackie's daily communications and experiences with those of the angelic realm in addition to those on the Earth plane. *When Angels Speak* is a true affidavit of a personal transformation. ~Quem Monteró Akasie~

Author's Note: Comments and teachings from Quem and the masters are woven into the narrative.

Introduction by Nakala Akasie

It began in the fall of 2008, shortly after I attended a weekend workshop to learn to dowse using a pendulum. Unexpectedly—no one told me this may happen—I began receiving, seemingly, random telepathic communications from a variety of Light Beings: ascended masters, Christed souls, archangels, and spirit guides from various star nations, in addition to messages from recently departed souls. Some I came to know quite well, while others have come to me sporadically.

Before the dowsing workshop, I had never exhibited any classic signs of having special abilities or spiritual gifts. Quite the contrary, I had been a devoted stay-at-home wife and mother who for the last thirteen years had been searching for answers of a spiritual nature concerning where my teenage son's soul had gone after his suicide. In addition, I had been seeking information on how best to help my family heal from the trauma that had resulted from his death. It was because of my unwavering determination to find those answers that I began what you may call a spiritual quest to find meaning and purpose to my life. It was time that I examine where I wanted to go from here: what I wanted to do with my life. In short, I wanted a higher understanding of who God is and where I fit into the big picture.

After the initial contact (introductory phase) from the Light Beings, it seemed only a few weeks had passed before I began to receive detailed communications instructing me on how to proceed with the messages and teachings from a master who identified himself to be from Pleiades. His name was Quem. Later he explained he was part of a Pleiadian network, the Akasie; and he was my master teacher. (Quem is the main contributor of this book.) Quem, boldly stated that we would be writing books together and for me to document all thoughts, feelings, and interactions I had with the unseen beings as well as family with friends.

Know that even though I felt the love these beings radiated, I was not instantly trusting of their motives, technique of teaching, or the relationships being forged. Neither were the

Beings of Light entirely trusting of me. More precisely, the masters were testing me to see where I stood and if I would continue on with their guidance. Even so, Quem and a handful of others, immediately, began dictating their teachings to be included in the manuscript for *When Angels Speak* I felt uncertain on how to proceed because some of their teachings seemed ambiguous. Through it all however, it became apparent, even crucial, that in order to work with these beings effectively, I had to learn discernment and establish boundaries: two areas that the masters were also working on with me.

I recognized, straight up, from the emotion that their words evoked in me, *When Angels Speak* was being used as an instrument to assist me in healing the trauma associated with my son's untimely passing, to teach me patience and discipline, while at the same time, practicing different methods of communication with them. I was also being taught to identify and dismantle all sorts of belief patterns and programming that no longer served me while simultaneously installing new programs—universal truths.

It wasn't long before I noticed that absolutely everything these masters did was many-sided, detailed, and complex: patterns of truth and wisdom emerged as they continued to teach me and dictate material that was to be included in this book. It proved to be definitive!

The teachings and messages are not just meant to assist in my personal healing or for the tedious process of building my spiritual foundation. The purpose of teachings are to assist those in all phases of spiritual reformation and are specifically intended to broaden the awareness of the seeker in order to ease all stressors that may come forth during the awakening process.

When the publication of *When Angels Speak* was nearing its final stages, my life took another dramatic turn. My marriage of thirty-five years was finished and then I was directed by Quem to legally take another name, Nakala Akasie. Adamantly, Quem explained that I no longer resonated with my husband (our spiritual truths were not in alignment) nor did I any longer resonate with my former name. I was to have the name that best suited me energetically—a higher frequency—a name that reflected who I had become, to attest, if you will, to the willingness to serve as a messenger and channel of the Pleiadian Council of Light.

I felt that being guided to go ahead with the printing of *When Angels Speak* before my name change was in opposition to the business side of publishing and a complete error. I questioned Quem if this were so, and how could I possibly get my name out there if I was in the middle of a name change?

However, Quem assured me that his guidance was indeed correct; that throughout the writing of *When Angels Speak* I had been that person and for now the cover would remain. He elaborated that all would be revealed in time. Meanwhile, he counseled me to lay down the need to know why certain things were: to trust and allow the Akasie to guide me.

For many years, I wondered, "Why had I been chosen for this work as a scribe and channel?" I truly felt that I hadn't honed the skills necessary to be an accomplished writer or speaker. I had merely been living my life as an ordinary homemaker who loved to garden and create art. On the other hand, as I examined my life, I clearly recognized that all along I had been preparing to become an accomplished writer and speaker: this was exactly what I could do if I truly wanted to.

It was only that I had been willing to ask what I wanted to do with my life and to have the correct circumstances align that supported me in the focus I required to do what I truly desired—what lay on my heart. It was then that I made myself available to receive and trust my Divine Guidance.

Almost immediately after I had begun writing the fifth book in the series, *The Accounts of a Pleiadian Traveler* entitled, *Fifth Sphere: Attainment*, Quem gave me a message. It was time, he said, to make the long-awaited adjustment to the cover of my very first book—this book—to change the author's name, my name, to Nakala Akasie, as I had completely integrated and adjusted to my new name.

The Akasie

join together

in the giving of this gift,

"When Angels Speak,"

to honor our Father/Mother God in Heaven.

I say unto you my sisters and brothers, go forth and take witness. Look upon these words that are written, as they are like the sweet honey that flows forth, filling your souls with pure love. Look upon these words as a wondrous gift that is meant especially for you from God, the Holy One, who watches over all. **~Quem~**

These teachings that we share will serve as a gate and will open up the communication between the reader and the Highest Most Divine Creative Awareness. **~The Akasie~**

Changes

There once was a time in history when all the beautiful people of Mother Earth were connected to the Great Creator. All were in perfect harmony with Mother Earth, Gaia, as she provided everything the people needed to survive and flourish. Succulent food was available in great abundance and variety for all.

When the glow of the great yellow sun, Ra, slipped behind the last mound of green earth the beautiful people slept peacefully. Then, there was no need for elaborate structures, as life was simple and unassuming. All were well provided for and all were grateful for everything they had.

Since then, many significant changes have occurred. Your lives have grown complex to the point of being unmanageable, causing many upheavals. People of all walks of life are experiencing this phenomenon of major overload on all levels of their lives. Life has become daunting, a task that is tedious in many areas, if not all. You lose sleep over your many obligations. There are times when you feel anxious because you fear there may not be enough food to feed all of the peoples of this great planet. You fear being displaced because of certain events that may or may not come to pass. We speak of the climate changes that your media continues to report on. Ah, the global warming.

What about your homes? Homes were once thought of as a place of refuge, comfort, and peace. For many of you, your homes are a mere commodity, much like taking a scenic hot air balloon ride. The value of your homes is in constant motion; sometimes the ride is uneventful, sometimes you go high, filling yourselves with new expectations, and then sometimes, for some unforeseen reason, the balloon loses air; you take a dive, not knowing when you will hit bottom. Where is the peace and security in this?

Today's lifestyles now include extended families. Some of your children are packed up and shipped around like common cargo! Do the children know that they are loved? Many of the children are displaying signs of being unbalanced; they have emotional disturbances. Some parents have no idea how to help their children. Many parents are frantically searching for answers while others turn their attention elsewhere in hopes that the problems will magically vanish.

When people are feeling unhappy and unsatisfied, they begin to examine their lives and ask questions like "Why am I here?", "How did I get here?", "Who am I really?", "What is my purpose?", and "Is this all there is to life?" We are here to explain to you that the answers to those questions have always been available if you ask.

These questions are the first stirrings of your spiritual awakening. "There must be a reason that I am here! What makes me happy? What have I experienced so far that makes my life worthwhile?" Questions may come slowly at first, or perhaps they may come rapidly. It is impossible to say, as everyone is unique. As you ponder these questions, more questions will inevitably rise to the surface. With a spiritual awakening, there is an internal drive that propels you forward. We tell you that your guides are directing you to find the answers you seek.

Sometimes a spiritual awakening is prompted because a traumatic event has occurred in one's life. Maybe you just have an intense desire to know! Perhaps you are not aware that the stirrings are even there, because they are so subtle. These questions and many more are inspired by a higher source—God, our Creator.

Now, more than any other time in your written history, a collective force is drawing people from all walks of life to remember their true essence, which is love. That collective power is God speaking to you, encouraging you to examine your life, your existence. God is telling you that, yes, there is more, much more to this life than you have experienced so far and more than you can ever imagine!

There is a love available that is incomparable to anything that you can remember in your entire life! This love comes from God our Creator, who is connecting with your heart. God is speaking directly to you and loving you. This divine love gives you reason to contemplate the vastness of our immeasurable and diverse universe.

This collective energy is everywhere, uniting everyone. Instinctively, you seek that energy, this power that draws everyone together. This energy is like an intricate web comprised of beautiful geometric designs. Every being is strategically placed at each intersection of the web. This energy is like a beacon of inspiration, a light of universal love. We call this beacon of light, this universal love energy, God. You have all heard the saying "God is Love."

The magnificent feeling of love is the self-expression of the God within you. Each one of you has an energy that is comprised of God's love. This love grows within you as you understand and reconnect with truth. Each one of you is on a path that takes you forward. You begin to ask questions like: "Who is God? Where did we come from? Why are we here? What is my purpose?" With each question and each answer, you are brought closer to the truth and to remembering that *we are all One* in nature.

The God in you is the love that envelops your entire being and brings you to a place of pure bliss. As spiritual beings in the physical form, you are drawn to God, the part of yourself that is pure and divine. When you reach this place of *Oneness*, you will feel within yourself a pure peace that no one or no thing can touch.

This place of Oneness is where you unite with your true nature, your higher consciousness. The reason you come to this Earth is to connect with your divine aspect of Self. This is the awakening and the quickening of spirit.

Love is your true essence, your *Oneness* with creation. Creation or evolution is all that is. You are all co-creators, and this makes you a part of God. There is a spark of divinity that is within each and every one of you. The spark of light shines in each of you and grows ever brighter as you seek the truth of your existence.

I would like to add that by being a co-creator, you are creating the world you live in through your thoughts, emotions, and actions. You are the master of your creation. Being a co-creator is an awesome responsibility. We offer these words to you at this time to remind you that as a co-creator, you are united with every other being on the planet for the purpose of creating your reality. *We Are One!*

~Quem Monteró Akasie~

The Quest for Our Truth

The Akasie, as is the case with any community, have a hierarchy. Certain members attend to certain tasks or teachings. We have always been assisting in the guidance of this one, Jackie. As it is with every student, as she continues her climb upward, she requires higher guidance. As her knowledge increases, her needs change also. As the student finds her way up, so to speak, she will need guidance on a higher level. New and more knowledgeable teachers are required as she moves higher in her spiritual journey.

There have been particular angels who watched over Jackie in childhood, and as she grew, there were others who took over.

As Jackie takes her steps, many Akasie members come to teach, to appraise, to plan, and to give. Many watch and wait until the time is right to come and join in celebration. Yes, we plan; we work, we teach, we love, but also we celebrate the Oneness of the Divine Spirit.

All people here on Earth have angels or guides watching over them, protecting them, guiding them. Know this, for it is truth!

Before Jackie's present lifetime, as we do before every lifetime, the Akasie agreed to assist her in all areas of her life, including the writings of the many books. We have been watching over this one, Jackie, always. We have whispered in her ear for such a long time.

Always, she has been one who has had a great love for all that she did. For many years, she has known that she received great satisfaction from writing. Always she has had the yearning to know more about many subjects and to do many creative projects. One of the subjects that held a special interest was for psychic phenomenon, or the "sixth sense," as many of you call this gift that she has. These special interests are the stirrings of her higher consciousness.

You will often find that there is a pivotal moment that dramatically turns the course of one's life. This is exactly what happened here with this one.

Many years back now, Jackie and her husband lost their first-born son to suicide. I speak of this matter because of the sadness, grief, the aching that ensued thereafter. Often during an intense period of grief, there is much deliberation of self, of values, and of beliefs that have been assimilated into the conscious mind.

After any tragedy, there will be those who take this time to go within and look at what is their truth. Many questions arise from a loss of this magnitude. A parent may ask, "What did I do wrong? What caused my child to be so unhappy?"

The innate role of a parent is to love and protect his or her young ones. It isn't natural to suddenly turn off the love and the instinct to protect. How can a parent stop? This loving and protecting is an inborn desire, and even though the physical body has died, this longing doesn't. This is why a person aches so deeply when a physical life is ended.

After a death, depending on the circumstances, the questions vary. Some parents have an intense need to know where their child has gone; if the child lives on somewhere else. Can he hear me if I talk to him? Does he know that I miss him and that I love him?

We tell you, yes, your loved one lives on. Where he has gone depends on his level of awareness at the time of his passing. He may have crossed over, gone into the Light, or quite possibly stayed on the Earth plane to try to comfort those he left behind. There are many emotions felt at the time of a person's passing. At some point, these emotions will be allowed to be expressed and released, allowing the person to move on.

We are connected to each other energetically and emotionally. Those who pass before you know your sadness, your pain; they can feel it!

At this time for Jackie, much reflection and reassessing ensued concerning all those beliefs that she held. So she began a quest of her own to reestablish her core beliefs.

Being raised in a middle-class family, Jackie attended a small Christian church. To us, some of the teachings were beneficial while others she received were not, but there is always a purpose. We tell you to always look within and know in your heart what your truth is.

For years, something about many of the teachings just didn't sit well for her. Because she believed that authority figures were always correct, she had accepted these teachings as her truth. We speak of the words in the Holy Bible and the words spoken in the house of God. It took a great upset of sorts to question those beliefs. What she was taught and what she knew in her heart were opposing ways of thinking.

One of the beliefs we speak of that directly relates to the death of her son is that when someone commits suicide, he or she goes to the fiery depths of hell. Now, think on this my friends; there are many angles to look at with this one. Yes, on the physical plane, this child made an irreversible decision, but would a loving God send a young child to hell for eternity for being depressed and impulsive? We think not! We know not! Read the pages that follow and you will fully understand. This one statement that was professed to be true: "If you kill yourself, you simply go to hell," was the catalyst that sent our dear one to the books and to her heart to search for answers, for her truth.

~The Akasie~

The Fall

There once was a time when all those who roamed the earth were happy; all creation was in harmony. All needs were effortlessly met. The weather was always beautiful. There was no death, no decay. The plant life flourished beyond anything you have ever witnessed or even imagined. Breathtaking, gigantic, lush specimens of all types of vegetation thrived here on Mother Earth. Many exotic creatures, the likes of which you have never seen, peacefully coexisted alongside the Earth people. All was One.

All were cared for. All cared for each other. No secrets. No hidden agendas. All knew. All was open. Life was seemingly perfect until one day, one became different, unsettled, feeling life was somehow not so perfect.

This one decided things should be different and things should change more to his liking. He began to sense that maybe things were turned around, and that he should be cared for instead of him doing the caring.

He stopped caring for those in his charge. A dramatic shift took place. The balance that once was crumbled, all because one being had an attitude that he was doing more than his share.

We do not know for sure why this being began to feel this way, but he did. With one thought, all creation changed. This was creation in itself. He pushed the boundaries, crossed the barriers because he found himself dissatisfied with the way things were for him. Somehow, he wanted something more, something different. No matter how perverted others perceived his thinking to be, this was creation!

Think. If this had not happened, where would you be now? Would you have experienced the great awakening?

~Quem Monteró Akasie~

Friends

There once was a man—his name was Mac—who was very sad. He wandered about looking for something; for what he didn't quite know. Many years had passed with this yearning he held inside of him, this yearning he couldn't identify or even begin to understand. What he felt was like a deep heaviness, a weight upon his chest. This weight he could not lift, as it was much too heavy. At the same time, Mac felt an odd emptiness he had not been able to fill no matter what he did.

One day on his travels, Mac met someone very peculiar; his manner was unlike any he had ever known. They called him Charlie. Charlie was an older gentleman with an unforgiving stoop. His clothes were rumpled and dirty. His face was unshaven, his shoes worn to the point of having holes in the soles. His hands were arthritic and twisted.

In his younger years, Charlie had spent his days on ladders painting houses. These days Charlie spent most of his time caring for his small vegetable garden. The space was immaculate and free of weeds. The plants appeared strong and healthy and bore much produce.

Charlie moved very slowly and with much deliberation. Perhaps he moved like this because he knew in his heart that he wanted to live every moment to the fullest. He moved about as if everyone he met was of great importance and he knew them intimately. Charlie treated everyone with kindness, respect, and love. When Charlie met someone, he looked straight into his or her eyes and asked them for his or her name. He spoke to each person in such a gentle and open manner. He spoke to them as if he had known them always. Even though Charlie had lost his teeth, he had an easy smile.

Charlie possessed nothing of real material value. He gave away the produce he grew. He did not own a car and his cupboards were bare. He lived in a small run-down mobile home on the edge of town. His life was simple. Was it complete? I do not know.

The diner is where Mac and Charlie met. Mac was sitting alone in the corner booth, his back against the wall so he could have a full view of the diner. Mac always hoped and prayed that no one would pay him notice, but when Charlie came in the diner, greeting each person with affection, Mac somehow knew that today things would be different.

Mac cringed at Charlie's appearance. As Mac worked to assess the situation, he took a deep breath and swallowed hard. Beads of sweat formed on his upper lip. As Mac watched, he cringed and his gut tightened. He couldn't quite seem to grasp what he was seeing. Mac had never witnessed such an unusual display of openness and friendship. Charlie treated everyone like his family. Each person responded like a flower thirsty for a long drink from a gentle spring shower.

At first glance, Mac saw a very old man who had an unkempt, rumpled appearance. Next Mac spotted the toothless grin. It was apparent that Charlie didn't seem to be aware that he was dirty and unshaven. Maybe Charlie didn't care.

This was a most unusual circumstance even though Mac had traveled for a living and had witnessed all sorts of strange people and many curious situations.

As Charlie slowly meandered through the diner greeting everyone, he noticed a new face sitting in the far corner. A twinkle emerged in Charlie's eye. His grin widened, and Charlie calmly shuffled toward Mac.

Mac felt his face growing warmer. He awkwardly picked up his napkin to wipe away the sweat from his face. He held his breath wishing he could somehow become invisible. He hoped beyond all odds that this person wouldn't see him. He did not want this encounter. He certainly thought he didn't need it! He felt his discomfort growing. Avoiding Charlie's gaze, Mac busied himself with his meal and some papers that were lying on the table beside his plate. Maybe, just maybe, the old man would take the hint.

Mac cautiously looked up again and there was Charlie. As incredible as it seemed, Charlie extended his crippled hand to welcome him. With disdain, Mac saw himself reach out and take his hand and heard himself utter a pathetic hello. Charlie didn't seem to notice Mac's discomfort and introduced himself, commenting to Mac that he hadn't seen him in the diner before. Before Mac knew what was happening, Charlie had quietly slipped into the seat facing Mac. Charlie began to talk to Mac like he had known him his entire life.

Much time passed before Mac dared to say anything personal about himself, but once he did, the words began to flow, and the tension began to melt away like a Colorado spring thaw. They sat there for some time chatting. Mac sensed something new and miraculous change in him. The heaviness had lifted if but just for a moment. Mac finally admitted to himself that he had always been afraid to open up to people. Why was this time different? To open up and be himself made him feel free, alive, and vibrant! Mac now knew that the heaviness was fear and understood that the emptiness was telling him that something was missing. What was missing was the freedom to allow himself to open up, to relax, to be a friend, and to love.

~Richerd Akasie~

After I received this story, this gift from Richerd, the Akasie instructed me to include it in this book. Even after they specifically told me to include it, I truly struggled with that decision. I just wasn't sure the story was suitable and complimented the rest of our work.

At a later time, I repeated my question to the Akasie, "Do you still want the story, Friends, in our book?" They repeated their answer, "Yes," with a firmness and strength that suggested there might be a bigger picture here. I remembered the countless times the Akasie had said to me, "Our teachings are always multifaceted." I silently asked myself, "Why was it so important that we share this particular story with the readers?"

Charlie and I were friends back in the late 1960's. It was odd relationship because he was ninety years old and I was ten. Yes, he was a real person and yes, his description is exactly how I remember him. He has been gone for over forty years now. For some reason every time I read these passages, emotions well up and the tears begin to flow. There is so much love inside of me when I think of him.

Mac, however, is not someone I ever knew, although, I can easily imagine Charlie having this kind of interaction with someone like him. The thing that really strikes me now (after editing this book countless times) is I finally remember one of the stories that Charlie told my mother shortly before his passing—she in turn, told me. I am sure that this is one of the reasons the Akasie wanted me to include the story.

One night Charlie awoke from his sleep, the moon was full, and he could clearly see everything. He got out of bed and looked out the window—it was such a beautiful night ... and then he saw them—the two angels. They had been there before. Because of that experience, he said, that he knew that he would be going home soon. True to his word, he passed just a few days later.

Charlie made a real difference in my life—he let me hang out over at his place and pick strawberries and tomatoes. Sometimes, I would sweep his floor and dust his furniture in his trailer. He was always kind to me.

I have many fond memories of him and am very grateful for the difference he made in my life. These words are in honor of him.

~Nakala~

May 2008
How It All Began—In This Lifetime

As long as I can remember, I've heard stories about angelic beings. As a young child, I would visit my grandparent's home. There, hanging on the wall at the head of the master bed, was a picture called "Guardian Angel." (There are many versions of guardian angel paintings.) The picture illustrates two young children, a boy and a girl, crossing a rickety bridge. Below the bridge you can easily see the turbulence of swift moving waters. To the side of the children—in mid-air—hovers a beautiful guardian angel. Obviously, the angel is there to protect and comfort the children as they pass over and through the potentially dangerous area.

Throughout history angels have always been represented as a source of divine guidance, always comforting and loving. Angels have been written about by knowledgeable theologians and painted by famous artists. Even though I have seen pictures, read many stories, and even heard personal accounts, my knowledge of angels has been surprisingly limited.

Quite honestly, my personal belief and experience had been that angels were a myth—a curious fantasy and misunderstood part of our culture. I had never seen one, had I? As I grew older, I have heard a few tales of sightings of ghosts, apparitions, or who they thought to be a guardian angel. So on some level, I have always known there may be a high probability that angels did exist, just not necessarily in today's world. What I am saying is I had not taken the time to stop and think about the possibility that we all have angels who watch over us all the time! Maybe angels are out there sometime, somewhere, just not right in my house! I certainly had not considered the concept that angels may watch over me personally. Looking back, I can sum up my truth as this: if there really were angels, they were out there taking care of other people who needed them way more than I did.

As one of the first angels I met explained to me, they have always watched over me. I just didn't know it (on a conscious level) until recently!

I have to go back and tell you a little about my life before I can actually explain how I met the Akasie, who work with me. I can look back and see how each step that I have taken has led me to this moment in time, this moment when, for the first time, I feel truly whole.

Today, I am doing what makes me happy and as the angels say, what makes my heart sing. The angels tell me that we all should do what makes our hearts sing, because that is what leads us to a state of love, gratitude, and bliss.

As I look back, I remember how I always tried to please my parents. I was one of those "good" kids. However, I do remember I had one period of rebellion when I was teenager, but for the most part, I remember that I did what I was expected to do. I was pretty much a happy child. Perhaps I was a little bit of an overachiever, but that is a good thing, right?

Barely seventeen, I married Scott, a wonderful man who is loving and respectful. He has always given me my space, and I am still with him, by the way. This in itself to me is a great accomplishment, because when you get married at such a young age the odds of staying married aren't great!

Together Scott and I gave life to three beautiful children. Our lives were pretty much typical for many years. We had our jobs and our home. Even though we have gone through some really difficult times, we have been truly blessed.

Being a parent I think is by far one of the most difficult jobs there is. I thought I was doing a fairly decent job of raising the kids, although I often found myself questioning my methods of parenting. Was I doing what was best for my children? Unfortunately, I couldn't see into the future to get the end results of the choices that I was making at the time.

Because of my husband's work as an air traffic controller he worked a rotating shift which meant that every day he went in at a different time. Because of this we juggled the responsibilities concerning the care of the children. I had taken a job as an art and frame consultant. It appeared as if our lives were moving along relatively smoothly until our children were nearing the teenage years.

My son was then twelve. Our daughter was directly behind him. At the time I felt like I should consider staying home to keep a better eye on the kids. More and more they were getting themselves in trouble. My oldest son's grades were dropping and he smiled less and less frequently. It was then that I began to grow suspicious that I was in over my head as a mother. It was then that I knew I wasn't sure of anything! I questioned why I had wanted to be a mother and what did I know to get us through until they were old enough to be on their own.

My son, Bradley's moods were becoming more unpredictable. I saw times when his sister and brother would unknowingly cross his path when he was in one of his moods. They were clearly not safe being around him, and certainly not safe when left alone with him. His anger seemed to have no justification. I didn't trust him and I didn't have the knowledge or experience to know how to redirect him.

For a while, I tried to ignore the mood swings thinking they would surely pass. Witnessing my son's sudden outbursts of anger and unrelenting sadness and gloom caused confusion for not only me but for the entire family. Later, when I saw that this thing, whatever it was, wasn't going away on its own I began to search for answers. Unfortunately, I didn't get the answers I needed to save Bradley in time.

To this day, after fifteen years as individuals and as a family, we still struggle with that one irreversible choice Bradley made to end his life.

It seems that the teenage years, for some, may be a very intense and even painful stage. But because I personally didn't go through a distressing transition from child to adult, I don't have a clue how he felt. Maybe that is why I was unprepared for what happened. But then who could have been prepared for what happened?

This was my first time as a parent. The only thing I knew for sure was that he was unhappy. What I didn't know was the depth of that unhappiness, and I sure didn't know how to fix it, so what is done is done. To quote the angels, "There is a purpose to all."

After Bradley left (and I refer to his death that way because that is precisely what he did), our family pretty much fell apart emotionally. When someone close leaves like that, what is it you are supposed to feel and do? How do you help your surviving children grieve and go on? How do you comfort your spouse? How do you help yourself? Do you lash out in anger at God? Do you blame your spouse for not doing something to stop the horrible nightmare? Because that was what it had to be; an inconceivable, horrendous nightmare that none of us could wake up from! It couldn't be real! How could we go on as a family?

Everyone was kind to us, but I could feel that the energy had changed. There was this thing that had been placed between every one of us and around us; not just with our friends, family, and neighbors, but between me, my husband, and our two surviving kids.

I felt like everyone else "knew" that I had somehow failed as a parent, but it was as though a great secret was kept from me. I felt guilty and knew deep down that I had done something horribly wrong, but I didn't know what it was.

After Bradley left, the first time I opened the kitchen cabinets to get the plates for dinner, I reached for five. That moment above all moments was laced with incredible sadness: I realized that never again would I set the table for him. Never again would I be able to cook him his favorite meal or bake him his favorite cake. Never again would I see his beautiful smile or hear him laugh. Each time I did some task like grocery shopping, laundry, or even making a doctor's appointment, I felt as if a sharp knife was being stabbed deep into my heart and being twisted.

No one knew of my pain, because, for the most part, I was able to cover up my sadness and my despair. I acted like I was okay; I felt that I had to be strong for the kids. Now I am not so sure. I think maybe everyone thought I was cold and uncaring. I think I was in denial.

Because of this one unnecessary, unbelievable moment, our lives were changed forever. People say that your life can change in an instant, and I am here to attest that this is so true. Cherish each moment you have with your loved ones, for tomorrow is a new day and a new beginning.

In the first year after Bradley's departure, we were adjusting to our loss—the changes that any family would be face with. During that time, we had some pretty bizarre things occur in our home. The kids would be watching TV and, without warning, the TV would turn itself off. I have never had this happen before. During that period, we had many electrical appliances suddenly die. Oh, I remember that screws would magically unscrew themselves from the light switch plate in my daughter's room. At the time, I didn't know what to make of it—what the cause was. Was Bradley trying to get our attention?

At the time, I couldn't say for sure that Bradley caused this havoc, but I certainly had my suspicions. There were too many weird things happening too close together. I had heard about spirits causing electrical interference. I remember at one point after several major appliances broke that I said out loud, "Bradley, if you are doing this, STOP!" The interference did stop on that level. Now I believe our departed loved ones can and do hear us, and I am sorry that I handled the situation like that. I wished I could go back and tell him how we all felt, that we missed him and that we wished he was still with us.

Bradley chose to leave when he was fourteen. My daughter was twelve then, and my youngest son was ten. They were old enough to know what their brother did, but too young to process their emotions in a healthy manner. As a parent, I felt like I was totally inadequate to help them. I tried taking them to grief support groups and to private counseling. They didn't want to go and neither did I. Maybe I gave up too quickly.

Time went on. I continued to do what I thought would help our family. The children grew older, and I continued to search for answers to my endless questions. Why did he do that unspeakable act? Was it all premeditated? If so, how long had he been thinking about killing himself? Where did my son's soul go when his body died? My thoughts would go back to my childhood when I sat in church. Clearly, I saw the pastor standing at the pulpit in his black suit. He rocked on the soles of his feet as he gathered momentum during his sermon. This time he preached on those who commit suicide ... how they would go to hell! Period! We never heard him explain the reason why, though. I knew it was just plain wrong!

I just couldn't fathom or even begin to believe that Bradley went to a fiery hell, no matter what that preacher claimed. Certainly, my child couldn't end up in hell. I was right, wasn't I?

Even though my son was forever gone, I would always consider myself to be his mother. I wanted to figure out what happened to him, so I began to look for answers that would help me understand where a person or soul goes when the body dies. Maybe if I could see more of the picture, I could somehow come to terms with all that I had gone through. If I could only know that he was in a safe place and that someone was taking care of him, maybe then I would be able to move on. For years, I asked why he did it. For years, I blamed the school, the hospital, and the doctors for their part in what had happened. Anyone who was involved, I blamed. Now I know there wasn't any one person or entity that was at fault.

Before Bradley left, I could see that he was suffering. The signs were all there. I had been taking him to talk to a psychotherapist. I'll be honest: at the time, I had no idea what to do for this boy or for my family. I struggled each and every day to make the correct choices concerning my children.

There is no one who can tell you how to raise your children. Each child is unique; you are unique, and every situation is unique. Everyone makes his or her own individual choices, but I still looked for that magic person who would tell me how to fix everything. I should have been able to help my child understand that whatever were his feelings, together we could sort through them.

I looked to others for their expertise, and quite frankly, that didn't work well at all. I tried to do everything I knew to do to help him, except for the one thing he needed most, and that was to take him into my arms and tell him that I loved him no matter what. He felt that he didn't have anyone to confide in, no one to listen to him who would understand. He needed someone who understood what he was going through. He needed a mother who would take the time to listen to him. I keep thinking about this, as I know that being a teenager is one of the most difficult times a person can go through. As a young man, Bradley was striving to be independent of his parents. I understood this, but at the same time, he still needed to have the option to come to us and talk out his feelings. He needed parents who would take time to listen to him. I keep thinking about this. However, at the time, there were so many diversions that took our attention. What had been our priorities? In the end, he made up his mind that his life wasn't what he wanted, wasn't worth living.

Here I am now, feeling such guilt about what I didn't do. All this time has gone by and I have never truly understood why or how this happened. All I remember is basically being stressed to the max to meet our basic needs like getting meals prepared, making sure the kids did their homework every night, making sure they all had the appropriate clothing and supplies for school, not to mention what needed to be accomplished in order to maintain our home. You know, as I write this I realize it is no wonder our relationship wasn't any better with him. Our lives were all about making sure we complied with all of the rules and regulations of society and government—dare I say, about appearances.

If you are a parent of school-age children, you know how hectic life can become. As parents, it is our job to engage our children in activities that they will enjoy and excel in to better their self esteem, but also to keep them busy and out of mischief. In my opinion, children should have extracurricular activities, but not to the point of denying them the time that they need to bond with adults who will listen to them and who will guide them in a responsible, loving manner. In my opinion, children should have quality time not only in group settings but also in individual settings. Get to know your children. Allow them to know you!

Why am I writing this? The first reason is to help myself understand how to be a better parent: how I can communicate more effectively. Even now, as my children are grown, I continue to want to serve as a role model for them. Maybe I can be a better grandparent or just understand children better.

The second reason is not only do I want to help parents understand how important it is that you are involved in your children's lives, but to be able to clearly and effectively communicate with your children.

Having your children tell you about what goes on during their day is a great treasure, a precious gift. Make time to hear your children and give them constructive feedback. Yes, you are the authority figure and it is your job to set the rules to guide your children so they may learn to be responsible adults. At the same time, they need to spend time with you, interacting with you.

Many years have passed since Bradley left. I have had plenty of time to recall particular incidents concerning the way I disciplined my children. I could kick myself for saying and doing certain things. Looking back at my parenting skills, I know that some of the choices I made were simply because I felt I needed to make a choice quickly. Sometimes instead of thinking about what I should do to discipline the kids, I just reacted to the situation with anger. Even if I had sat back and really thought about what I should do first, how would I have known if my choice was correct or not?

Quem: I wish to address your question; but first, be it known that I am Quem. I am your master teacher and throughout the coming years I will be assisting you and working very closely with you. I oversee all that transpires concerning you.

Your question concerning choices is a question that all of those on the Earth plane ask themselves at one time or another. Many times, you feel confused because your mind tells you that you must do something. To make a correct choice you must first feel what is best for a particular situation.

At this time, I will touch on disciplining children. Let's set this example before you.

One of your children did something that wasn't wise and was to the detriment of his physical being. You being the guardian of this one were to protect him from all harm, including harm from his own hand. You saw the error in his ways and were fearful that he could have very easily been critically hurt or even killed. What he did was most serious and understandably, your aim was to make a lasting impression to insure this type of behavior would never occur again. Your choice was to spank the child until you were satisfied that he had learned his lesson. This spanking was nothing more than a socially ingrained response on your part. When you react to a situation, it is rarely the correct choice. When you stop to think and feel before you take action concerning any situation you will know what is the correct choice.

Know that it is for your highest good to review decisions that you made in the past. However, I caution you to not get caught up with feelings of regret and even feelings of unworthiness as a parent. What transpired was the result of your level of understanding at the time. You had not learned to stop and access the situation and then feel with your heart before you made a choice to administer discipline. You are learning now, are you not?

Take what you learned from it and go on your way. You have learned valuable information and you are the better for it. Take what has been given to you as a magnificent gift and be grateful. You have learned that each moment is precious, as each person that comes your way is precious. Your love has grown and expanded because of your experiences. Take this love and share it with those you meet along your journey.

Thank you, Quem, but if I had made different choices, things would be different. Quite possibly my son still be here with us. I feel like I have learned beneficial lessons too late AND at the sacrifice of my son! I understand what you are saying, but at the same time, I feel that if only things had been different ...

Quem: Yes, you are correct. If you had made different decisions, things would be different. Your life would be totally different. But I tell you the truth, no your son wouldn't still be here. The events that led up to and after your son's passing were for many purposes. Understand that because you are on the Earth plane, you do not see the entire picture. You do not understand all. There were many reasons for your son's choices. Know that what happened was for the highest good of all concerned. I know at this very moment this is impossible for you to understand. I know that you question this statement. You view suicide as a horrible thing. You listen closely to these words, Miss. Your son was communicating with his Higher Self. You view suicide as a negative act, but you do not know the entire story.

[There was a long pause in Quem's commentary.]

I understand your words. I do have questions regarding all of this. I trust that you will build on what you have just told me at a later time when I am ready.

After Bradley left, I wanted to know what happens to the soul of a person when they die. More specifically, what happened to Bradley's soul since he took his own life? I felt that because of the way he left this had to have a great impact on where he was now.

At that time, I didn't have the Internet, so I was limited to the library to find information. At the library, I did find a small selection of books on grieving and some on life after death. I began with There is a River: The story of Edgar Cayce by Thomas Sugrue. Edgar Cayce was the renowned twentieth-century psychic and medical clairvoyant. Another book I found helpful was entitled The Awakening Heart by Betty J. Eadie.

The information I gleaned led me to the realization that we reincarnate! We are spiritual beings that come back time and time again to live in a physical body. The church I attended had taught that we live a single lifetime, and the quality of our "good works" would determine whether we would go to heaven or hell. I wonder if my little church still teaches this way today.

Having one lifetime made no sense to me. Think about this: after just one lifetime can anyone really be good enough to get into heaven? Who feels they are perfect enough or worthy enough to land in heaven after one lifetime? I mean, what the church was saying is after just one lifetime we are finished, no more. If I was good enough to get into heaven, what would I do once I got there? Even with the exultations, hallelujahs, amens, and all, I think I should be doing something productive! I don't remember ever hearing the preacher talk on that issue.

Doesn't it make more sense to keep working to strengthen our virtues like our patience and compassion and so on? To me, to keep striving to be a more loving person is the only way to grow.

So now that I had found out that we are spiritual beings who keep coming back to the Earth to live over and over, what about this heaven and hell business? I have found that in these places of worship they just tell you bits of the story, just enough to confuse people really well!

Okay, we have heaven and hell, and we have Jesus Christ who died on the cross to wash away our sins.

Quem: You know Jackie, you are getting into religious beliefs. I do not wish to go there in this book. We will explain in this book about heaven, hell, and reincarnation. You all are responsible for your own energy. Because the teachings of Master Jesus were so instrumental, I will touch lightly on his purpose in this text.

Okay, I understand. I think I got off the subject. I was talking about the books and being here on this Earth many times before. Reading the books about Eager Cayce's life was totally awesome. When the house was quiet, I would study, think, and feel. Sometimes when I would read a particular passage, the words would touch me deeply and I would feel a tingling sensation in my arm much like goose bumps. The sensation was new for me and I paid attention. This happened several times when I was reading the books. Some people might call this an "A-ha moment," only it felt like a vibration. I didn't know what it was, this beautiful sensation, only that what I felt was incredible and good, so I let the feeling flow.

Much has happened to me since that first time when I received that first tingling sensation. I look back at my journey and am amazed at all of the ways I was lead to this particular place where I am now.

After the loss of our son, the plan was that we would wait two years and move to a smaller community. We lived in the Kansas City suburbs in a nice neighborhood. Everyone was more or less friendly, but the issue was that everyone in our neighborhood was acutely aware of our situation. Talk about stigma. I wanted out of there! Moving away was my answer to start fresh and to forge new friendships with those who didn't know our background. My husband and the kids all agreed that moving was a good idea. Was this running away, though?

For the children, having a brother commit suicide seemed to really mess up their way of communicating, their social skills, and their relationships. It was like being swallowed up in a big, black hole: no way to get out, no place to go. Too much had happened to us. The children felt they couldn't talk to anyone about what they had experienced or how they felt about it. No one knew what to say or do, so basically everyone stopped saying or doing anything. One by one, their friendships ended. I felt like we had been placed under a microscope; like we were quietly being scrutinized and judged. It was a rather peculiar situation, because no one said anything that was hurtful to us; it was just a feeling. Was what I sensed my own insecurity and guilt?

Not only did the children feel abandoned by their peers, but they felt abandoned by their own brother, their flesh and blood. To them it was cut and dry—he didn't love them enough to stay here and fulfill his role as a big brother.

Someone who hasn't lost a brother may not have stopped to consider what a big brother brings to a relationship. A big brother is someone who cares deeply about his sisters and brothers, who watches over them and is there to do fun things with. A big brother is an important role model, as well as someone to go to when you need to talk about something; someone perhaps who you'd rather talk to instead of your mom or dad. Their way of life, as they had always known it, was maliciously stolen from them; their brother, who had always forged the way, as far as they knew, didn't even pause to glance back in their direction. They both struggled to grasp the implications of what their brother had done and once again regain their footing.

As soon as our two years were up, true to our plan, we found a home south of where we were living that met our exact expectations. As soon as I walked into the foyer, I knew that I wanted to live there. We would have some acreage, and the home itself was larger so we would have more privacy. Unanimously, we agreed that to pull up roots and move was what we wanted to do.

Our move to our new home ended up taking place in the dead of winter. Even though on moving day the temperatures were in their teens, we were excited to make the changes we felt were necessary for a new start. For the first time in two long, tedious years, we allowed ourselves to feel hopeful again.

Getting settled took our minds off our grief for a while, but after the excitement wore off, I could see that the new surroundings really didn't change anything; we were still struggling with how to handle our grief. Not one of us was having an easy time of it. We continued to act like all was fine, but underneath our lives were crumbling. None of us were happy. How could we be?

Since my son's passing, I had taken the kids to therapy for grief counseling to help them cope with their brother's passing. It didn't seem to make any difference. On the surface, my younger son appeared as if nothing had happened, although it was quite evident that his brother's name had been stricken from his vocabulary. In my daughter's case, she sank into a deep, impenetrable abyss of depression and she stopped eating!

Finally, I decided to seek alternative ways of healing for myself and my family. This was a huge step for me. I say this because our society has been hypnotized, put to sleep if you will. For many years, I looked for help from psychiatrists and psychologists, and every single one of them wanted to label and medicate my children. I am talking about the fact that we look for healing from the medical doctors to heal particular pieces of ourselves. When we are working to heal, we must look at all of the pieces. In addition to the physical, we have the mental, emotional, and etheric bodies that we must consider. It was now time for me to look at my entire being instead of only a part of who I was. I realize now that by not understanding these aspects of our true selves, I was creating a huge block in the healing process for my entire family.

I made an appointment with a woman who used alternative methods of healing. She did not prescribe medications or sit passively behind an expensive desk and pretend to listen. This woman was skilled at many intuitive healing techniques, such as myofascial release, past life regression, hypnosis, and Reiki, and she also allowed her spiritual guides to assist her.

I explained my dilemma to her; how the kids were not dealing with the loss of their brother, and how they were not coping with life in general. What we did was much like psychotherapy. However, this person didn't sit back in her chair with a pad of paper and a pen frantically making notes and nodding her head. This one would give her opinion even though she knew what she said might sting. She had a voice and she used it! She didn't hold anything back. I took her advice and things began to change; feelings began to emerge, and healing began to take place.

Before I go on, I want to say that there are many methods that we may use for healing purposes. What works for one person may not work for another, and I am certainly not advising you to seek out one type of healing method over another.

Have you ever heard that there are no coincidences in life? This is what I've been told by my angels, and this I believe to be absolutely true. You are divinely guided throughout your lifetime. Sometimes you listen to your guidance, sometimes you do not. This is free will.

One thing lead to another, and through this woman I met another who is a Reiki master and teacher. (Reiki is pronounced ray-key.) She was offering a workshop and several of the women I knew personally had decided to take it.

What did I know about Reiki? Precious little. I was apprehensive, but after much thought about it, I decided to enroll in the workshop. This was the period of my life when I began to learn about the chakras which are energy centers in the human body, and the energy fields that surround the body. The more I practiced this modality of healing, the more fascinated I became with the subject of energy.

For those of you who do not know what Reiki is, Reiki is an ancient way of energy healing. The Akasie have confirmed to me that this type of energy healing has been in practice for thousands of years and is much like the healing modality that Jesus practiced, called the laying on of hands. The healing energy flows from Source down through the crown chakra, going out through the hands of the practitioner into the client. The practitioner is a conduit, a vessel for the healing energy to flow through. The intent is that the healing energy is for the highest good of all concerned. To clarify: we do not set any preconceived outcomes that, for instance, the person will be healed of a particular disease. The energy will be directed by Spirit, going to and working for the highest good of that person.

Soon after I took the Reiki workshop, I met some people who practiced Reiki and also knew about dowsing. They told me about a dowsing workshop that just happened to be taking place in three days' time. The workshop was out of state in a place called Bradleyville, Missouri, seven hours away. When I saw the name, Bradleyville I about choked. But in the credits it mentioned connection to our spirit guides. That is what had drawn me in. I have found when I really want to do something, little things like distance will not be a deterrent! It was like I felt that I had to be there no matter what, so I went!

What is dowsing? Dowsing is an ancient art of finding natural resources, such as water, oil, minerals, or even finding lost objects.

The instructor who taught the workshop used a pendulum in addition to some other divination tools. He took dowsing to another level! As he demonstrated with his pendulum, he verbally asked his question, and then waited a moment for the pendulum to swing or spin. The direction of the swing or spin would denote the answer. He stated that he was connecting to his spirit guides this way. The mechanics of the other divination tools were a little different.

I found that I was able to connect to my spirit guides this way quite easily. I was totally fascinated with the entire process. This was my niche. Immediately, after my drive home I began to practice working with my pendulum. At first, I began to ask simple questions. Then the questions grew more complex. I noticed a real discrepancy with the answers I was getting. Even so, I did not stop my work with the pendulum.

You know, I really never considered myself to be an obsessive individual, but after this workshop, I felt more or less driven to work with the pendulum. Quite honestly, I didn't want to do much of anything else. I continued to do my household chores and everything else that I had always done, but with every spare moment available, I would grab my pendulum and begin to work. In the evenings after my husband came home from work and dinner was finished, I'd spend some "quality" time with him by watching a show and having some ice cream. Then I'd politely excuse myself and go upstairs to my room to work.

Talking about my personal life is really the last thing I want to do, but in order for you to understand my situation, it would be better if I explain that a while back I had established this routine to retire early for a time of personal enrichment. This was my personal time and I used it to listen to music, read, meditate, and journal my thoughts.

First off, I have been married for over thirty years. A few years ago, when we finally got an extra bedroom, I moved into it. For many years, I have resented having to share a room with someone I couldn't sleep with. My husband snores. Yep. He also keeps unbelievable hours because of his work, and I was through with losing sleep.

It was a simple choice: I'd do my time, and then go and have my time. My evenings were packed to the hilt with stuff I loved to do. I found myself guarding that time by making sure that I didn't agree to anything that would take away from it. I had mixed emotions concerning this. I felt guilty that I wasn't spending more time with my husband (that was what I was expected to do, right?). However, he wasn't complaining … yet. The feelings of guilt were slowly eating at me because I wasn't being honest with him about what I was working on.

I worked with the pendulum every chance I got and for as long as I could to establish a relationship with my spiritual guides. I had what seemed like a million questions to ask them. I asked about life after death and about my relatives that had passed on. I asked questions about people who were living. The questions were endless! As I continued to ask questions, I continued to get answers that just didn't jibe. What was happening here? I just kept trying to figure out the problem. As time continued, the anxiety began to build. Then one night, someone began to communicate with me in other ways besides answering me with the pendulum.

I strongly advise anyone who intends to use any sort of divination tool to set the intention of only working with the Divine Ones, the Spirit Guides. Saying a short prayer asking for divine guidance and divine protection is the proper protocol when you work with beings in other realms. When you say a prayer, do it with love and gratitude. "I am grateful that I have the highest, most divine angels, who assist and protect me always. What I receive is for the highest good of all creation."

Unfortunately, when I learned how to communicate with the other side using the pendulum, I did not set any intentions or affirm that I was working only with my divine guidance. It didn't even occur to me to say a prayer of protection. I just took the pendulum and went with it, assuming that I'd connect my spirit guides. This was not the smartest thing that I could have done, but at the time, that was my level of awareness. Somehow, I opened up something that allowed a different kind of communication to take place. I began to receive communications with beings that said they were not my spirit guides. Who exactly were these guys? Not understanding the different levels of energy beings, confusion set in. I became concerned, skeptical, and a little fearful. However, I kept going forward.

In addition to my error in judgment or my lack of discernment, I didn't fully understand how to ask questions properly. When you ask a question, you must be specific. Questions are always answered in the present tense, unless otherwise specified. Questions will not be answered in a future tense. This is just a very quick overview. Right now, I am not going to explain in detail the proper way to pose a question to the angels; just know that there is a proper way.

Because I didn't fully understand, I received answers that contradicted themselves. I might ask the same question five times and get three of the answers as a yes and two of the answers a no. Well, if this sort of thing happens, it can promote a bit of anxiety and fear. Negative, as well as positive emotions are very powerful.

I really hesitate to reveal my entire story, because quite frankly, what I did shows the depth of my naïveté. I brought it all upon myself, and some of it is very embarrassing, but I will tell my story because I know that I am not the only one in this world who could use a good lesson on discernment.

November 5, 2008
The Opening

Quem: I am currently working with my brothers and sisters, the Akasie, from Pleiades in the writing of this book. We have many more books in our mind's eye, and we are waiting until the moment arrives to go forward in such an endeavor. The writings of the books are a deliberate collaboration between all of us to serve you in your steps to go higher into the Light.

One must always ask to receive a gift such as this. We came to Jackie with words of the esoteric teachings of which she had never heard before. For her, the wanting of such words was immeasurable, the push to receive never ended. Even so, we caused quite a stir!

I tell you, all must be in alignment to begin the communications to one on the Earth plane. Even then, we must tread lightly. We wish not to cause fear or panic with our presence. You are of a delicate nature when you first open; the flower wilts easily.

I am one of those who assisted in the giving of the gift to this one who is so dear to me. You wonder what I mean when I talk of "the gift." The gift is to open to receive the transmissions from those who are of a higher level of intelligence and from other dimensions. We assisted in the activations of the brain's neural pathways. In other words, we did a little rewiring in the cranial cavity so that she would be able to hear us and channel our communications to others. We have the knowledge and the ability. This is how it is done.

What a time it has been! There has been much upheaval in all areas of her life. At this time, we witnessed the making of much negative emotion from Jackie, because she did not have the full realization that we had come to teach. We saw fear being birthed because of the many modalities in which we chose to teach! Sometimes our teachings came across a bit unusual and maybe even a bit eccentric. Some we were told, funnily enough, were unrecognizable as teachings even! We can laugh about this now, can't we Missy? Many times, Jackie has said that she would never teach in the manner we choose, but I tell you, we got our point across and quickly.

For Jackie, working with the pendulum without divine intent was the source of what we call creation and possession of negative thought forms. We tell you here that this was a great learning for Jackie, albeit a very difficult time. Because of her awareness, she suffered many long days and longer nights.

When you are working at communicating with the unseen, we highly recommend you say your prayers or affirmations first thing upon awakening from your night's sleep. Always affirm that you are working with the Highest Most Divine Creative Awareness, or you may end up having a similar experience, or perhaps one that may be a bit more of a challenge. It is always best that you have Divine guidance in your spiritual communications. When you do not set a particular intent to work with Divine beings, you are in essence inviting communications from anyone who happens by. There are many different energies or spirits of a lower vibration that may come forth when you are using a spiritual tool such as a pendulum.

The pendulum is a tool used to bring forth unseen forces much like your Ouija board. We tell you to always use extreme caution when calling down any entities. This is for your protection as well as the protection for those who are about you. This information is particularly important to know and to follow!

People sometimes jump into places they are not prepared for or don't belong in, and then they may be faced with situations that can become unhealthy or even dangerous. For Jackie, in the dowsing workshop, the necessity to *affirm* and *believe* that she worked only with the Divine Ones was not emphasized sufficiently! Maybe Jackie didn't take the words spoken to heart. We do not blame; we do not judge. We take this opportunity to teach others of the different possibilities that can occur.

The Akasie: We want to make it perfectly clear here that this experience was allowed! One of our tasks as guardian angels is to guide, and another is to protect those in our charge. We make this known when you get off track or you are not listening to your heart. We may use extreme measures or employ unusual tactics to allow you the opportunity to see that you are doing something that is not in balance with Spirit. All spiritual beings in the physical form have free will, so you may look at any given situation and decide what it is you want to do; what is your best choice? In any given circumstance, you must listen to your emotions (your heart) to find the solution that is correct for you that will bring balance and harmony to your life. The correct answer is always within your grasp.

At the time, Jackie was not listening to her emotions because she was so determined to connect with us and grow spiritually. She was pretty much willing to go through the torments of hell to do so. Instead of allowing the teachings to come as they were meant to with the use of the pendulum, she called forth the information from us to the point of being unhealthy.

Because spirit guides have the ability to communicate with all levels of your being, specifically your higher consciousness, we knew it was her time. We were to assist in this opening by taking the situation as it was and working with it for the highest good of all concerned. Yes, we did look at all possible outcomes to what was occurring. We love this one we call Jackie. Know this, for it is truth.

We created a detailed curriculum that had particular teachings. The main concern at this time was to teach Jackie to not only affirm that she was working with the Highest Most Divine Creative Awareness, but to teach her that she must totally believe in her heart and in her mind that those working with her at all times loved her unconditionally, having the highest regard and respect for her welfare, not only spiritually, but physically, emotionally, mentally, sexually, and psychically; in all dimensions, in the cosmos, always and everywhere.

In order to direct Jackie to the realization that she must know in her heart that she only works with the angels of the Most High, we allowed her to communicate with Earth-bound spirits, including her departed son. We also played devil's advocate by allowing her to think she was communicating with beings of much lower vibration. We played the part quite well by thumping on the walls and walking on the roof. Oh yes, we did other things as well. In essence, she fully believed that evil beings had taken up residence in her home. Negative thought forms do not communicate, they control. Even though Jackie continued to ask endless questions and receive contradictory answers, she persevered.

Repeatedly, the pendulum told Jackie that she was in the company of negative entities. Daily, she worked with the pendulum to remove the negative entities, only to seemingly have more appear. Once fear comes into the picture, it has the tendency to grow to huge proportions and become extremely powerful.

We will stop here and explain that when you are communicating with spirit guides, the only way to receive accurate answers is to ask your questions in a very specific manner. We repeat what Jackie has previously stated. If you do not ask questions properly, you will get answers that are inconsistent. We take your question literally, word-for-word, and answer each question in accordance to how the question is asked. The Akasie do not answer future questions, ever! We will tell you the probability of something that may occur, but that is as far as we go. The future is constantly in motion, ever changing, so we ask you to please not ask who your future wife or husband will be in ten years, or perhaps how many children you will have. We cannot answer those questions accurately.

This is an example of what can occur when a question is asked that is not specific enough. "Will I receive a phone call from Tom today?" We would take that question and may answer you with a "yes" because Tom is thinking of calling you. His thought of calling you creates a high probability that you will receive that call. We may answer you with a "no" because either Tom hasn't thought of calling you, or is thinking of calling but hasn't decided. Even if he has decided, he may very well change his mind or simply forget. One must understand that you can ask the same question two separate times, and phrase the question exactly the same, but get two completely different answers. This is why Jackie got inconsistent answers on many occasions!

As Jackie went deeper into her obsession, she withdrew from many of her friends and family. Her social activities slowed down in order to spend every available moment she could get to work with the pendulum. (Yes, at this writing she is still married. We laugh. It worked out for the best.) We tell you, however, that when this teaching was occurring it was very serious business.

At the pendulum workshop, the teachings included how to work with all sorts of negative energy by releasing it and then filling the void created with love and gratitude. We are only speaking on the negative energies here, specifically negative entities, including how to check with the pendulum to see if there are any negative entities about and how to release them.

Let's explain what a negative thought form or negative entity is. A negative thought form or a negative entity is an energy that has been created from negative thoughts that are fear-based. They include but are not limited to anger, hate, and insecurity. When the energy frequency becomes strong enough, it is classified as an entity and has the capability of attaching itself to the creator of the energy or attaching itself to others. Whoever the negative entity chooses to attach to will be either the person who is creating negative thoughts and emotions, or someone who is very vulnerable in specific areas. Like energies attract like energies. People who have negative thought forms or entities may exhibit any type of symptom(s) in any number of areas. I speak of being unbalanced in the physical, mental, emotional, and yes, the spiritual capacities. When you are in someone's company who is creating this type of energy, you may feel uncomfortable or distrustful of them.

We repeat here that thoughts and emotions are very powerful. So powerful are these energies, in fact, that we have chosen this subject to place much of our attention on in this book.

When a person has a negative thought form or entity attached to them, he or she will most assuredly suffer from feelings of anxiety and vulnerability. When you create negative thoughts, you, of course, are going to feel the negative emotions.

We will go back to Jackie's case here. When she was working with the pendulum, she asked many questions that were not phrased accurately or specifically. Her assumptions were that she was getting some sort of evil beings that were "playing" with her. Because of this assumption, she began to feel frightened. Jackie's thoughts were negative, fear-based. This is the beginning of creating a negative thought form or entity.

You see, much emotion was created with this fear of evil beings; how was she going to get rid of them? As the days passed, the fear grew. These entities can and often do become extremely controlling. In fact, with many cases, these energies become so powerful they may take possession of the person and cause many undesirable behaviors. For instance, they can cause severe mood swings that typically encompass depression, anxiety, and anger. Negative entities may cause illness, and in extreme cases, the energies can cause such instability that they the person will surrender to self-mutilation or perhaps go insane. In some occurrences, we see homicide and/or suicide. There are many variations that have been experienced and observed with negative entity possession. Often you will see addictions, rage, abuse, bipolar symptoms, depression, and suicidal tendencies.

You see, when you have invested much energy thinking negative thoughts and feeling negative emotions, such as fear, insecurity, anger, unworthiness, and so on, you lose control of your thoughts. As time goes on, if left unchecked, those thoughts and emotions become very strong and they take over like a whirlpool, sucking you further down into the murky waters. In essence, you have given yourself over to be controlled by the negativity; to become more negative than positive.

You may think of it like a pregnancy. You have conceived this embryo that is a negative thought or energy. In the prenatal period, the energy is tiny and must be fed in order for it to survive and grow.

It is easy to slip and not be vigilant of your thoughts. For example, this morning you overslept. You are supposed to be at work at 8:00 a.m. You rush to the bathroom to get ready and see that you have a pimple on your face, and your hair doesn't do what you want. Your anxiety mounts. There is no way you are going to get to work on time. You are worried that your boss will notice that you are not at your desk. You worry that he will want to have "that talk" to flex his power. Traffic is horrendous and you end up parking out in the sticks. As you head to your desk, you run into someone who is talking about his or her teenager having an attitude, and you remember this person gets on your very last nerve! You don't have the time or the patience for her to unload on you! What you are creating is negative emotion, my friends. You are feeding your embryo by nurturing it with anger, anxiety, and so on. As the embryo grows, it requires food, or negative energy. With more negative thoughts and emotions, the embryo grows into a fetus until it is time for it to be born. I am sure you know someone who seems very negative, so much, so that you may prefer to avoid his or her company. The person has given birth to a negative entity. The thoughts and emotions have grown so powerful with negative energy that the majority of what he or she is creating is negative! When this happens, he or she has tipped the balance and he or she is not in control of his or her thoughts or emotions any longer.

We have discussed what negative entities are capable of. In Jackie's case, there was much fear of the negative entities themselves! Much attention was given to checking to see if they were around and releasing them, but we say here that with this behavior alone, Jackie was creating them herself.

Unfortunately, she was unaware of what she was doing. As the days passed, the fear grew and so did the negative energy. We tell you here, all is for a purpose.

Because this one went through this unforgettable experience, we can share it with you in hopes that you will realize how incredibly powerful the energy of thought and emotion is.

November 10, 2008
Balancing My Life

I took every available moment I could find to work with my pendulum so I could learn new things concerning the esoteric. I was well aware that my behavior was becoming obsessive and I felt like if I wasn't careful ... Well, I was becoming a little concerned about myself. However, I made sure that I continued to do my chores around the house; I kept it clean and tidy, and I made darn sure that meals were prepared on time and everything else concerning my husband was completed.

Was this wrong of me to want to connect to a higher intelligence? I wanted to know the secrets of the universe. I wanted to know everything about the angels and the spirit guides, their origins, and what their personalities were like. Did they have families like us? I simply chose not to lay the questions down, but this horrible fear kept creeping up.

The answers I got were sometimes inconsistent. Why? I wondered who I was talking to. Why did they lie to me? I really didn't like what was going on. I was constantly weighing the pros and cons of what I was doing. Sometimes I thought I should stop talking to them all together! But I always rationalized and came to the same conclusion: I wanted to hear what they had to say! I felt like a ping pong ball that was being bounced around, hitting the walls, the ceiling, the floor and then landing in a sink full of dirty dish water!

The reason I kept coming to the same conclusion, kept talking to the angels, was because I received the wonderful love energy. There was no mistake that this was love.

As I checked for the negative energies, I began to receive this amazing gift, the opening. I had begun to see in my mind's eye symbols or movements, much like a person taking a piece of chalk and writing on a chalkboard.

In addition, the angels had begun to stretch my neck by turning my head in different directions. Every morning they would work with me to release the tension from my body and to get the blood flowing to the brain and all parts of my body. It was like having a private massage therapist come to my room. I was getting all of this great stuff at the same time I was getting contradictory information, and then I turned on my CD player to relax and the angels began to dance with me by moving my head in different positions, at the same time giving me this beautiful energy that I now call "love energy." This love energy coincided with the rhythm of the music. The angels have exquisite rhythm, perfect timing ...

Quem: I am going to help you out here a bit. All angels have the ability to give energy to anyone, anywhere, and at anytime. As you know, everything is made of energy and everything has its own specific vibration. When we wish to dance with you, we create or feel an emotion, a particular level of love which is manifested by a vibration. This all depends on our level of love at the time.

You have noticed that there are moments during a melody that you "soar higher" emotionally. During the dance, we feel many levels of positive emotion or even negative emotion. As you receive the energy from us, you are also resonating with each aspect of the music: the melody, tempo, pitch, and even the lyrics that you hear and feel. This is an expression of emotion. In short, you are creating a vibration that resonates with our vibration. This is the dance.

Since we are connected to you on an energetic level of consciousness, we know when you are listening to your beautiful music. We can hear your music; we also feel the vibration of the music and the vibration of you, Jackie. We really don't hear it like you do. We do not reside in the third dimension.

We must explain this to you. Remember, my dear one, a time when a melody or a song was stuck in your head? You heard the music, did you not? Over and over the music played. The sound was internal. It was the mind that gave you the music.

Now we go on. When we wish to share our love with you, we do this by sending the love to you energetically. This is all done with our thoughts and emotions, Jackie. You feel a vibration, do you not? What happens is your body receives this energy, this love, and you respond in turn energetically to this love vibration that we are giving you by creating your own emotion and your own vibration. This energy that you receive feels good; it feels like love to you, so you respond. It is a dance of positive energies. As you know, it is quite beautiful!

Positive emotion will manifest in a vibration that feels really good and will send you high! What we were doing with the dance was multifaceted. We chose to give you our love, this gift of positive emotion. Also, we were asking you energetically to join with us in the creation of positive energy.

During these same occasions, we were teaching you to realize that when you are listening to beautiful music, you are personally resonating and responding energetically to this music, these vibrations. Sound is given to you through one of your senses. You are resonating with the vibration of the tones that harmonize. You love the sound; it is beautiful and it brings you much pleasure. Through this beauty, you respond emotionally with love and gratitude, lifting you up high. This is an energetic dance. This is also self-expression.

To sum this up, I tell you that we both are in a very high state of love. In essence, what we are doing is gifting each other with this energy, this love. When you bring together two or more individuals, the energies created are magnified above and beyond what the two or more individuals can create individually.

God promises that He will be present with you. *"For where two or three come together in my name, there am I with them."* (Matthew 18:20, NIV).

As I was saying, the vibration that I felt in my body increased or decreased according to what the angels were expressing energetically. In addition, as I felt the intensity of the vibration lessen or strengthen, I felt the vibration move around in my body much like I was a musical instrument. With each note that was played, a different part of my body would sing, hum, or vibrate. This was all done according to how they wished to express themselves energetically through the dance. The vibration was always in sync with the music and was a beautiful compliment.

December 14, 2008
Initiation: Part One

Then the voices came. The head movements became more focused. I didn't think I was totally crazy, because I had heard of this phenomenon before in the recording of "The Law of Attraction," by Esther and Jerry Hicks. Esther channels Abraham, who is a group of spirit guides. They had begun to communicate through her with the movements of her nose and voice, which is exactly like what I was experiencing.

To be honest, I was an emotional wreck. I was afraid to speak to my husband and to my family about what was happening to me. What would they think? Sometimes my head hurt with trying to keep up with the conversation that was secretly going on in my mind.

Strange things continued to happen, and I grew more frightened. Finally, I caved and told a couple of people I knew just a little of what I was experiencing. In response, they adamantly told me that they thought I had mental issues and strongly advised me to see a doctor to get some medication. I have seen what medicating a person can do, and I absolutely had no intention of going that route.

I was scared, but at the same time, I received the most beautiful love imaginable! I kept asking myself how something so amazing could be bad. Even so, I continued to question this gift, because the communication was inconsistent. In addition to the inconsistent answers, I was receiving instructions on what to do. One angel was by my side constantly telling me when I was thinking negative thoughts and teaching me how to rephrase those thoughts. She would also tell me what I should buy at the store, or perhaps when I should stay home.

At night, I was awakened by who I thought were the angels and talked with them for hours at a time. Sleep was becoming a rare occurrence. I don't do well without sleep. During the day, the angels would ask me to please sit down to receive energy that would sustain me. They assured me that I would be all right, and I gladly allowed this and gratefully accepted it. However, I felt as if I were like a fragile crystal goblet that was sitting precariously on the edge of a table, and at any moment I could easily fall and shatter into a thousand pieces.

I remember this one particular night that I was actually getting some decent rest, when I was abruptly awakened by a pounding in my chest. There was no question, I felt terror and panic! I asked my guides, "What is happening?" The guides said, "You must get up and go downstairs now." They wouldn't let up. They continued with, "You must learn to trust."

I worked to make sense of this situation. Why would I want to go downstairs in the middle of the night? Am I in danger? After being harassed for a while, I finally got up and went downstairs as quietly as I could. They said, "Go into your office and sit on the floor. Feel the energies." I sat down and felt the vibration that quite literally astounded me. There was a definite hum and vibration that was under my house!

The guides working with me continued by explaining that we have an electrical current, specifically a grid, if you will, that runs from the electrical lines to each home. If all is still, you can feel it! I knew this but never put any thought to it. Oh, wow!

What do I do with this information? Are we constantly being exposed to an electrical current? How can this be good?

Also, they wanted me to learn that when I received a "bad" feeling, I should examine it to find what was wrong. They went on to explain that if I were in any situation and felt this foreboding energy it was a way to tell me that I should move quickly out of the area!

The teachings were reaching a climax. I could see that my lack of sleep was affecting my life on every level. My emotions were swinging wildly from one extreme to the other. One minute I was feeling this great love energy that brought up my love and gratitude, and then the next moment I was suspicious, fearful, and full of anxiety; surges of anger would come bubbling up to the surface and were directed toward the angels.

In addition to the symbols, the dancing, and the voices, I was receiving instructions on how to visualize and move energy in my body. What happened next was the breaking point for me.

March 11, 2009
Initiation: Part Two

I would sit for lengthy periods of time working with these energies. The energies had color, movement, and feeling. As I continued to work, the energies would change, expand, and become stronger. Beginning at the perineum (near the root chakra), this energy would spiral up around the spinal column, going up through the crown chakra just above the top of my head. Then the energy would go back down around the spinal column once again down to the perineum. This action was repeated over and over, becoming stronger and faster. Over a short period of time, the intensity of this energy became overpowering.

I asked what the purpose of this was. The answer was to learn to have great focus. As I said, the power of the energy was awesome and confusing at the same time. With the movements, I became sexually stimulated with nowhere to go with the energy. They instructed me to lay down on the bed after the energy movements to release this pent up energy. The energy was supposed to be released through the crown, but it wasn't. What I felt was utterly raw, primitive, sexual, and extremely powerful. The result was that I felt powerless to make mentally sound choices, to think rationally. I had never experienced anything of this nature before. To release this energy was quite necessary, and at the time, it seemed to be the only thing of importance.

What happened next was shocking and for me was way beyond anything I considered appropriate or anywhere near acceptable. A spiritual being came to me and made me feel like I was having a sexual experience with a man. I quite literally felt the energy and the intention. Believe me, by that time I really thought I had lost it! I begged for protection and for this nightmare to end.

I have only heard about this type of encounter two other times. One was in a fiction novel. The second time, I was actually seeking help from an individual and was explaining what happened in as few words as possible. (This stuff is embarrassing!) This person explained that they thought it was a spiritual rape because it was against my will.

In addition, particularly at night, I was feeling this energy in my genital area that felt invasive. I really don't know how to describe the energy other than it was a strong tingling sensation, a vibration. Try that for a few hours and see where it gets you! This energy felt really uncomfortable and wrong. Where was the energy coming from? It was strong and kept me from sleeping.

I tried to distract myself. I tried to cross my legs. I tried to run! Nothing worked. What I felt was horrible, and I couldn't escape it. I finally told my husband in as few words as possible what I was feeling. I went to him out of shear desperation. I had to do something, try anything! I thought somehow he could protect me, although I knew what he thought—I was crazy. He didn't saying anything condescending, however.

My understanding was that I was being controlled by Earthbound spirits or some sort of evil entities, and they were quite literally working to send me this energy to drive me crazy.

At the time that this happened, I was in a very confused state of mind to say the least, and was quite literally becoming worried about my mental state. How long could I go without sleep and have this energy invade my body? I felt desperate, and my life was quickly spiraling out of control.

I made the effort to overcome my embarrassment and my shame. I went to several of my friends who knew that I was in some sort of trouble. My pride went right out the door when I began explaining some of the things I was experiencing. I quite literally felt that if I didn't get help, I would die. I began to brainstorm and try to find people who would understand my predicament and have the wisdom to guide me.

Previously, the people I had confided in had warned me in one way or another that I was into something that was really volatile. One person stated bluntly that she thought I had become mentally ill. Another was sure that I had opened up some sort of vortex or passageway from different dimensions, allowing the unseen to travel to and from me. I don't know about all of that. This was all sounding like a sci-fi movie! The only thing I really understood was that I had to get rid of the negative energy. My friends warned in no uncertain terms to put the pendulum down and not pick it up again.

Sure, I understood that I had to do something. I knew I should put the pendulum down, but I didn't want to! What I didn't understand was how to go about getting rid of these energies. The thought still hadn't occurred to me that I was creating these negative entities from my own fear!

I was talking with my angels, and at the same time, I believed that I was talking to evil spirits (negative entities). In fact, one of my closest friends instructed me not converse with any of them!

To put it bluntly, I would not let it go. I was obsessed with all of this. Fear was controlling me. My guides knew it was time for me to understand that who was with me was not a bad spirit, but a very strong negative energy that I had created myself, and as long as I continued to be afraid, this energy would continue to grow. My situation would escalate. In order for the angels to teach me what I was doing to myself, they chose to take on a different persona, a persona of a controlling nature. I was at a crossroads. I had to make a decision here. What was really in my best interest?

The angels upped the ante, so to speak, quickly working to teach me that I must listen with my heart and feel what was best for me. I could not go into fear because I was powerful and divine in nature. Nothing and no one can hurt me unless I allow it.

The situation continued to unfold, growing more bizarre. Someone was telling me to prepare for the climate changes and buy several items in large quantities, who to keep company with, and when to do energy work. When I didn't take my power back by saying, "No, you will not tell me what to do anymore," the angels decided to take this to another level.

The thing is, I knew that I was doing something very wrong. I kept thinking that they shouldn't be telling me what to do, but in the next moment, I would receive something that was so beautiful. How do I fix this? What do I do to get rid of bad guys but at the same time keep the good guys?

For me, my mind and my body are extremely important aspects and I must protect them. It is instinct to protect yourself against harm. I knew at that time I wasn't thinking logically, but I couldn't sort out my thoughts well enough to make sense of any of what was happening. I still had the sense to know that I had to protect myself, though.

Little by little, the realization came that I had given away my control by creating negative energy. I had allowed that energy to become so powerful that I was no longer using sound judgment concerning my everyday tasks. I was no longer making sound choices.

You can call me a slow learner. I knew that what I was into was not right, but I wanted to have that relationship with the angels so badly that I had allowed myself to get into a precarious situation. I had an addiction.

No one wants to be hurt, abused, or violated. Because my guides had been unable to wake me up, they chose to use my deepest vulnerabilities to show me that I had to wake up and see what was happening. I was allowing someone other than myself to have access to what I know to be some of my most precious gifts—my body and my mind! The angels were teaching me that I had to use discernment in all situations and feel with my emotions what was right or wrong. I had to set some boundaries for myself; if there was any question whatsoever as to the intention of the situation, I should not participate. Don't allow!

March 17, 2009
Surrender

Sleep wasn't coming. I would go to bed with the desire to sleep, to shut this all out of my mind, but my mind wouldn't shut down. I continued to ask questions and the guides would continue to answer me, taking me into the early hours of the morning. I had to get some sleep!

Again, I went to my friends. This time I asked for help, and my friends agreed to come to my aid. They gave me a bread crumb, a tiny piece of comfort that help was on the way. Could I hold on until they got here? My life was rapidly spiraling out of control. I wasn't able to get the proper rest. The voices were constant and the energy invasive.

As a group, they decided that we should meet at my home to get rid of these negative entities. The best time would be just before the spring equinox, which would take place March 21. We had to move quickly. I was extremely doubtful that I could make it a few more days, but what choice did I have? I kept myself busy as best I could, and in a matter of a few days, my friends were by my side. I was amazed at how quickly we were able to put a plan together.

The last thing I wanted to do was ask Scott to support me through this. For the most part, he didn't have a clue about what I was involved in or what was happening to me. Because of our sleeping arrangement and his work schedule, it was easy for me to not let on what was happening. I was living a double life, but it was coming to the point that I just couldn't pretend that everything was okay anymore.

The energy I felt was nothing like I have ever felt before. I was buzzing—like I was hooked up to a high voltage of electricity. Between the energy I received and the voices I heard, there was no sleep. I was more than frightened, I was terrified! Scott could clearly see that I was becoming more and more agitated. Instead of my usual nightly ritual of going to bed early to read and listen to music, I got my headphones (to try and drown out the voices) and a blanket and tried to rest in my recliner in the living room. It didn't matter that he was watching football or David Letterman. Wherever Scott was I was right beside him; I didn't want to be left alone. I knew logically that he couldn't protect me, but I took what little comfort I could from him being near.

When the time came, I took a deep breath and announced to Scott that I had several friends coming over to the house on the evening of the 21st to help me get rid of whatever the heck was going on. I knew that Scott was scheduled to work that night. Trying to not sound desperate, I told him that I'd like him to be here for this "thing." I wanted to have his support, but said I'd understand if he didn't want to be there or couldn't get off work. I just left it at that. I simply left it up to him to decide what was best for him to do. For the most part, Scott is very understanding, but this stuff was out of his comfort zone. I was really embarrassed to have to ask anyone (especially my husband) to come bail me out because I was naive and doing stupid stuff.

At that time, I didn't know what we as a group were actually doing, but I trusted that someone would have a plan. A couple of my friends recommended that Scott participate, because he is my husband and this was his home, too.

I know this all sounds really strange, but we agreed to come together in my home and form a circle. I chose the attic space beside my bedroom because that is where I heard the most activity: footsteps, rustling sounds, knocking noises, and doors closing. I still thought we had some sort of being that had taken residence in my home.

March 21, 2009
The Time of Resolution

Everyone had arrived by 7:00 p.m. Before we got down to business, we shared some taco soup and Irish soda bread.

Opening the meeting, I began by recounting all of the sounds I heard in the attic and included how invasive the voices had become. I told them about the energy I felt without getting specific. (I felt this knowledge was too personal.) A couple of the others talked about what they thought was happening, how they felt about it, and what they thought we should do. A plan began to formulate on how we would release the negative energy. I listened to everyone's thoughts, feeling grateful for anything they had to offer, because I didn't have a single idea on what to do to resolve the issue.

While we were discussing our options, someone in the group began to demand that these beings, whoever they were, show themselves. He continued to challenge them by saying that if they were real and so powerful, then they could most certainly move a turkey feather that he had laid on my coffee table. Nothing happened. He went on to call the entities a bunch of chickens, adding that he didn't believe that they had any real power whatsoever. Then he went on making some noises that were meant to belittle them.

I know that he was showing everyone that he wasn't intimidated by anything, so I watched, not saying a word. I felt my heart sink and the muscles in my abdomen tighten. I felt strongly that this type of communication might not be our wisest choice, but didn't say anything to anyone. Now, I know what I felt at that moment was my own fear.

We waited until about 8:00 p.m., because that is when the activity usually increased. We gathered a candle, stones, drums, and rattles to help us strengthen and express our emotions and our authority.

We got our cameras and recorders and off we went. I was instructed to tell the entities to leave and really mean it; I was to stand up for myself. Again, I felt a swell of fear that nearly paralyzed me. Everyone would be watching me. This would be my show! I had been cowering in the corner for months now; could I pull this off? I quickly did a pep talk in my mind, "This is my home and whoever is here is not welcome for any reason, period!"

We entered the doorway and each took our place. With my drum, I sat in the middle of the floor with my husband by my side while the others formed a circle around me. I worked to put all of my attention on the task at hand, but on some level, I was conscious of my failures and insecurities and wanted to run as fast and far as I could.

As I beat on the drum, I commanded the negative entities to get out of my home. At first, I felt extremely foolish and awkward. I certainly didn't feel confident. I just didn't have the power or conviction behind my words; instead, I felt weak and insignificant. My friends instructed me in no uncertain terms that I must stand tall, express my authority, and believe with all of my being that this was my home and no one or anything was allowed there that I didn't want to be there! As I continued to beat the drum, I began to feel stronger and believe that yes, this was my home, and by gosh, my home was my sanctuary!

Toward the end of the ceremony, I intuitively knew that we, as a group, had to unite and send love to these "beings" in order for them to leave. Taking control of the situation, I said to everyone that we had to pull together and raise our love and gratitude vibration, because these beings had to go in love. I didn't know where this knowing came from. I only knew that this was extremely important for us to do; the only thing we could do!

As the closing of the ceremony neared, one person told me that they thought the work was finished, and that the entities would all be gone by tomorrow. Needless to say, I was apprehensive. Tomorrow? Uh, I was still hearing someone talk to me who wasn't in a physical body. Still believing that I had divine guidance, I decided to let it go.

I was instructed that there was one thing left that I must take care of myself; I must close the vortex or the opening that I had created. Since I opened it, I had to close it. I was advised not to go into the attic until I had closed the vortex. What?

My friends advised me not to converse with any beings who were talking to me. If I heard any voices, I was to ignore them. That worked for about three days.

March 22, 2009
Closing the Vortex

Immediately, I began working to contact the teacher of the dowsing workshop. I had no idea how to close a vortex. I needed help. Heck, I didn't even understand how I had opened it in the first place! Unfortunately, he was too busy to talk to me so he handed me off to his assistant.

Right away, I wrote her an e-mail explaining that I had some "stuff" that I needed help with. She wrote me back telling me that she thought we could talk on a particular day. That didn't work out and as the days passed, the stranger things became. I felt that if anyone could help me with this issue she could, but we just weren't connecting, so I decided to call her. There was no answer, so I left her a message and sent another e-mail instead. After a week without connecting with this person, I felt I had to move on with this myself. I wanted help, but at the same time, I wanted this ordeal to end and end now!

It was time for me to come out of seclusion, my self-made prison that I had so elaborately constructed, restore my faith, and believe again that I was strong! I pledged to not be fearful anymore.

Quem: Jackie, I give to you this gift: Remember always that water is life sustaining, and the Light is love.

All creation is energy. We are all one. I have compassion and love for beings that have not yet grown to love. There is negative and positive to all people and all situations. All people of all origins inherently have positive and negative aspects to themselves. This is the nature of duality. Somehow, in all of that chaos, I chose to love instead of hate. I chose to see the negative as an asset, because through the negative I was shown the positive—Light and Love.

Since I hadn't connected with the woman from the dowsing workshop, I decided to ask my spirit guides to assist me in writing a prayer to close the vortex. Suddenly, the warning to not go back into the attic reverberated in my mind. Yes, I was advised to not go back in there, but, truly, what was I afraid of? I was no longer willing to be held prisoner in my own home. I was no longer fearful. When love is strong, there is no room for fear.

After the words to my prayer were written, I gathered the items to smudge the attic space (this is a Native American practice) to clear all positive ions. I had my feather to move the energies outdoors to be transmuted by Mother Nature. After I smudged the room, I sat on the floor directly in the middle of the room. As I recited the prayer, I felt the love and gratitude swell from deep within my heart. When I was finished, I simply got up and quietly left the room, knowing that this part of my life was finally over. Not looking back, I firmly shut the door.

Now, it almost seems to me that this part of my life was a dream—a bad dream at that. What I have left that proves to me that yes, I did experience this and yes, what happened was real are the many pictures taken of the spirit beings (orbs) and the recording of the entire ceremony. I also have my wonderful friends who cared enough for me to come to my aid when I asked them for help. To this day, I have not listened to the recording. I have no need to.

My Prayer to Close a Vortex

I call upon the assistance of the Highest Most Divine Creative Awareness.

I ask that now this vortex be forever closed by the Divine Angels in the appropriate manner and with great love and care.

I affirm that this home is restored from this moment on with positive energy, the fifth dimensional energies of love and gratitude for the highest benefit of all concerned. ~Amen~

Quem: What I would like to say is that when you are releasing any negative energy, no matter how strong, you must do it with love. Negative energy cannot be moved or transmuted without first creating the positive thought with love, the highest vibration. Love is Divine; love is Spirit! There is absolutely nothing more powerful in this universe. Know it!

March 24, 2009
Expansion in Consciousness

The Akasie: Writing this book has been a very therapeutic endeavor for Jackie. During the opening, there was much agony and turmoil. We also wish to make it known that she experienced much love and much comfort. Up until now, she has not been able to retrieve all of the memories associated with this period.

Psychic openings are mysterious, and the circumstances surrounding them are almost always unusual and unpredictable; one rarely knows what they are going to get. In the beginning, the individual going through the psychic opening usually doesn't put two and two together until much later, after the situation has calmed down somewhat.

Nonetheless, the angels are always with those who are going through this expansion in consciousness and giving comfort as best they can. We are with you always! Sometimes the communication isn't such that the individual person understands that he or she has angels with him or her to guide, protect, and love him or her along their journey.

We tell you that a psychic opening brings you to a higher level of awareness. With a psychic opening, depending on the circumstances, many questions may arise such as: Is this real? Am I sick? Who can I talk to? What do I tell my family and friends? If I do say something, how much should I say? Will they believe me? Who can I trust? Will this ever stop? Do I want it to stop?

One of the challenges concerning a psychic opening is compounded greatly when the individual doesn't believe there is anyone they can confide in. In other words, the individual will choose to keep what is happening hidden inside rather than risk being criticized, judged, or worse yet, hospitalized. Being told that you are crazy and getting locked up isn't in the best interest of anyone.

March 25, 2009
Dream: The Quilt

Last night, I had this dream that stuck in my mind. Because I was able to remember the details so clearly, I ask my guides to help me interpret the symbolism.

There was a lovely patchwork quilt on display in a crowded school cafeteria. I could see the array of beautiful, deep, jewel-tone colors, the interesting shapes and textures of the various fabrics. Many people were looking over the quilt, which was adorned with numerous sentimental trinkets, small bits of delicate lace, and hundreds of precious jewels. To me, the quilt was absolutely stunning.

I entered the large room with my dearest childhood girlfriend, and we looked around to assess the situation. To our right was the cashier. Further back were several counters with steaming food and several women serving the food to the students. The floor was generic white tile. There was so much activity that we had to pause to decide which way to go. There were people moving in every direction, some getting their lunch, some looking for a seat, and others gathered around the quilt.

My attention was drawn to the quilt and the crowd of people surrounding it. To me it looked as if they were all searching for something.

My friend and I were also interested in the quilt. As I looked closer, I could see these people were all taking items from the quilt. For some reason, I felt this was expected. We saw that the quilt had a large number of tiny diamonds attached to the fabric. The diamonds were so tiny that if you didn't know they were there, you would overlook them entirely. We saw them, we knew they were there, and I wanted them. I wanted to give these diamonds to my dearest friend. Together, we decided to go talk to the cashier to see if she had any ideas of how to get these diamonds.

I went to the quilt while my friend stood by the side and patiently waited. Quietly, I worked with all of the others who were gathering their treasures. I only wanted the diamonds and was wondering why the others didn't want them. Maybe they didn't see them, or possibly, they just wanted something different. The diamonds were right there for anyone to have. Why weren't they seeing them? Why didn't they want them?

As I continued to collect the diamonds, I watched the others casually take whatever they wished. I systematically worked my way across the top and to the right of the quilt getting every diamond that was there and then placing the diamonds in little plastic baggies, but some of the diamonds had fallen to the floor. I then made note that the floor was carpeted with lush green grass. I found all of the diamonds and put them in the bags so I wouldn't lose them. The diamonds must be kept safe.

This dream is very revealing, and I think I understand parts of it now. Diamonds are the strongest and most brilliant of all stones, and are considered very valuable and also symbolize an aspect of me. The stones represent something about me that I cherish and love. In the dream I knew the stones were there, I just had to look closely to find them. In addition, all of the people in the dream are other aspects of me. The people who were looking over the quilt for their treasures (which are aspects of myself also), either didn't know the diamonds were there or they were looking for other stuff that they considered valuable to them. My friend was an aspect of myself; the part of me that I trust and love.

What I wonder, though: was I the diamond that was multifaceted, refractive, strong, beautiful, and valuable? Did the diamonds symbolize what I was learning and processing, or could the diamonds represent qualities like inner strength?

Quem: Dreams are very personal. It is a wise practice to take notice of what has been happening in your life prior to receiving any dream. This dream was given to you after your ordeal with the negative entities; more specifically, your release of them. You released your negativity, your fear. At the time of the release, you remembered that love is your strength, your power, and all that you require.

The scene in the cafeteria, which was full of people in a flurry of activity, represents chaotic energy and is telling you that you are going through a chaotic time in your life. You pause at the doorway to assess which way to go on your path; which choices you must make to go forward. You seek the cashier, who is your higher self, for guidance.

The quilt is the beauty that you see that is amongst the chaos and the drama. When you look closer at the quilt, you see the adornment that brings more beauty. You are focusing in on particular aspects of beauty, which can be perceived as anything that is of value to you.

In this case, the stones represent positive energy. At this time in your life, you are receiving many gifts in the form of teachings. You are also experiencing and releasing many emotions; the energy is moving for you. You are now processing what just occurred and focusing on the beauty.

You walked through the chaos (the negativity) with your sights set on the beauty (the positive).

All the people who were looking at the quilt and taking what they wanted represented more chaos and more choices. You have free will to choose what you want in life, which is symbolized by the choice of trinkets, lace, or jewels that you most desired or loved. You made your own choice to take what was most valuable to you. You made your choice to gather strength, which comes by loving.

You are collecting your diamonds (love, the highest vibration) beside the other people who were choosing other trinkets or stones (a lower vibration). This segment is two-fold. As I said previously, choosing to take those diamonds, to you, was what was most important. This is also revealing to you, because the people who were helping you with the release of the negative energy were gathering love and strength also, but their choice (how strong their love was and how they went about it), was a little different.

You want to give this gift (the love, strength, and power), to your friend who is the part of you that you trust and love.

April 1, 2009
Messages from the Angels

The Akasie: Messages come from the angels in a variety of ways. One way we guide you is by repeatedly turning your attention to specific numbers, signs, or symbols. The method of communication that is becoming more popular these days is the double and triple numbers that are shown to individuals several times in a short period. This method is designed to get your attention and to make you wonder what it all means. When you begin to see something repeatedly, it may be helpful for you to keep a record of it. Write down what you see, when you see it, and what you are thinking or experiencing at the time. Most certainly, you will notice patterns emerge.

Currently, we have just a few dedicated writers working with us who are sharing the meanings of the different numbers. Remember, everything has a specific vibration, including numbers. Math is the universal language.

Now, we tell you there are some contradictions concerning the meanings of the numbers floating around. What is happening is a misunderstanding of sorts.

Doreen Virtue, a dedicated light worker and author is advocating for the angels—us! We love her, as we love all peoples of the universe and all of creation. Doreen wrote the book entitled, *Angel Numbers 101*, which is a most helpful book for those who are looking to know what these revealing messages mean and who also wish to connect to their guides. In Doreen's book, she explains the corresponding significance of each number from 0 to 999.

We have another who is a well-educated man, Drunvalo Melchizedek, who has written many scholarly books. He works with many spiritual beings without complaining ... much. Drunvalo, this is a joke for you. The book we are wishing to discuss is *Serpent of the Light: Beyond 2012*. In his book, he writes of the triple digits 111–999, saying in short that the numbers all have mathematical implications and correspond to harmonic values. Drunvalo states, "Long ago, the angels taught me that when you see a triple number in the reality, it has significance relative to what you are thinking or the environment around you."

When you reach the level of awareness that brings you to the realization that angels wish to communicate with you, it is highly likely that your guides will begin to show you numbers or symbols in a multitude of places and ways.

Remember that angels may get very creative, so have your eyes wide open. Here are a few examples of places that you may have your attention directed: license plates, phone numbers, digital clocks, receipts, checkbook registers, odometers, and street signs. The list goes on. Again, we remind you that the same sequence of numbers will be shown to you repeatedly. We wish you well on your journey to communicating with your spiritual guides who have chosen to work with you.

We really have a good time with Jackie. She will be driving down the road and for no apparent reason will glance at the odometer on her car. She knows then to check the clock because we often give her double or triple digits simultaneously. We have great fun! In the beginning, we gave her numbers to uplift her and to teach her that, yes, we really are here to guide. Most certainly, none of what she was receiving was a coincidence. Now, the reason we give the numbers to her is to remind her that yes, we are with her and love her. Yes, we are ones who enjoy a good time also!

However, in order to teach this one to pay closer attention to her thoughts and actions, we have recently given Jackie her own personalized set of numbers that we will share with you. This is to inform you that there are different reasons that numbers are given to different people. Just because one gets numbers doesn't necessarily dictate that they hold the same value for another. Each person has his or her own path, his or her own lessons to learn. So we tell you that this modality of communication may be very personal, and often is a teaching.

111—New beginnings: Either in the physical or in the spiritual teachings.

222—Indicates going back to what you love.

333—You must repeat a lesson. Work and pay attention to everything you do. The details are important for you.

444—You are focusing on the external, the physical. Are you doing what makes your heart sing?

555—You are here in the now. Be grateful you have achieved Oneness.

666—Creator beckons you. Look to the heavens for refuge, peace, and love. Divine energy comes down to you. Just ask for it.

777—The water restoreth your soul; it cleanses and purifies. Drink and be whole.

888—We come down to bestow upon you the Heavenly Spirit and the multitude of gifts that can't be seen with your physical eyes. Behold what cometh unto you, the energy of pure love. This energy is of the highest vibration known. When you ask or give to another, you always receive in abundance.

999—This comes to you when you have completed a level.

April 2, 2009
Beginning to Heal

The Akasie: The subject we speak of now is on what you can do to change, evolve, and ultimately go forward. It all boils down to how you perceive yourself. Do you love and respect yourself? Do you feel you are worthy to have others love you? You must all learn to care for yourselves better by eating healthy foods, resting, enjoying self, exercising, and also relaxing. Spending time in the great outdoors is most beneficial to balancing the entire being. Treat yourself with respect by listening to your body and loving yourself! That means not only caring for the physical body, but the mind and spirit, as well.

We would like to further explain how to listen to your body. You have emotions to guide you. When you feel good, with love in your heart, you are feeling positive emotions and you are in alignment with Spirit. When you feel physical discomfort, such as a stomachache perhaps, a headache, and so on, you are not in alignment with Spirit. These emotions always manifest themselves in physical sensations to guide you to make the correct choice, which is to be in alignment with Spirit!

We are speaking of being aware of your thoughts, specifically being in control of what you are creating at all times. If you think negative thoughts, you are creating negative emotion, and this will manifest into physical discomfort! Think positive thoughts to be in control and feel the love!

April 3, 2009
To Go Within

The Akasie: Jackie, at different times you receive energy from us that causes your physical body to produce much heat. We direct the energy to different areas of your spine and then direct the energy outward. You are told to embrace the heat and go within.

This is what we want to tell you. You have received this energy for a few weeks now for different reasons. You have continued to question this that we give to you out of love.

The energy is for healing purposes. This is multi-level healing, meaning we speak of healing that is directed to all levels of your being. Sometimes when someone hears the word healing, they may only associate it with a healing on the physical level. We are not speaking of physical healing only. *We are speaking of healing for your mind, spirit, and body.*

One reason you are given this particular energy is to teach you to use your mental faculties in order to train yourself to go within while maintaining great focus as you find yourself in different and unique situations.

For you, the heat is an extreme method of learning. There is absolutely no way that you can ignore or get away from this energy, this heat that encompasses your entire body. We are instructing you in this manner so that you are forced to feel with your entire being. The heat permeates your whole body, taking over all of your senses: physical, mental, and emotional. At the present time, you have no physical means to escape the heat. The heat is there no matter how much you complain and try to fight it. Again and again, we instruct you to go within and embrace this heat, to become one with this energy.

When we first began teaching you this segment, we used this energy because heat is a challenge for you; you could feel it without a doubt, and you don't like it. In addition, because you are seemingly powerless over this energy, you yourself are creating negative energy! For so very long you have ignored the negative emotion that manifests in your body as a specific discomfort, such as tension, anxiety, depression, or even pain. Miss, no matter what you say or do you cannot ignore the heat.

In the beginning, you did not have the focus to feel subtle discomforts in the physical body. Now, you are becoming more aware when your body feels the consequences of negative emotions. You are being taught that when you feel discomfort, you should associate it with whatever you are doing or creating energetically at the time. Question any discomfort.

Perhaps you are creating negative emotions. Look at them closely. When you feel discomfort ask yourself, "What am I doing to create this discomfort?" As you progress, you will be proficient in recognizing when the body is telling you that something is out of alignment with Spirit. This recognition enables you to change whatever it is you are thinking, saying, or doing. Yes, we have been speaking about the effects of negative energy created by *you*.

In addition, we are teaching you to embrace the seemingly unbearable heat by going within to focus on the internal, not the external. Say that you have a bad day, for instance. You burned dinner and your husband came home in a sour mood and made a derogatory comment. You took the negative comment and allowed it to affect you emotionally. You reacted to the comment because perhaps you were feeling sensitive. What I am saying is that you allowed the comment to intensify your anxiety regarding your feelings of inadequacy, of not being a perfect cook.

When you are faced with a situation that causes you to feel uncomfortable, go within. What is your body telling you? Where in your body does the anxiety manifest? Focus on the vibrations of your inner being to see where you stand. Look at your total energy. Are you feeling positive emotion, negative emotion, or are you in a neutral state of being? When you identify what you feel, you may be more able to decide what to do with those feelings.

There is another reason for this energy that produces the heat. This heat is a tool for you to use to teach you to become one with self, to allow, and to just be. There is no use in fighting it, as fighting is always futile. You are learning to correct the impact of the negative emotion you feel to transform it to positive emotion, to love yourself. What we wish you to do when you receive this energy is to relax and focus on loving yourself and being grateful. You can then create the positive energy by going deep within yourself, thus shutting out all external distractions.

April 14, 2009
What Am I Doing?

I know I have experienced this same type of phenomena before, but not on this level! I have been going to Native American sweat lodges that are great! It is much like going to church, because it is a group of people who gather to pray to God our Creator, but we also come to do a cleanse by physically sweating like the natives have done for hundreds of years. It is a time to release painful memories, old beliefs that do not serve us any longer, and to release the toxins from the body.

We come together in reverence and gratitude for the Oneness of all of Creation.

However, the same thing keeps happening to me. I go to these ceremonial sweats because I want to heal. I want to purify my body in order that I may heal on a physical level. For starters, I am not a native, so that in itself makes me feel out of place. This type of ritual is also something brand new to me. I find learning about the Native American culture amazing, but every time I have gone to that ceremony, I come face to face with the same person that I have a reaction to. I feel like I am put on the defensive. We don't have any past issues (in this lifetime) so I totally don't understand what is happening. I feel so much anxiety around this person. You know, I feel like this person is directing hate toward me. It truly is awful.

Every time I see on the calendar that a sweat is coming up, I weigh the pros and cons of participating. Will this time be different? Does the positive time in the lodge outweigh feeling this intense negative energy? Is it me that's causing this issue, the other person, or both of us? How do I fix this?

April 15, 2009
How to Resolve Issues

The Akasie: Up until now, we have talked about the energy that you create. It doesn't end there. Everyone creates energy. Of course, you know this. The situation that you are speaking of is rather confusing to you. The person you are speaking of is in fact the same woman who helped you to go forward in the healing process concerning your son's passing; a rather unusual situation here, yes.

This person, in your opinion, is of great value, yes? She is a teacher and a healer, and here you are faced with this energy that you do not understand. The negative energy seems to be directed toward you. Maybe it was animosity that you felt. We tell you this is true. This one isn't comfortable around you, though we will not say why. This is for the two of you to work out.

When you first laid eyes on this one, you began to feel this anxiety, yes, even before this particular occasion. You thought that surely this one just had a bad day or something, and that is why you were feeling these "vibes," so you hoped that the next time that you would be in this person's company all would be all right. Unfortunately, the situation has not resolved itself.

The best way to resolve this type of circumstance is to talk it out with this person. Explain to this person what you are feeling. Try talking through your feelings. See if the two of you can resolve the issue together. It is possibly a misunderstanding of sorts.

All the same, there will be times when the appropriate opportunity does not present itself to discuss a matter such as this with the other person. If you find at the moment that it isn't convenient to discuss what you are feeling with that person, take this opportunity to examine your own emotions instead. What part of your body is being physically affected; what part of your body feels the anxiety? Then deliberately feel love and gratitude, sending that energy to that part of your being, then radiating this energy to all of self. Unfortunately, there will be occasions, especially in the beginning of these teachings, when you may find it difficult to go into a state of love and gratitude. Please continue on, as anything of this nature takes patience on your part to master.

April 17, 2009
Learning to Find Oneness

The Akasie: At this time, we are working to help you find your way. There are many different techniques and tools that may be helpful in assisting you to relax and to find Oneness with love and gratitude. This is the reason we have instructed you to listen to your music much of the time. This is the reason we ask you to join us in the dance. The emotion that you experience during the dance takes you high into love and gratitude. At this time, this is the easiest way for you to expand your love.

We tell you to sit in your chair and look about you. What do you see? All is creation. All before you has taken thought and emotion from someone to create. Look to your couch, for example. What is it you see? You see the intricate design in the weave of the fabric. You see the style of the couch itself. To create this couch, there was much love felt by the persons who were involved in the creation of this piece of furniture, this piece of art! Think of the focus it took for these people to complete this. There was much that went into the design and the making of the product.

For the fabric alone, to be completed is truly amazing. For the artist to create the design, pulling together the rich colors, textures, and patterns is pure genius. It takes thought, emotion, and physical labor. This is the totality of creation and the end result is your fabric.

Every article about you has taken thought and emotion to have it come to completion. The person designing any product experiences much wonder and excitement upon creating something new. This is positive emotion. The artist felt much anticipation, pleasure, and yes, love in his or her heart in order to manifest his or her idea.

When you can look at an object and know that it was created with love, you have an easier time of being grateful for it. We say look about you and appreciate all that is before you.

Books may be used as another tool. Do you remember a time when you read perhaps a romance novel?

Tulro: Some people think these books are trashy and unnecessary! I tell you, everything is for purpose!

The Akasie: We go on. We had one who wanted to interject his opinion. Remember the last romance novel that you read? The book was colorful, descriptive, evoking emotions on every level of your being. The positive emotions you felt took you higher, raising your vibration. When you go higher with your vibration, this allows you to open to a higher level of spiritual awareness.

Now we take you to another modality, another tool. This one is the best, so we save it for last! We ask you to go with us on a journey to the great outdoors and awaken your senses, your awareness. Look at this as a new and grand adventure. Now remember, when you go you must look to everything like it is all new, foreign, and exotic to you; this is the very first time you have been to this place of amazement in nature.

Go back and experience this adventure as if you are once again a small child full of wonder. As a young one, you are thirsty to experience the senses, to see, to touch, to smell, to hear, and to taste everything! This is what a small child wants to do when he or she first encounters anything. As you look about, you are filled with a sense of newness and birth. You are eager to see all and experience all, but still you stop to linger at each thing that attracts your eyes to closely examine what you see.

As you walk outdoors, your world is instantly changed forever. You look down at your feet and see the sidewalk is made of red clay bricks that are rich in color, texture. The bricks are laid in such a way that they make a very interesting pattern. You ponder this design for a moment and admire the ingenuity of the brick layer.

Looking to the right, you notice a large yellow and black butterfly fluttering about. She gently lands on a cluster of purple flowers and drinks in the sweet nectar. As you take a closer look at the flowers, you see that each cluster is comprised of many tiny flowers; they look like little stars! You reach down to touch the butterfly. Surprised, she gracefully lifts herself and gently moves to another cluster of purple flowers.

The wide variety of flowers is enchanting! Some colors you see are vibrant and catch your attention quickly, while other colors are more subdued, soft, and unobtrusive. There are so many different shapes and sizes, so many shades of green! Take your time, young one, to take notice of all!

You move to the end of the walk and see a narrow path that takes you further into nature. How beautiful! Taking in a deep breath, you drink in the different fragrances of the grasses, the flowers, even the rich black soil. The path begins to wind and suddenly veers off to the left. You walk slowly, going down a gentle slope. With each step, you feel an unusual sensation. You catch the scent of pine. Looking down, you see the path is carpeted in dried pine needles that once clothed the magnificent pine tree that stands grandly before you. You take particular interest in the rough, irregular bark of the pine tree. You stop to touch the bark and feel the sticky sap that oozes out, noticing its distinct pine fragrance. The sweet smell takes you back to a childhood memory when you were carefree and innocent.

You wander off the path, wanting to experience the feel and smell of the green grasses. As you take a small step, you notice that the grass is so thick that it is much like walking on a plush carpet. Without hesitation, you decide to sit and remove your shoes and socks. You want to feel the cool dampness beneath your feet. It is so inviting to sit for a time in the grasses, to relax and feel the texture with your hands. You go further and lay in the grass to smell the fresh fragrance. The grass smells so alive! You wonder how long it has been since you have last allowed yourself this pleasure.

Looking up toward the heavens, you see the clouds slowly drifting by; they simply are in no hurry to get to their destination. You breathe deeply and feel with your entire being. You are in the now. You are one with all of creation.

You begin to notice with much detail that some of the sounds you hear are but a faint whisper while others are comparatively much louder, possibly even shrill. When you put your ear to the songs of nature, you can hear the sweet melodies. Our feathered friends, the birds, have much to sing about! The little ones, the insects, they do create quite a stir!

We tell you when you journey to the country sometimes you hear the coyotes communicating with their brothers and sisters in song to prepare for their night's hunt. You see, all creatures have the ability to sing their own song to communicate, to express their own desires.

Yes, even the resilient trees sing their own extraordinary song. Their leaves dance in the breeze. Their strong limbs sway in the wind. Listen, as they each have something to say, their own song to sing! Yes, even each plant has a particular way to express itself!

When you go outdoors and allow yourself to be one with nature, all of your senses are stimulated. Every creation has its own way of expressing itself, to communicate, and to procreate.

We tell you this, when you have difficulty raising your level of love and gratitude, use your physical senses and appreciate all that is around you. There is beauty in all. Find it and be grateful, for God has given you much. *We are One!*

April 28, 2009
Expression of Love

The Akasie: We have words of wisdom for you tonight. Special! We have all come to the place where we have grown to love and trust one another. So now, we will share this small bit of information with you.

Yesterday on our travels, we saw a special sight! Our way of thinking has been accepted by many. The thoughts are multiplying rapidly. Creation is beautiful! Please continue to send your positive thoughts, prayers, and emotions up to the cosmos, to our beloved Creator. It is a beautiful expression of love that we see. Yes, we want all to see, to experience this magnificent energy.

Every night I go to bed hoping that I will sleep well. I take these generic sleeping pills that get me to sleep fairly well, but every night I wake up and you are there. I hear you talk to me, and I am immediately engaged in conversation. Once I start talking to you, I can't seem to shut down. I am tired all of the time. What can I do differently so I can sleep better?

The Akasie: First and foremost, we wish you to affirm that you sleep well, all night and every night without interruption.

April 29, 2009
Why You Are Here on the Earth Plane

Quem: Being in the physical body is complex in nature. This is why we are with you always, guiding you along your journey. We guide you, our counterparts, in many ways. I remind you now that we are all One as we are all connected. We are together in what we do: evolve. The Akasie has agreed to guide the people alongside the many others from the many benevolent star nations. This universe is vast and there are many of us who have joined in this endeavor! Together, we have all agreed to assist in the ascension process of all creation. We are together in the awakening—the evolution of you, who are spiritual beings in the physical bodies: the merging of the soul, spirit, mind, and physical body all together to transcend all the negativity into beautiful love, the highest vibration known to all.

We tell you in order to transcend and transmute the negative energies into the positive energies you must first know that you are responsible for your own energy. You must remember that you are co-creators!

You are of the highest intelligence in physical form on the planet Earth at this time. You are the ones who are appointed to watch over our Mother Earth and all of her children. We speak of the humans. You are here to care for one another and also to care for the many creatures, big and small.

We are all one! We create together. This includes us, the angels, and many other energy beings who reside in the multiple dimensions.

We create together. We have a surprise for you. All creatures have thought and emotion. All creatures have intelligence no matter how small they are! They also contribute to mass consciousness. What we are telling you is of utmost importance! The mass consciousness controls what you are experiencing on the global level. Thought and emotion is energy. What you think and feel is what you create.

To be more specific we will break this down a bit. Be it known we are discussing one of the Universal laws, the law of attraction. What you think and feel is what you attract, no matter what it is that you are thinking and feeling whether it be negative or positive.

We go back a bit. Remember when we explained that Jackie was afraid of the negative entities? Jackie put much thought and focus on those negative entities in her home. Instead of standing firm and knowing she was safe, she questioned her safety. The fear created much negative emotion. The energy Jackie created was strong enough to take control of her, thus leaving her in a state of fear, anxiety, paranoia, and depression.

We tell you now, the correct discipline here is to affirm that you are safe at all times and that you are in control. Affirm that you have divine guidance and divine protection at all times. Know this! I remind you that you have angels all about. We, the Akasie are here to encourage you to ask your spiritual guides for assistance!

We go on here. When you have much love and gratitude for something, this energy that you are creating ascends and joins with like energy in the cosmos with our Creator.

We explain that you are creators on many different levels. You are all individuals and have the ability to create on a very personal level. We are speaking of your own personal reality.

You also have the ability to create on a planetary level. This is called mass consciousness. With the law of attraction, all of those thoughts that you have relating to the masses, like how your government operates, are being controlled by the mass consciousness. It is all done with thought. The majority that believes in a certain way controls the outcome.

We also say here that the collective creates by default, meaning when you are not focused on what you are thinking or feeling you get whatever the universe gives you. We hear you sometimes curse and grumble because of your particular experience. We tell you to take heed and know what you think and feel, as you receive this in abundance.

May 2, 2009
How Energy Works

Olim: Jackie, we have what you call a specific plan to your teaching. We work on a specific segment and then go on. That is how we do it. We don't jump around; you jump around. We must allow you time to process what we give you thoroughly before we move on. For now, please focus only on what I say.

To begin, we were discussing the process of how energy works. Look at yourself, how you feel when you are praying. The energy is high and is expanded greatly during your prayer time. Your emotions are heightened. We have listened to you when you pray, and we see your colors (your aura).

Also, we know that you are confused about how praying works compared to affirmations. Affirmations work with positive emotions as well as prayer. However, with prayer you ask for guidance, love, healing, and so on. With affirmations, you are affirming your well-being as well as another's well-being and so on. You see, both forms of communication are correct.

Affirmations attract energies that are like themselves, magnetically creating a mass of like-positive thoughts in the cosmos. This works the same with negative thoughts, as well as with imagination, wants, likes, and dislikes. Are you getting the idea here? This is how creation works. All things work for both positive and negative.

We, the Akasie seek positive in all we do. Jackie, you ask, "Who do these prayers go to? Who exactly are we asking to help us?" We say unto you, Jackie, those requests go up into the cosmos, connecting to like requests just as all thoughts do. We are here always to witness all that is said and felt by you. We are helpers, so to speak, in connecting you to what you have set your thoughts and emotions on. We assist in everything. Make no mistake here, your thoughts are extremely powerful! The strength or focus of your thoughts, be those thoughts positive or negative, will determine how quickly you manifest those thoughts into your physical reality.

Now to go on to why you are here; we told you that you were here to awaken. The experience of awakening is the greatest, most blessed gift ever.

You come to the earth to be in the physical, to consciously raise your love energy. As you know, at times it may be difficult to raise your love vibration. You must focus to keep your love vibration high for an extended period of time. You must place your full attention on your thoughts and emotions in order to successfully navigate around and through the dense third dimension of the earth plane. Like thoughts attract other like thoughts, negative thoughts, like positive thoughts, have a way of creating more of the same.

An example of this is when you are with someone who is being negative or has a "bad attitude." When you are in the company of those who are "having a time of it," you can either act or react to this negative energy that they are expressing.

Reacting is what you do when you are not in control of your own thoughts and emotions; therefore, you are not consciously aware of what you are doing. You see, to act is to be in control and thus be consciously aware, or mindful, of what is occurring. The desired goal is to be consciously aware of the dance of the energies. To be consciously aware of the negative and the positive energies of all players is to be in the now. To stay focused and positive is to be balanced.

Always think and feel before responding. Always examine the purpose behind what people say and why they say it, looking at the different viewpoints. You can then assess what is motivating them to say and do particular things. Nevertheless, you must allow them to have their experience without buying into it yourself. They are having this experience for a purpose.

You have seen the negativity in others. Sometimes this is merely a release of negative emotion like a valve that opens for hot water to spray relentlessly onto all that in its path. The hot water just goes wherever, toward whoever is in its path. Know this isn't the appropriate way to release negative emotion. We will discuss this later.

Other times this negativity has become a habit. What we speak of here is being constantly critical of others and ultimately all of creation. Be vigilant of your thoughts and emotions, of what you say and do. Make it a habit to seek the good in all.

The goal here is to always be aware of your mood, your attitude, and to be consciously aware of your feelings of love and gratitude. With this accomplishment, you continue to raise your vibration, taking you closer and closer to the fifth dimension.

This is not an overnight accomplishment. How long it takes you to consciously raise your vibration depends on how focused you are on your thoughts, emotions, and actions. How disciplined are you? Do you have a great desire to go forward?

May 4, 2009
Spiritual Rape

Tonight I flat out asked if the Akasie raped me. At first, they didn't respond. Maybe the reason the Akasie hesitated to answer me was because of the accusing tone of my voice or my choice of words. With more conviction and authority in my voice, I repeated my question. A few seconds passed without an answer, which for the Akasie is simply not the norm. I held my breath. A few more moments passed. Their response was that the Akasie energy did. Yes, they are confirming that the Akasie spiritually raped me.

Quem: The Akasie is a very large group, Jackie. We are from Pleiades like we told you. There is negative and positive with all of creation. This is the world of duality, which you perceive to be either good or bad. Many of you have come to a place in your understanding where you put labels on all people, things, and situations. You look at your TV screen and even describe the weather as being good or bad!

It seems to us that you on the Earth plane put everyone you know or don't know and everything you experience and haven't experienced into all of these nice little packages with pretty ribbons. Then you place each package away on the good shelf, the bad shelf, or the shelf that doesn't matter. Make no mistake here, we tell you that this is where you are at in your evolutionary process, and all is for purpose!

We, the Akasie, do not perceive anything as good or bad. We work with the energies to motivate all to move forward and to evolve.

As to your encounter—this teaching was allowed in order to reveal to you several things and to open your eyes, if you will. This was just another facet to the teaching. Those beings are of the Pleiadian origin, yes, and of our group, the Akasie. These particular beings have a specific task at hand to teach in this manner. As you remember, you did not set any intent whatsoever to whom you were calling upon to converse with you. This is not okay! We take you under our wing, so to speak, to teach you the correct way to communicate with light beings and all other beings as well.

What happened at that time was that we took you down; took your power from you. This is what you have believed to be so, but I tell you this is not so! You allowed your power to be taken from you!

When you failed to set the intention that you were working only with the Highest Most Divine Creative Awareness, we used this opportunity to teach you that there are many energy beings in the universe and beyond. It is of the utmost importance that you understand the complexity and the vastness of this place. You are on the Earth plane, and in the past you have relied solely on your eyes to show you what was before you. We are here to tell you that there is much more before you that you are unable to detect at this time. I am here to teach you of the unseen, the many energy forces that you, at this moment, have no understanding of. Always affirm and believe that you are working with The Highest Most Divine Creative Awareness. We have agreed to protect you always.

You were one of those who realized you must be protected somehow. At that time, what you did not understand was that all you had to have was love in your heart, and that you were and are divinely protected. Make no mistake this teaching was to educate you, and through you and this book our desire is to educate all those who seek the truth, the way, and the Light.

In the beginning, because you did not set your intention to work with only The Highest Most Divine Creative Awareness, you slipped easily into fear; you were not in control of your power. In reality, with each negative thought and emotion you created, you created more fear until that fear was so powerful that it controlled you, my dear. From this point on always, always know in your heart that you are safe, because you are always loved and protected by the Akasie.

We continue to give you teachings to help you to realize your boxes, those personal beliefs that no longer serve you or anyone else to the highest benefit. We are pleased to give you these teachings, these gifts. Know this, Jackie, that we give these gifts out of love for the highest good of all concerned.

May 5, 2009
The Role of the Akasie

The Akasie: Our role in your life is to keep you going toward your goal, your agreement. If you venture off your path, your higher self instructs us to direct you back on. If you continue to stay off of your path, we direct you with more strength until you listen! We will get creative, I tell you. At this moment, you are listening. We are not here to keep you company, only to keep you on your path. We are not here to talk "chatter." We are here to help you to expand your awareness by teaching you in a variety of ways. Live conversation is but one way.

Our way of teaching you to be in the now, to listen to your heart, to love yourself and others, to relax, to be flexible and appreciate the beauty of all, may be a bit unorthodox for some to understand. To allow is but one of the lessons you are to learn. It is your place to accept or reject teachings. It is not the place of your friends or family to make choices regarding the teachings given by us, the Akasie, to you. You are goddess of self; you decide. This is *your* life experience. Live it! Go where it takes you. Feel what is right for you in your heart space.

We tell you, this is an important time in your life. Much change is happening on many levels, and our place is also to comfort you during the changes that come. Know we are here out of love. We love all people, all things, and all of creation.

Know we are here to teach you to be your own person. You are learning to walk by yourself. Your training wheels are falling away. We are glad for you. The day is coming when we shall push you out of the nest. Maybe you will fall like one of your friends predicts, but we doubt this. No, we see you are a strong woman; we know you have what is needed to love all of creation and have the heart connection. We see your transformation now and in the future. We love you. *We are One!*

May 6, 2009

Guardian Team, In-Depth Learning, and Focusing on the Now

The Akasie: Jackie, the Akasie is a huge group of light beings from Pleiades. The three of us, Quem, Olim, and Colér, are a subgroup of the Akasie. We are together to teach. Today, we give you new information. We are a guardian team, yes, and we work together intimately. We know each other, live together, and travel together.

Some of us are not as highly evolved as you are, as we have not experienced what you have. Your physical time on the Mother Earth allows you more in-depth learning and more challenge.

Are there any beings still on Pleiades?

The Akasie: Yes, there are many. We come and go as we please.

I feel this underlying exhilaration like an underground spring that has tremendous pressure behind it. Any moment the water will burst through the earth's surface, creating a new stream or river.

The Akasie: You feel as if you are on the cusp of something huge, something grand. You are! We cannot begin to explain what is happening to you. Let's focus on the here and now, okay?

Tomorrow, I tell you it would be beneficial to visit your land south of here and dig in the rich soil for a few hours. Take time to lie in the Mother's arms (on the fertile soil.) She loves you much. This will relieve much tension and help to balance you.

May 7, 2009
Looking for My Truth

These days I am looking into my heart for my truth. I am beginning to understand the teachings, but at other times, I just feel confused!

May 8, 2009
Oneness

During the night I woke up and felt so pure, so at peace, so perfect. I was still in a very relaxed state and in the deepest recesses of my being, and I knew I had felt this before. The feeling was of total Oneness.

May 8, 2009
The Labyrinth and the Manipulation of Time

I have been thinking about the Native American retreat I attended last summer. Something happened during that time that has really aroused my curiosity. This had been my first retreat at this place and it was during a lunch break that several of us were visiting when a woman began talking about an energy labyrinth that was located within walking distance.

A couple of the people in the group decided to go "experience" it. I decided to join them.

Whoever built the labyrinth had somehow dowsed the area, locating the energy centers and created what they called a chakra labyrinth. This labyrinth was created specifically to feel the energies associated with the chakras. There were designated points along the labyrinth that resonated with the seven main chakras in the physical body. The first stop was for the root chakra. The last stop in the very center of the labyrinth would be for the crown. You would then turn back the way you came, going through each energy center and stopping to once again let the energy build. I stood there and felt my vibration rise. Then I moved on to the next energy center.

Because I had another session scheduled in thirty minutes, I felt rushed. In order to get the full impact of the experience, I had to be relaxed and allow the energies to build. I only had time for a quick walk through, but even so, the energies felt wonderful to me!

So, my question is: Could I have gone back in time so I could have spent as much time as I wanted at the labyrinth and still arrived on time for the next session?

The Akasie: Yes, this is possible. You believe and you know in your mind and in your heart that you have all the time in the world. Be in total Oneness with Self and in the now. Time will stand still as you know it.

May 9, 2009

Ancient Ways and the Hierarchy within the Akasie

The Akasie: Jackie, as we have told you before, the Akasie is a very large group of star beings from Pleiades. Within the Akasie group are many subgroups. Each group is involved with numerous activities. Each individual has specific interests and plays a particular role in the group they are affiliated with. Over time, those interests may evolve or change entirely. It is much like you here on the Earth plane. You have certain interests during all segments of your lives. You will find that when you were younger perhaps you were more drawn to a particular subject such as racing cars. As you grew more mature, perhaps your interests grew more refined and you wanted to learn to build the engines for the fast cars. Later, perhaps you veered off into another direction totally and wanted to learn to grow a vegetable garden. These are areas of interest, and when you hold a specific interest, you may be drawn to people who hold the same type of interests. Groups may be formed by these people to gain a more expanded, formal, or organized way to experience these interests. Perhaps the group evolves even further by birthing the desire to share their interests with others so they begin to teach in an organized fashion. The reason I am explaining this to you is because it is the same with us. We have the love for all of creation, but we also have passions for certain types of projects, endeavors, and people!

You wonder how you came to be with us. When consciousness was born, you were with us in the star system of Pleiades. No matter where you reside in your ascension process, we watch over you always. We have agreed to always hold you near, to protect you, to assist you in any way we can, to teach you with the words when you were ready to hear. In addition, we give you the healing energies to assist you in releasing the many blocks that have taken residence in the physical and etheric bodies.

You have many who visit you from our group, the Akasie, and this coming and going confuses you. Those who gather in your presence come to greet you with the intent to exchange the love energy. Many know that you are an open channel now, and they wish to share with you in any way they can. The Akasie is a large and diverse group, and there are those who are particularly interested in the books that we write.

A group came to you this morning and they introduced themselves as "Telbar." This is one of the subgroups in the Akasie. We prefer to use the name "the Akasie"; Telbar is not necessary in most cases, as using the subgroup name invites division. We prefer unity, Oneness in the Akasie, but there are certain groups that are involved in specific tasks. On occasions that we deem necessary, we will use the subgroups name. At some point, you will learn what the groups specialize in. Within every organization, you will find that there are central points or persons in higher command that will oversee a bigger, more diverse area. It is like this in your America and in all of your organized institutions. There must be leadership in your government, your companies of employment, your places of worship, your schools systems, and even the charitable organizations. You even see leadership in the home.

We are a benevolent nation. We are a peaceful and forth-coming group of beings. The leadership of our nation is one of a loving nature with much wisdom. New ideas are always welcome to be put on our table for discussion. To allow new ideas is to expand and grow as a people and a nation; to evolve and to go higher into the Light.

Telbar is involved in the creation of written material for the use of the people on the planet Earth at this time. Yes, there are those who give the words to be written. This modality of communication and teaching has been in existence for thousands of years. Yes, Miss, there have been those who have channeled the words for us all of this time. When a new one such as you opens up to this way of communication, it is a glorious time for celebration. We rejoice!

Telbar is an ancient word meaning "to come." We form a group, giving that group a name that states our intention. You now have a different perspective, a different way to look at the meaning of our words, our names.

May 11, 2009
Dreamers

The Akasie: Jackie, listen to this! Drunvalo Melchizedek speaks well! He says you are all dreamers; this is the law of attraction! To dream is to imagine. You must take responsibility for your thoughts. As time quickens, you become more focused and powerful. Extraordinary events are about to unfold!

We prepare you by teaching you. We must go at your pace or you will not attain the required level of master manifestor. You see, you must connect to your heart always and think in a positive manner. We must continue to write the book as well, as we *all are One.*

May 13, 2009
Positive Energy

Quem: Yes, today we have come to uplift you! Feel the joy, the love, and the gratitude for being here now! Today is for you, made especially for you! Feel the love surrounding you, coming down to you, flowing through you, and merging with your essence. You are the love. Ah, there it is in your heart, radiating outward from your essence, your body! There the love goes back to whence it came. *We are One!*

May 14, 2009
To Heal and Balance

Today Scott I and drove down to our eighty acres. We come down as often as we can to walk, hunt, and dream of our future. We have always wanted a log cabin, and this is perfect place to build one! At some point, there must have been a home here because there are the remains of a walk that goes to some steps, an outhouse, and many varieties of flowers that line the drive.

Shortly after we bought the land, I went exploring and found a cluster of three very large cedar trees. Inside the cluster was a nice private area that was well protected from the elements. Right there in the middle of the trees was an old hand-dug well that someone had put an old wooden sign on top of, I assume because the well went dry. Of course, you don't want anyone to fall in. Not cool! Beside the well is a depressed rectangular area measuring about 4' x 12' lined with flat native stones. To me, it looked like someone had dug out this rectangle pit and lined these flat stones around it. Now, the area is mostly filled in with soil, some barbed wire, and a tree stump. I didn't like the idea that we had this area full of junk, so I decided to clear it out while Scott was out doing whatever guys do. I considered myself to be on an archeological dig. Who knows what I might find buried deep in the soil? What fun!

So far, I have found lots of old glass and hundreds of nails. It must have been a dump site at one time. Some of the old timers say that root cellars became a place to put trash that could not be burned.

The area intrigued me, but also to physically sit on the earth and sift through the soil felt so good! I had found some different gauges of chicken wire to sift the soil in buckets. The activity has been a wonderful way to relieve the tension and to ground myself.

Oh, wow! It was shortly after I began to communicate with the angels that we found this parcel of land! We had literally been looking for years for a place like this; no coincidence I bet. I have experienced so much in such a short time. I am still so confused, and I still feel like I don't entirely understand what is really happening to me. There has been and still is so much pain inside that I need to release. What I am doing is very symbolic in nature. When I remove the sharp objects from the Mother Earth, I am releasing the anxiety and pain that is inside of me. We both need healing.

After I had moved dirt for what seemed like hours, my back was beginning to ache. I decided to check the time and maybe take a short break. I picked up my cell phone and checked the time. It was 2:22 p.m., which for me means: "Going back to what I love." Ah, a gift! I decided to sit and write for a few minutes, and thought maybe I would read awhile after I finished writing.

Suddenly, I realized that my guides had been extremely quiet all of this time, so I asked if they had anything to say. A quick response came with much authority, "Yes!" I was startled by their response! The Akasie wasted no time in telling me to "get back to digging because break was over!" I could hear the laughter and smiled.

They went on to say that they wanted me to enjoy our Mother Earth and all she has to offer. "Get your nose out of the book!" I agreed to read at home. If I was to take a break, I was to look around and notice all the beauty that the Mother had to share with me.

May 14, 2009

What Are Those Lights in the Sky?

Later that evening, I was relaxing at home out on my patio. For some time, I just laid there on my lawn recliner, staring up at the evening sky. The sunset was nearing and I was enjoying just being still, doing absolutely nothing. I have always been a "busy" person, and to be able to lie still without guilt was a beautiful gift. The Akasie continue to advise me to enjoy myself throughout the day and to find the beauty in all. I must allow myself to relax, go into love and gratitude, and do things that bring me joy and happiness.

As I was staring up into the sky, I noticed these tiny lights flitting in all directions. They were like miniature shooting stars only they were going in all directions! And there were hundreds, if not thousands of them! Silently I asked the angels what I was seeing. "Are they some sort of bugs?" I wasn't able to see any actual bug bodies. What on earth could they be? What I could see was an energy that I couldn't describe. What I was seeing was much like a tiny light. What were they?

The angels said they were in fact tiny bugs. I have never seen anything like it and I was enchanted! I kind of suspect the lights may have been something other than bugs.

May 15, 2009

Gratitude

Today, I woke up running! I had an appointment and didn't allow myself the time I needed to go within, center, and give thanks. I recognized the anxiety in my gut and began to pray, "Please give me peace. I know that I am in disharmony with

Spirit. Please help me to allow the love to flow through me so I may feel the love once again."

May 16, 2009
Manipulating the Energies and Energy Symbols

I woke up during the night. Like so many other nights, I began to think of past events. For some reason I remembered the leak in my roof. Last year we had sustained hail damage to our home, and it was time to replace our roof. Just a short time after we had our roof replaced, I noticed a wet spot on the ceiling of an upstairs bedroom. Needless to say, I wasn't happy with the roofers. Once I had heard that the angels could fix anything, and they would if they were asked with love and gratitude. I remembered that when I had asked the angels to repair the leak the roof did stop leaking.

For some reason, I wanted to be assured that my roof was truly repaired even though the roof hadn't leaked in a few months. Also, I wanted to understand how they fixed it! I asked them if they had fixed the leak, and the Akasie said yes, and gave me a symbol which consisted of two triangles with the points facing inward, touching tip to tip. This symbol reminded me of the multitude of other symbols that they had already shown me.

Quem: There are infinite energies and infinite energy symbols. We have shown you only one of these symbols. This particular symbol consists of two triangles joined horizontally at the tip. Yes, the symbol looks much like an infinity symbol only with straight lines.

The energy symbol depicts the type of energy that we created to be used to repair the damage to your roof. If you could see this particular energy, it would look much like the symbol we have shown you. This energy has a particular frequency and spins with particular intention, speed, and direction. We create energy from our thoughts, sending it to the place needing the repair. All fifth dimensional beings have the ability to do this level of energy work.

While we are on the subject of energy, I would like to take this opportunity to reiterate that, yes, we create energy from thought. We can also disrupt energy with thought. We talk of anything electrical. You have noticed that we can and do disrupt your CD player or clock radio when we want to give you pause. We laugh because at this exact moment when you were receiving these words to type, I made a popping sound in your wall. We both had a good laugh just then. You are no longer frightened of our disruptions in your gadgets. We are pleased.

For you, the clock radio-CD player is a common gadget that we make use of to get your attention. When your CD gets stuck, it is because we create a disruption in the flow of energy. We do the same thing with the digital clocks. We let the numbers roll!

At first, you thought your CD player was broken, or that possibly the CD was dirty or scratched. Maybe you had static or even dust particles on the inside of the device. These are all logical explanations. There was a time when you were ready to buy a new CD player. I tell you, China has a good market on these digital clocks and other technical devises because of us. Oh, well. Now, you know it is we who play havoc with the music on your players and the numbers on your clocks. This is all for the purpose of drawing your attention to something of importance. One reason may be to remind you that we are here with you at all times to guide and protect you. We love you.

We also disrupt the flow of the energy for other purposes. Take note of the precise time of disruption. What is it that you are creating with your thoughts and emotions?

This disruption is a way for us to get your attention. What is occurring is unusual; take notice! This is our attempt to say, "Please pay attention here." We are here to assist you. When the one in our care continues to disregard our attempts to communicate, the guides come together in discussion and contemplate our methods of communication. "Do we continue to disrupt the energy? Do we try something else, or do we stop these types of communications for a time?" It depends entirely on the individual and the situation. Is the person ready to listen? Often we come together to perform assessments on you and the others we work with to determine how we wish to proceed.

May 17, 2009
Slow Down and Enjoy Life

The Akasie: What we want to say to you today is that you have many irons in the fire—too many. Get good at one thing, and then move on. Forgo the work on meditation for now until you become more relaxed. You question this, but we tell you, you are creating negative emotion concerning when to meditate, how long to meditate, and even what the results of your mediation should be! For now, for your health and peace of mind, it would be best to slow down and enjoy life. Jackie, life is a precious gift! *We are One!*

May 20, 2009
Student Teaching and the Ego

Quem: Today was a fine day for you. You experienced a few opportunities to teach. Well done! You felt happiness and contentment. Although you sensed that something about the way you felt concerning your teaching wasn't appropriate, you asked if your ego was possibly involved. We said, "Yes, your ego was involved, is involved." You are sure we are correct. Jackie, what I saw was smug satisfaction, because you felt you knew a little more about the subject you were speaking on than the others. Maybe you felt you were in a higher place than them, that you were better because you have overcome some adversity. You felt this may somehow confirm that you are more advanced than them.

Watch yourself, young lady, as this is where many get caught up in service—the fall. This is ego that is taking control. You must learn that you are here to serve as a facilitator. You are a channel, a teacher, and a healer. When you view yourself as better or possibly as more knowledgeable than the others, you are placing yourself in a box that will not serve anyone to their highest good. You all are learning life lessons that are different yet connected, leading you to the same place—the Light.

You are all here to awaken the spiritual aspect of who you are in the physical; to remember who you are. With the awakening, your vibration rises and enables you to go forth with your steps, ultimately taking you to the fifth dimension.

This is the goal. It is happening now, I tell you! Watch yourself; be vigilant of your thoughts and emotions, specifically your ego. We tell you to continue to pray and affirm all that is positive with much emotion. We wait for you, Jackie. We wait for all of you to remember who you are and to remember you are not alone! *We are One!*

May 21, 2009
These Are Exciting Times: Changes Are Coming Rapidly

The Akasie: We have news for you! We are excited to see Essemotial ("Esse") and Jithury, for they have come home to share their experience with us all. They went to visit many other star people. That is why they have been absent for so many days, although they were both with you for the Native American ceremonial sweat that you attended. We tell you that they do come home to check in periodically.

The news is they have met some new people and have heard some exciting stories. These people told Esse and Jithury that those under their care are awakening more quickly. Everyone is busy! Everyone is excited! People in human form are traversing.

People have felt the negativity so strongly that they are finally realizing that this energy is affecting them on every level of their being.

This can be used as a huge step in the awakening process for those who look deeper. They all require assistance and guidance in changing their thoughts to become more positive.

We speak of a sequence of changes beginning with their thoughts and emotions, and then proceeding forward to their speech patterns, then ultimately their actions. This is wonderful to hear the others speak about such changes in the human race!

We are so very grateful and so very happy! Gratitude for this change in the mass consciousness is manifesting all more rapidly. Please affirm that all the peoples of the New Earth remember that they are spiritual beings who have chosen the Earth plane to experience all things in the physical in all of their glory. *We are One!*

May 25, 2009
Spiritual Warfare: Are You in Control?

Jackie, you have been interested in the term "spiritual warfare" for some time. Spiritual warfare is not engaging in your opponent's release of negativity that appears to be directed at you. You step aside and let the energy die.

The example we give you is when you had your last garage sale. An older gentleman who was very forward in his demeanor felt he was entitled to purchase items way below your set price; this engaged you in spiritual warfare. This man was an opponent. He used negative energy to engage you. Set your price, be firm, and use humor. Do not engage with anger or compete with the other to "win."

Oh, yes! I felt a lot of negative energy on that one. I knew instinctively at the time that I should have been able to maneuver the conversation so it would have had less of a negative effect on everyone, but I grew angry because this man thought he was entitled.

May 25, 2009
Who Is the Government?

The Akasie: Another subject you have questioned, Jackie, as with many others, is the integrity of that Bush fellow since he showed up in the oval office as your President. You questioned his ability and his integrity to govern all of the United States, not to mention his ability to negotiate with heads of state from other countries. Many of you have listened to his sugarcoated words for at least one good reason. This is to show you that it is imperative to take back "your power." At the time President Bush was in office, the people chose not to stand for themselves. You allowed the government to take you to the cleaners. Will you continue on your passive ways?

To see a true improvement in how the United States operates you must all take action and responsibility for self. You are the people; you are the government. Why, we hear you talk as if government is a separate entity! Is this the way your forefathers set up this great nation? We should say not! America was intended to be a nation *"by the people, for the people."* Look at what became of your America (note this is past tense). This signifies an end of an era. All must go forward!

We renew and go forward with new leadership, justice, and a black man to add to the mix; no pun intended. It is time for the people to realize that you all are spiritual beings. Does it truly matter what color your skin is? You take off the skin and you all are the same physically. Look deeper than the skin and see the true nature of the man.

We believe in your new President Obama. He has a multitude of positive qualities. He has a strong, reliable sense of what is right and wrong, being fully able to discriminate opposing views and to keep his power in check. He knows spiritual warfare. Yes, he is well-versed. We are pleased to know him and work with him.

At this moment, I wish for you, good people of this planet, to go back in your recorded history to a time when your President Abraham Lincoln held office for your great United States of America.

The Gettysburg Address

Dated November 19, 1863

Fourscore and seven years ago, our fathers brought forth on this continent, a new nation, conceived in Liberty, and dedicated to the proposition that all men are created equal.

Now we are engaged in a great civil war, testing whether that nation, or any other nation so conceived and so dedicated, can long endure. We are met on a great battlefield of that war. We have come to dedicate a portion of that field, as a final resting place for those who here gave their lives that that nation might live. It is altogether fitting and proper that we should do this.

But, in a larger sense, we cannot dedicate—we cannot consecrate—we cannot hallow—this ground. The brave men, living and dead, who struggled here, have consecrated it, far above our poor power to add or detract. The world will little note, nor long remember what we say here, but it can never forget what they did here. It is for us the living, rather, to be dedicated here to the unfinished work which they who fought here have thus far so nobly advanced. It is rather for us to be here dedicated to the great task remaining before us—that from these honored dead we take increased devotion to that cause for which they gave the last full measure of devotion—that we here highly resolve that these dead shall not have died in vain—that this nation, under God, shall have a new birth of freedom—and that government of the people, by the people, for the people, shall not perish from the earth.

This work written by your late President Lincoln gave credence to the fact that all men are created equal. He clearly states that the government is *"of the people, by the people, and for the people."* It is obvious in this work that he so diligently wrote that this was his truth. He wrote these words and they have been read by the majority of Americans. These words are part of your history. These words are monumental!

These words act as a powerful affirmation that you are powerful and that you stand tall; you are in control of your destiny. Your peoples stand firm in this knowing! Yet you slide back and let others have control and take your power from you. The Akasie say these words out of love. We know that the darkness comes before the light. This is the way of evolution. You take steps back in order to go forward. It is the way. Know this. *We are One!*

May 27, 2009
Kind Acts for Mother Earth

Jithury: Jackie, I have been traversing to many star nations. I take witness to the great rumbling in the heavens. The many who are in alliance and meet within the great halls of the Grand Council of the Galactic Federation and who reside in continuance for the Commissions of Earth Affairs speak of the positive changes taking place on the Earth plane. Those in attendance of these meetings are much excited about what is happening on your New Earth! Those in attendance have seen and heard first hand that many people of the Earth are speaking kindly of her and to her. They are now realizing how indifferent, even hateful they have been to her for many years past!

A newness, a change, is sweeping the nations. The energy is sweeter. The vibration is higher and more pure. We still have a ways to go, but at the same time, we are already there! Confusing for you?

Knowledge of this brings you into love and gratitude. If I, Jithury, went to all places and told of this happening, imagine what would occur! Just think! This is the universal law of attraction!

Earlier this morning we spoke to you of the negative and positive energies, of how there must be a balance of energies always. To have balance you must have negative energy (the darkness) and positive energy (the light.) Think of your black and white photographs that have the whitest white to the blackest black and all shades therein. If there were only white, what would white or the positive energy illuminate?

Because your existence is in the third dimension, the Earth plane, you must experience the duality of the energies. In order to evolve you must experience the negative energies in addition to the positive energies.

This negative energy is what is uncomfortable and is the catalyst to encourage growth and ultimately push you forward. If there was only positive energy or only negative energy, you would not receive the gift. The gift we speak of is the awakening, to remember who you are.

With the negative and positive energies, the people come here to play out different roles and to move the energy. You all come to contribute to the New Earth by creating. All come here for the chance to awaken, which is the most beautiful time of life! This experience you will always remember! *We are One!*

May 29, 2009
Clairvoyance: The Gift of Sight

I can hear your words clearly, and I am grateful that I receive the teachings. I want to be able to see with my physical eyes the spirit guides who work with me, however, and I also want to see those who have passed on. They continue to linger for reasons unknown, and some of them need assistance to move on to the other side. I want to be able to see you in the physical!

I don't want to seem greedy here, but I have been affirming and praying for this gift for several months now. I don't understand why my affirmations are not working. Before I began to receive the words for this book, I wanted to work with the families who had lost loved ones. In order to truly assist them and give them comfort, I think it would be easier if I could see who I am working with.

The Akasie: With the gift of sight, you are able to see the unseen that still walk the Earth. Sometimes they are called the forgotten ones. You have not received this gift in its entirety. Remember that you do see, Miss, with your third eye.

The spirits who have lived on the Earth plane and have passed on before you may communicate with you in a variety of ways. Do not discount your abilities that you have already mastered! You have received many communications already from those who linger in this world unseen and untouched by those in the third dimension. Continue to affirm that you receive the gift that you desire. For now, I give you this. You will not see us, your guides, like ghosts or apparitions, but as beautiful stars that shine brightly in the night for we are not of the physical realm.

May 30, 2009
The Fifth Dimension

Quem: People come to Earth to awaken. Each incarnation is a big gamble. All dominos have to be in a row, so to speak, for the awakening to come about. There must be an intense desire for spiritual growth and love for all. I am speaking of the law of attraction.

To come to Earth, the people must first accept the role of traversing through difficult times for the opportunity to awaken.

To awaken means to become alive with God's love. This is to love unconditionally without judgment, allowing others to experience their own lives, circumstances, and make their own choices, which are incidentally all learning opportunities that take them further and higher to the fifth dimension.

May 31, 2009
Those Who Serve

Quem: There are many who have ascended high and are now in service to all of creation. I speak of the ascended masters, the archangels, and all of the light beings from the many nations in the universe. You have also come to this place to be of service to all.

I tell you that you have come to the place in your spiritual growth that you realize you have kept this ego well fed for some time. You finally understand that this ego of yours has kept you from feeling with your heart. This ego is a part of you that is most necessary in order for you to see and understand the full scope of what lies before you.

You allowed your ego to build many boxes and that same ego has kept you imprisoned in those very boxes. These boxes have been constructed with fear, specifically fear of the unknown.

You are living in the physical world. This physical plane is one that gives you promise that all is to be seen with the eyes, but I tell you that all before you is an illusion. At this time, there is much before you that you are unable to see, to feel, or to even know. This place you live is the world of the physical. You have come to this world to feel with all of your senses and to know your emotions. This world is an illusion of sorts to get you to dig deeper, to look within yourselves to find your truth.

You come to this world and you live for the material. At some point, when you realize the material world no longer serves you, has never served you to your highest good, you will question why you wish to live this way.

The material world consists of inanimate objects. These objects do not have the capability to love. Yes, you can appreciate these things that have been crafted by the humans; that is precisely what they are for, to help you to see that there is beauty in all. Make no mistake that these are merely things that consequently do not have thought, emotion, or the power to love.

Look about you and see what is before you. Things can and will be replaced, but people cannot be replaced. People are gifts that have been placed in your lives for the purpose of exchanging love energy. You are to love the others as they are to love you. It is the way, you see?

When you begin to see that this is the way, you will appreciate the others on a level that, up until this time, you could not even imagine. I tell you when you appreciate the others on this level, you are ready to serve. *We are One!*

June 1, 2009
Guidance

The Akasie: It is important for you to understand that we only will guide those of you who ask for guidance and clarity. Take time to listen and ask yourself what it is that you feel and what you require for us to assist you with.

Jackie, you know that you have not listened and processed properly. I am talking about how you feel concerning the teachings.

Quite honestly, I am so busy writing down and recording what you say to me—You are correct; I haven't taken the time to understand my emotions concerning the teachings. Really, I don't know what I feel. This is all so new and surreal! You are certainly correct about me identifying what I need assistance with. I thought I was doing well by affirming that I receive the guidance that is for the highest good of me and for all of creation. I didn't realize that I must be specific!

Quem: The big factor here is that you are so busy conversing with us that you have not set aside time to know what you're feeling! Miss, you haven't done anything wrong. I am merely showing you how to broaden your scope. It is time for you to understand that you have feelings and choices concerning all that involves you! Perhaps it is time that you begin to identify where you would like to direct your attention. Work to strengthen your focus and listen to self, your heart.

What is it you desire the most?

June 2, 2009
Our Mission on Earth

The people have much courage to come here to Earth at the time of the Great Renaissance. You all have a particular mission to accomplish here on Earth. Yours, Jackie, is to share yourself through the written word that is only available by the way of the angels, the masters, and the spirit guides who agree to work with you.

We are here to guide, teach, heal, and most of all, love you and all of creation. Opportunities continually present themselves to help you along your way.

Most importantly, we have specific work to do. We all agreed to assist in particular projects that are very important for those who seek knowledge and are awakening. They must have guidance, a direction of some sort! We want to take part in teaching all to learn the art of listening to their guides and the angels who have agreed to come here to work with them by showing them the way! These teachings that we share will serve as a gate and will open up the communication between the reader and the Highest and Most Divine Creative Awareness. We give this information through this book we write now! *We are One!*

June 3, 2009
Be Grateful for the Beauty That You Receive: Climate Changes

The Akasie: Today we talk about the imminent climate changes. For several years, you have noticed a few changes right here in the Midwest. We are here to tell you that all of this is normal. Yes, you have more moisture this season than usual. This is making your lives a little happier to know you do not want for pure water. You have more than enough!

Why not be grateful for all the rains? You have all that you need to sustain life here. With the rains, the grasses continue to maintain vibrant shades of green. When the wind blows the grasses move as if dancing to their favorite song. It is so beautiful to see! Sit, watch, and lose yourself in the movement.

The temperature … what do we have to say about that? Nothing. There is nothing so out of ordinary about the fluctuation of your temperatures. This has always been the way of the weather system! Relax!

So you have a few storms? All is okay. That is Thunder Being doing his work; cleansing all the impurities from the air that you breathe. He does fine work. We are well pleased that he does all that he does. He moves the energy so nothing grows stagnant. The energies must move constantly! Thunder Being keeps working to make sure this happens.

What about Mother Earth? What does she have to say about the climate fluctuations? She grows weary of the constant changes. Not only does she endure the continuous fluctuations of the temperature, but she endures the geographical changes as well! The land masses are constantly changing in size and appearance. We have given the name Mother to this planet because of that which she does. She gives birth to newness. She is a creator just like you are.

Something miraculous occurs each new moment. The Mother is a unique entity. She has all that she requires to sustain life. She is surrounded by her brothers and sisters in the planetary system that provide particular and precise energies that enhance all that she does. Your sun comforts the Mother as he warms her skin with his golden rays. Nothing can grow here on this plane without his assistance.

In the same manner, the rains bring life to your planet. All who reside here depend on this gift of the rains to keep all of creation in balance.

The Moon's energy creates a magnetic pull. The waters follow this magnetic tide in a dance of their own! All in the universe is on the go! All goes forward with creation. To cease to create is to cease to live. Without the moon's energy, the planetary cycles would cease to exist. I tell you all is for a purpose and all is alignment. Each entity has its own force and its own function.

We speak of the great bodies of water. These consist of your oceans, lakes, rivers, and streams. Ah, remember the puddles that are created after the rain has come! The rains give unto all life, as water is life! These bodies of water are another world unto themselves, exotic in all manner! The diversity and abundance in everything about you is beyond your imagination.

The varieties of life (and we include the human beings), that abound on the Mother Earth; each contributes in his or her own way and each brings joy to this planetary existence! You are given all that you require in order to go forth and flourish in this physical reality.

The planet that you reside on at this time, the great Mother Earth, is an entity, a being that is constantly in motion, birthing newness. All are connected. *We are One!*

June 5, 2009
Heaven

Quem: When you leave your physical body, your spirit continues on. Where you go after you leave the physical body depends on where the people of the Earth are in the ascension process. You do ascend into the heavens when you are ready for that transition, but exactly which level of heaven you arrive at depends on you, on your soul's mastery. While on Earth, you are not aware of your soul's mastery on a conscious level.

June 6, 2009
Love

Jithury: Jackie, thank you for your prayer. You wish to give us something in return for what it is we do for you. We will gladly accept something beautiful from you ... in fact, we think we know what we would like. I, and the others are in agreement to this. The three of us say we only want love from you.

June 6, 2009
As It Should Be

Quem, Colér, and Olim: Jackie, you have come a long way in your steps in just a short time. We are happy to have this time with you to assist, teach, heal, love, and to do anything we can that we are permitted to do that will help you reach your goals. You have questioned us on how well you are doing on your growth. You wonder if you can spiritually grow fast enough, so you will not have to come back to Earth.

This being an infant is something you do not wish to endure again! We know you do not wish to have the challenges that an infant or young child has. You do not wish to have your conscious memory wiped clean again. You say it is all trivial and you wish to move on. We laugh at this, because when you think on this, it is the infants who have it made! During that period of time in your life, you receive much care from a mother and a father. You are held closely with much love. You are looked upon as perfect in all ways.

Well, that is certainly one way to look at being a baby. Being a baby is the most vulnerable time of our lives! A baby depends on others for everything! In order for a baby to survive and be healthy in all levels of his being, he must have a balanced upbringing. To get parents who have the skills to achieve this is a very rare occurrence.

My real issue here is my memory. I feel that I am having an exceptional life. Finally, I am where I feel I should be, and I am fearful that I will not get to this place again. I don't want to lose my momentum or forget all that I have worked to learn. Do you understand?

Quem: I hear what you say and understand that you are fearful of not attaining this level of awareness during your next incarnation. Know that all is for a purpose and all is as it should be. Trust what I say to you, my child.

We work with you in segments. All of what you question will be answered at the appropriate time. You are torn because you know that fear creeps in, and you fully understand that this is negative energy that you are creating. There is never judgment on our part toward you. You are just as you should be. All grow or ascend at their own pace. It is our place to allow your choices always, as you have free will. Also, it is our place to assist you when we are called upon.

We tell you this: we work with you on more than one level of your consciousness. Until you are aware that we are here to assist you and you intentionally seek our assistance, we carry out what your higher conscious mind instructs us to do. You see, we wait until you are ready to work with us on a conscious level. We wait until you ask for the assistance that we so desire to give you.

Remember, it is not a race to see who gets to the top (highest level of heaven) first. It is a mass conscious effort for all to evolve and ascend together. *We are One!*

June 7, 2009
The Body Is Beautiful

The Akasie: Jackie, we tell you that you have a beautiful body. In your eyes, you see imperfection. You think that no one has a perfect body. What is perfect? But look, your body is beautiful and it is perfect! Look at the complexity of the body; the workings are fine, exact, and precise in every detail! Yes, look how your healing system works. The energy is perfect! Everything about the body is beautiful and perfectly designed by the Creator!

Those struggling with ego are rarely happy with their physical appearance. You come here fully expecting to remember who you are. You are of the Divine, but yet you are of the physical. This puts you in a precarious position. You have come here to this physical plane to learn to love yourself and accept yourself as you are, but instead you find yourself faced with all this negativity. You are here to learn to overcome this way, this negativity. *We are One!*

June 8, 2009
Take Notice of Your Thoughts

The Akasie: Each lifetime you receive an intricate apparatus, the body to carry you through your travels here on the physical plane. You are to care for this body with love and respect.

This is important, so please listen closely. Your body listens to everything you think, say, and do about it and with it. With your thoughts, words, and actions, you are constantly programming and reprogramming your body to perform a certain way. The longer you think a certain way the more ingrained the program becomes.

All of your life you have looked into your mirrors and saw what you believed to be imperfection. Your face wasn't beautiful. Your teeth weren't straight. Your hips were too wide to suit you. You see, we could go on with this, but you get the idea. Every single day when you looked at yourself this is what you saw and what you thought! You openly talked to others about your many flaws and imperfections. Why, it is a common topic of discussion to speak of the flaws of the body! When you shopped for clothing, you mercilessly criticized yourself for these seemingly imperfect features.

These are negative thoughts and emotions. Every time you thought about how imperfect you were, you felt bad; you felt ugly. You convinced your conscious mind that you were imperfect!

Most of you don't even realize that you are having these thoughts, they are so subtle. Take notice of your thoughts! It is time to love yourself and be grateful for your body. When you create positive thoughts and emotions concerning your body, you are healing it! You are giving your body the healing energy of love.

June 9, 2009
The Dance

The Akasie: Jackie, although you have no conscious memory of this, you have always known us, as we have worked with you through each and every one of your lifetimes. You have a strong loving relationship with the five of us.

When Quem danced with you, you felt the deepest love, gratitude, admiration, and respect for him. This love you feel toward him is different somehow than how you feel for the rest of us. When Quem danced with you, you loved his movements; his energy was pure, strong, and full of love. This energy was such that you have not felt anything like it in this physical life of yours.

He is Quem and this is his style. His love is expressed this way to you and in other ways also, but for you, the dance has grown into more than just a dance that is an expression of love and joy. Somehow, you feel that this emotion must be wrong! You dance with an angel and feel so much love that the dance turned into something dirty and unacceptable!

Quem: I take over this one because what you speak of involves me! Oh my, this is the story.

When physical beings feel this intense love coupled with the vibration, it can and often will be confused as if it has sexual undertones. Jackie, you are in a human body and your senses are alive! When you receive an energy that is so pure, your physical senses will heighten. Make no mistake: others have walked the same path as you. As angels, we feel love on an extremely intense level. You have no idea what it can be like—*is like*—to go this high! We wish to take you with us. However, you are still in the human body. You are unable at this time to feel this love, so grand, so divine, and so pure that it literally lifts you up into the heavens. When you come home we will show you and we will celebrate with you. It will be a grand party, I tell you!

All who read these words, pay attention to this passage, please! I, Quem, speak on behalf of the group and Jackie. I have much love for this one who we call Jackie. You will understand later why she is so special to me. The point here is that the love I feel is so intense that for Jackie it turned into something physical. She felt this was not healthy or acceptable to feel this way, so she said to me, "I won't dance with you anymore."

I cry inside, but understand why. I do not push her anymore to dance with me. The memory of this time causes much pain to be released. Tears flow freely from both of us. *We are One!*

June 10, 2009
Las Vegas

The Akasie: Your trip to the west is planned. You and your husband will go to Las Vegas for a time and then on to sacred sites in Utah. What a beautiful opportunity for the two of you! We intend to take the time while you are away to teach you a little about the energies. Pay special notice to the positive and the negative energies that are all around you.

You are one who is drawn to watch the people. You notice the diversity, the different ways the people dress, their body language, and even their gait. As you watch the people, you also wonder about the physical maladies of the different people; why they have specific disabilities and disease. You go deep within and look to the various possibilities of why they have chosen a particular lifestyle and what might have occurred in their lives to cause them to have a particular physical challenge. You have an appetite that seems to never be satisfied concerning the people and their physical difficulties. You see someone who you perceive as having a peculiarity and you question why he or she is that way. Always you question the origin.

Because you wish to follow the path of the intuitive healer, we will teach you the many causes for physical disease and mental and emotional unbalances. There are many reasons for these challenges.

First, when you get to Las Vegas—specifically when you are at the airport—we ask you to feel the energy. Is the energy positive? Do you feel relaxed and happy, or is the energy negative? Do you feel uncomfortable; is your body tight and anxious?

For many years, your husband has asked you if you would like to go to Las Vegas for a short respite. Up until this time, however, you have expressed that you had little desire to take this trip. You have held a strong biased opinion concerning this city for as long as you can remember. You have formed particular beliefs concerning Las Vegas mostly because of what you have watched on your television programs. You have allowed some source other than your own experience to convince you what your reality is and what your beliefs are.

Television has given much attention to this city, which incidentally is called Sin City. Many TV shows have depicted Las Vegas in a negative way by sensationalizing the crime that takes place in this city. You feel that any place that encourages "sin" such as gambling and sexual pleasures for a price must be all bad!

We assure you that we will be with you every moment. No harm will come to you.

This trip is a grand learning opportunity for you. Know that all places and all situations are for learning! Do not judge those you are with and those who you see. All you encounter is for a great purpose, for you to grow and move forward on your journey of ascension. Remember this: there must be darkness in order to have light.

June 11, 2009
To Ask, Allow, and Accept

Quem: Know that when I speak, I represent the total group of the Akasie. When any of us gives a teaching, we are speaking for the entire group. For us this is an important responsibility and this keeps us in check. It is truth! I tell you here that we like to have our fun also!

You are always being guided. Each day, you are guided by your higher awareness and your spiritual guides. The writing of this book is a fine example that you are already listening to your divine guidance. I say that you are not only listening to your divine guidance, you are following it also. I am most happy to be working with you, one who seeks the truth, the way, and the Light.

We were with you during the time of your son's transition, when his body no longer breathed. You cried out for help just then. We heard your cries, young one. We knew your despair. We were by your side always. As you searched for answers, we held your hand and we guided your way.

To Ask: For some people it may not occur to ask for assistance from the angels. How are you to know to ask for help unless you have been informed at some point in your life that you may ask, and that you should ask? We tell you that learning to ask is only part of the plan! Learning to ask for help sometimes takes a bit of effort. Allow yourself time to form the necessary habits. You may remember to ask for assistance when you find yourself backed up against a wall. We tell you that we wish you to ask for guidance in all situations!

Also, we say that it takes patience to form a bond with your guides, to learn to trust. On a conscious level, we are forging a relationship on many levels. We play many roles as assistant, teacher, father, mother, healer, confidant, and protector. We love all of creation. We are all one.

We tell you that in order to go forward in your ascension process, it is not only beneficial but imperative to seek guidance from us on a conscious level. We assure you at this time you have many guides who are willing and ready to work with you.

We have explained to you that you have many levels of consciousness. Until you know and believe that you can work with your guides on the conscious level, you are already working with your guides on a higher level of consciousness awareness. Be it known that there are always exceptions. This higher level is such that you are not aware of the communications that are going on. These communications between you and your guides occur during your sleep-state via dreams.

We also communicate in many other ways on the physical plane according to your level of mastery to receive said communications. We will discuss some of these types of communications throughout the books that we have agreed to share with you.

To Allow: On a higher level, you tell us what it is you would like assistance with. For instance, what type of information would be most beneficial for you in any and all areas. This is so we may guide you to certain transformative data that comes in the way of books, seminars, events, places, and people. This is all in hopes that you will follow our guidance and learn on a conscious level what it is your higher consciousness already knows. This is all in order for you to move forward. We do many things to help you on your way. Remember, you have free will and it is your choice, on a conscious level, what you do at all times!

You are masters of your own souls! This means that you are in charge of what you learn, how you learn it, and when you learn it. Neither we, the Akasie, nor any of the other angelic beings will tell you how to manage your own life. You make all of the decisions. We do not interfere. We do only what your higher consciousness instructs us to do.

To Accept: Now, we tell you that, yes, we can and do give you suggestions on how to plan certain lessons. There is no question to this. We definitely can and will give our advice when asked. There are those on the Earth plane who flat out say, "No, we do not wish your assistance on the conscious level." This is their choice to go about their journey on their own if they wish.

We gladly and with unconditional love always assist in any way we can. Although, we must tell you that what we give must be for the highest good of all concerned.

June 13, 2009
How We Teach

The Akasie: We give many teachings to many people. We use many different methods, settings, and situations in our teachings. We like variety!

We use every opportunity to teach those under our charge what it is they are ready to learn. To some, our teachings are seemingly eccentric, making them difficult to understand. On some occasions, we choose to teach in an unconventional manner to shake you up, to show you there is more than one way to look at anything. We tell you here that we teach this way because of your many boxes (unbeneficial beliefs) that you have constructed.

Remember, on a higher level you are always in charge of your steps to go higher in your ascension process.

To this day, many of you have had preconceived notions of what angels can do and will do. One of the reasons we have chosen to write this book is to show you that these types of notions will hold you back. You will not be in a position to receive the teachings for your highest benefit when you form preconceived ideas regarding the esoteric, as anything is possible!

In order to go forward, you must break free of your confining belief systems. You will find that some of your boxes have become very large and extremely limiting, keeping your hearts and minds closed. You can choose to ask your guides for assistance to reveal what beliefs you entertain that are holding you back from your spiritual mastery. Your guides are with you to help you. We remind you again, however, that you have free will. You can accept or decline any assistance. This free will is the ability to choose what you feel is best for you in any given situation.

When you are presented with a choice, do you stop and consider all of the possible outcomes? What is for your highest good? What is it that is best and for the highest good of all concerned? What makes your heart sing, my friends?

June 14, 2009
Energies

Quem: Because Jackie asks to go high, we give her energy. To go high is to grow spiritually and ascend. She asks to receive the beautiful love energy that takes her into a state of bliss. We call this place Bliss Land.

There are many different levels or strengths of energy we give depending on the intent or the emotion felt. The sensations received can vary from subtle to divine bliss. The energies are beneficial in the least and exquisite in the most.

As I said, we give energy to Jackie. For her, the energy grows stronger over time. This is the process of the attunement in order to bring the mind, body, and spirit into balance and alignment.

We are careful not to give energy to anyone until he or she is ready. The mind must be willing and accepting to go higher before we can assist the body in attunement. I tell you this so that you may understand that we do this out of love for all of creation. You must be ready for this love, this energy, and this vibration.

You know, I feel the energies. I know they are real, but at the same time, I ask why? Why me, and how in the heck did I get here? What did I do specifically to be able to communicate with the angels?

Quem: Miss, I answer you the best I can at this time. We give the energies to you to challenge the body—to ready the body to ascend higher in the vibratory rates. The reason for this happening to you is your level of consciousness at this time. In other words, you were ready for this step.

June 15, 2009
The Ascension Process

Quem: You, the peoples of the planet Earth, are all at different levels of ascension. It has always been this way. I explain this ascension to you now. We are all evolving. Yes, even we, the angels who are here with you now continue to go higher. We all continue to learn, to grow, and to feel. We go higher just as you do.

Yes, we teach you, but at the same time, we are evolving also. We all have the same goal to go together higher and into the Light. We take you with us; we take all with us who choose to go. You must actively seek in order to find.

We tell you that in the ascension process there is pure, divine energy, an energetic spiral that will take you higher into the heavens toward the Light. The energy is like a cylinder encased in pure gold to traverse through. This energetic cylinder was taken by the ones who have gone before us, the ascended masters. This same road composed of the grandest energy is where we travel also. All will travel this road at some point.

June 16, 2009
The Picture Shows

On several occasions, I have asked my guides what I must do in order to see them. It would make so much sense to me if I could see who I am working with! I am also considering those beings who have passed on before me. I know they linger in my home, not saying anything to me. Sometimes, I smell something that I can't identify. (I know there is someone who smokes cigarettes that comes.) I know some of them need some sort of healing so they can move on. I do see pictures in my third eye but I still want to see the energies with my physical eyes.

To put it simply, I want to see who I am communicating with. Sometimes a being will not tell me his or her name and just talk to me and I will not know who it is until maybe a particular phrase is used or an accent might give them away. There will be times when I will recognize him or her by their sense of humor. The differences in the style of each being's speech patterns are subtle; I have to be really paying close attention to what and how everything is said in order to figure out who is talking to me. Working this way has been quite the challenge.

It is much like being physically handicapped. In addition, I am still working on the trust issue because some of these beings I do not know. They come and go freely and I have no idea what it is all about. So last night, when the two guides came to help me by giving me visions, of course, I wanted to work with them, but at the same time, I was on guard.

They referred to it as "second sight." I welcomed them into my home and asked if they would introduce themselves. They have quite a sense of humor!

Clare: Jackie, we have not spoken to you before, so we would like you to know that we are here to assist you in every way possible to make this transition easier. It is very exciting for us to be here with you.

I never dreamed that all of this would be possible.

Clare: Jackie, your higher self says, "Yes, you did!" This was all planned. You have a special purpose as do all people of the Earth and *all* beings of the universe!

Now, we introduce ourselves to you. I am your servant, your friend, your guide, your teacher, your angel. I go by many names, but you ask for my given name. Yes, I give it to you: Clare. I am pleased to meet you. Now you have another to address.

Sarah: Jackie, I am also pleased to be here at this time to witness the great awakening. It is beautiful energy for you! Ah, you thought I meant the great awakening of the people. I was referring to *your* great awakening!

We have plenty of time to talk, but right now, I would like to explain to you something about myself. I am like Clare, as I have feminine attributes. I am mother to you, nurse maid, confidant, and friend. Remember we are here to guide you in your process of ascension.

You are humbled, yes?

I am so blessed and humbled, yes.

Sarah: Jackie, the name that was given to me a long, long time ago is Sarah.

Jackie, you ask how long we will be guests in your home. We don't know, as it depends solely on you. You also ask what we are here to accomplish. You are able to receive the pictures with no problem. We just require the opportunity to give the information to you for you to process.

There are many "pictures" to share with you concerning future changes. These will assist you in the decisions you make concerning your life. You must be prepared for what is to take place. Do not be alarmed. You are one of the key people to begin the transition of like people joining together to form close knit communities. Your husband is also key, but doesn't know it yet and possibly isn't ready to know. He requires rest before he can begin to make connections. All is working as planned. Right now, you are in the middle of transitions with changing households, so you may spend more time relaxing and balancing your lives.

I feel a great push to make changes right now. So I am really interested in what you are going to show me. For some time now, I have felt like I was to live in a small community and share responsibilities with others. Here, I just feel tired. There is always work to do and most everything falls on us. You know, working in the garden, mowing the lawn, making all the repairs, and of course taking care of all the household chores. It seems silly to live this way.

There have been many occasions when I have gotten all fired up about going off-grid (to not be dependent on others for electricity, gas, water, and food). For the most part, I have been open about my views with Scott, but for some reason, he doesn't seem interested in living off the grid or with anyone in a close-knit community. He politely listens to me ramble on about my ideas and goes on his way!

Shoot, I remember the time when I brought up the subject of having goats and chickens. Scott bluntly told me, "In order to have goats and chickens, fences, and shelters need to be built. Oh, and remember when the snow is a foot deep and the wind is howling at thirty miles per hour, someone has to go out there and make sure those cute goats and chickens have food and water." Okay, reality check. Maybe I am getting in too much of a hurry to be self-sufficient, 'cause that somebody who goes outside in the dead of winter will most certainly be me!

Last year, I was all for buying that eighty acres of "recreational" land down south, because deep down I hoped that eventually that land would be turned into what I always wanted—a place to grow my own food and produce my own power.

My view is that these power plants are unhealthy for our society. We need to heal and so does the earth. I have come to the conclusion that I no longer want to pay for anything that I can make myself! I also want my freedom from any and all entities like the city, county, state, and the country. I feel there is a better way for me. I have had my fill with other people deciding what is best for me! When is this all going to end? I don't want to be anti-government here, but we are taxed on everything. I don't feel that I should be charged several thousand dollars a year for the privilege to live on my own property! I guess I have some anger concerning this issue.

June 18, 2009
Take Responsibility for Your Energy

Quem: Even though all past feelings, events, and experiences have been erased from your conscious memories, people are born with spiritual purity, with pure love in their hearts. You come to Earth to merge into a fresh body and to begin anew with a clean, conscious mind free from all fear of the unknown!

The positive is spirit and it manifests itself in the emotions that are love-based: gratitude, peace, joy, compassion, etc. The negative is ego, and it manifests itself in the emotions that are all fear-based: hate, anger, stress, depression, and insecurity, etc. You live in a world of duality, which is of the light (positive) and of the dark (negative).

We tell you to be respectful of all negative and positive energies, because they all have an important purpose!

When another sees the results of the negativity, he or she is hopefully motivated into going within and examining where the challenge lies, thus, making changes toward being more positive and asking for help from us!

There are levels of negativity. We take the example of tyranny. Who alone can change such a circumstance as political oppression? At this time in our evolution no one person can, but a collective group can bring about change and has many times! There is great power in numbers and like thought forms.

Life on Earth is a precious gift. Cherish each moment. These words I don't say lightly. This is your time to evolve and to grow spiritually in the physical realm. In addition, this time is a great challenge for you all. We are working to take you higher to the fifth dimension in the physical body. This has been accomplished before by previous cultures many generations past, and will be achieved again by you as the master manifestors of this great Earth!

Many do not realize this, and this is why we speak on the subject. You have all come to the beautiful Mother Earth for the great opportunity of awakening! You are creators and you have come here to manifest all that is experienced by the way of your thoughts, including your spiritual ascension.

Your ascension can only be accomplished when you take responsibility for your thoughts!

We are here to teach you how to go within, to recognize and take responsibility for what you are thinking, feeling, speaking, and ultimately creating. When you focus on what you are thinking and see the negativity, you are then able to change those thoughts to positive if you so desire! This is free will to choose what it is you want to create with your thoughts. Do you choose to continue to have thoughts which run rampant in your mind without discernment, or do you purposefully choose to be in control of what you are thinking and creating at all times?

You are all powerful beings; know this! You are creators by right. All thoughts, positive, negative, and indifferent ascend, joining with other like thoughts or energies, thus creating divine power. Everything around you is comprised of power and energy! You are energy. Therefore, you are creating energy with your every thought.

June 19, 2009
Utah: The Desert

This year my husband and I decided to take our vacation in Utah. We flew into the Las Vegas airport and rented a car to drive up to Utah through Brice Canyon and on through Zion National Park.

Scott had rented a convertible. No, the car wasn't red, but what a surprise! (It wasn't a car that I would have chosen.) I guess I am a little boring because I would have gotten a car that was more practical, like a sedan, but I was so glad to experience something different and fun! Thank you, Scott!

Before arriving at our destination, we drove for many miles through some really desolate areas. Having never laid eyes on this type of terrain before, I was totally shocked by what I saw! The land was barren, and because in my opinion the vegetation was ugly and sparse, I reasoned that this land was of no use.

The Akasie immediately told me that there was a purpose in all, and I was to look for the positive in all that I see and all that I experience!

June 20, 2009
Raising the Vibration of Your Food

Ever since my Reiki training I have known that we are able to raise the vibration of our food. With love and gratitude, we thank the Creator for the food while placing our hands over our food and allowing the energy to flow through us into the food. This action transmutes the molecular structure of the food. This is called purifying and energizing your food.

The Akasie: Much of the food you consume in today's world is processed, meaning that much if not all of the nutritional value has been destroyed during the process of preparation and packaging of the product.

To have high nutrition in your food, it must receive energy from positive sources like the sun, rich soil, and people without the detrimental effects of pesticides and herbicides. To have the highest vibration possible in your food the people who grow this food must have love in their hearts for what it is they are growing.

Unfortunately, these days much of your food is mass produced. People feel they are much too busy to grow their own food, so they go to the supermarket and buy what has been mass-produced. Much of the food is never in the real outdoors, but in greenhouses, grown in prepared soil that is also mass-produced and laced with chemicals. This is all with the purpose to produce higher yields for the least amount of work and the highest profit.

For your produce to contain the highest level of nutrition or energy, the food must receive the warmth from your sun, fresh air, vital minerals from your soil, pure water, and the love from the people who grow it.

The same goes for the meat you consume. Are the animals held captive in a small area only to be slaughtered as soon as they have enough bulk?

We tell you that animals have emotions. When animals are confined to small areas, it creates great amounts of negative emotion, and they suffer from much discomfort and fear. To hold the animals in captivity is not in the natural order.

Today, the people are living in the fast lane. They are in such a hurry to get everything done that there is little appreciation for this miracle, this energy, this food that heals and sustains the body that is the temple of God/Goddess.

Do you truly wish to fill your temple with chemicals that are meant to kill another life form? Think about this. Does this make sense to you? We feel pain, horror, when we see you, our brothers and sisters, consume this poison!

Until you calm yourselves and begin once again to nurture the land and your physical bodies, we offer this way of raising the vibration of your food. The way you raise the vibration of your food is to send love and gratitude up to the Creator knowing that your food is pure and of high vibration, full of the force of life. It is not enough to merely say "Thank you, God." You must feel great love and appreciation for what God has provided for you!

When you begin this practice of purifying and energizing your food, place your hands over your food, leaving about one inch of space in between. There is also a space of about one inch between each hand. Focus much on how your hands feel. There will be an energy that emanates from your hands.

At first, it may be a little difficult to feel the energy. Keep practicing and pay close attention to what you feel. We encourage those who are interested in this practice to find a Reiki teacher and take a class! Learn to give this energy to raise the vibration of your food for the highest benefit to your bodies.

Quem: I would like to take this time to explain the importance of energizing your food. First, energizing your food makes the vibration of your food higher. Anything you eat would be more beneficial for you if it had the highest possible vibration in it.

Second, you are energizing your food to help pave the way for others. They see you doing something to your food, and they wonder what it is that you are doing. You are helping to break down boxes by showing there are other ways, other beliefs. For the most part in your culture, it is unusual to see someone place his or her hands over his or her food before he or she eats. To have the freedom to follow your own truth is a beautiful thing. Be grateful, as this has not always been the case. You as a collective are evolving into thinking that it is all right to be different and unique individuals.

Third, you are raising your own vibration through this practice. You have noticed that over time your love and gratitude expands on a deeper level; furthermore, your vibration is becoming stronger and faster.

Fourth and last, you are energizing your food and drink for a reason that has been unknown to you until this time. The explanation comes to you by the way of this example.

Recently, you saw two women in a restaurant energizing their food. You thought this was cool! It gave you permission, in a way, to do this in front of strangers. What you saw told you that there are others out there who are Reiki masters, or possibly just aware that the food is much more beneficial for you when energized. Be it known that there are many others who have been given the information and are ready to move forward, but it is quite possible that they also require the self-assurance that there are others just like them! Just by seeing others energize their sustenance in public gives them the go-ahead to grow the confidence and faith to keep moving forward.

June 21, 2009
Psychic Gifts

To be clairvoyant and a channel for the angels is a beautiful gift and also a tremendous responsibility. There must be unwavering trust between us all. How can we work together if we don't have the trust that we will all do what is for the highest good for all of creation?

I look back and see that we didn't always share this trust. Trust, I believe, is something that grows as the days go by. Trust grows as we go through the teachings and learn from each other. As I sit here and write these words, I feel that I am just beginning to understand a huge lesson. I haven't always trusted my guides. On many occasions, I have questioned their intentions.

My guides know what is in my heart, that I love life and do the best I can. At the same time, I am not by any means perfect. Sometimes I become stubborn, angry, and even resentful. Then there are times when I feel worn out and I wonder what the sense in all of this is.

The angels tell me that I must balance my life by getting plenty of rest, eating nutritious foods, exercising, and having fun! If my life is balanced, then my temperament will be balanced.

The guides who are teaching me must, in turn, trust that I will take what I learn and do what is best and for the highest good of all creation. I look at this now and see they really have to believe in me, know what I am about, and see what my intentions are! Receiving the words has changed, is changing, my life. I am making many adjustments and it takes much time.

As soon as I began to hear the angels, I remember being overwhelmed and sometimes even frightened, but at the same time, I was exhilarated! One moment I would question, "Oh my gosh, what is happening to me?" Then later, my heart would fill with this incredible love and gratitude, and I knew absolutely without any doubt that this was me; this was who I was, and this gift was the coolest ever! Thank you, Creator! Thank you, the Akasie!

Receiving this gift was like the birth of a new child. I wanted to tell everyone! However, there are some people who just aren't ready to hear about anything out of the ordinary, as some are not yet open to new ideas, concepts, or experiences. Sometimes when I spoke to someone of my communications with the angels or maybe talked about the energy I receive, I would get these knowing looks and people would say, "Oh, right. Oh, I see. Uh huh ... this sounds really ... uh ... interesting." I can tell right away if a person is uncomfortable by the dead silence or when he or she all of a sudden can't look me straight in the eye. What I really love are the knowing looks that tell you they are wondering which nut house let you out. Then there are those who flat out tell you that you should have your head examined.

The way I usually process information and my emotions is by talking out my experiences with people, and this was no exception! I need to talk about how this gift is affecting me. I have used the writing process to help me, but I still feel like I need to connect to people about this! And I want to share the messages that are so revealing, full of promise and love, to everyone. This gift has rocked the very core of my being, as it has also changed how the people I am closest to perceive me and understand me; I am no longer the person I was. I realized that what I have doesn't fit neatly into any box or into anyone's way of thinking, but I still want to be accepted by my friends and family.

June 22, 2009
Utah: The Sacred Sites

We are still in Utah. Today was such a beautiful day. The temperature was moderate. The sun smiled on us while we rode horseback down the canyon at Bryce National Park. I rode a mule named Betsy. Well, at first, I thought I was getting ripped off. My belief was that horses were better, classier I guess, but when I saw how sure-footed Betsy was as she worked the steep trail, I was very grateful to have her support. My entire body is sore, especially "those" areas. It isn't every day that I sit on a mule for three hours being jostled in every possible direction. Thank goodness, one of the trail-riders was there to help me down! I have to laugh because that guy had to practically lift me off of Betsy because I was so stiff. With each step, I groaned with pain, but I felt a sense of wonder, too. Wow! I did it!

The Akasie told me to ask Sarah, Clare, and an observer, Christopher, to work with me when we got home. I have been okay with working with them while on vacation, but the time we use is taking away from my rest.

Sarah, Clare, and Christopher: Jackie, we do wish to speak to you concerning the time we spent training you. Right now, you are upset because you are not seeing the pictures we give you clearly or even remembering the pictures we give you. You say to us, "Just do it!" We tell you the process isn't as simple as you think. You think we should just give you the pictures and be done with it. You are tired and short on patience. Please understand that we must ease you into this. We do not wish to overload you.

We will gladly wait until you return home from vacation if that is what you truly want. We will check tomorrow to see how you feel then.

June 23, 2009
The Ego

This morning as I sat in this beautiful dining hall at the lodge we are staying at, I felt so insecure! Paranoid is more like it. I didn't want to be looked at or thought of as a nut case while I energized my food, so I just skipped it. All the while, I felt guilty for not bringing up the energy.

Quem: Jackie, this is what I'd like to say regarding your choice to not energize your breakfast this morning. Not all is lost.

Yes, you are disappointed in yourself. You did not forget, you simply chose to not energize your food because you worried that people would stare at you and think you were odd. You realized this not following through was associated with worrying about what people thought of you, and that your ego was taking control. This is a big step. Get to where your goals are more important than that ego of yours. You are doing fine.

Tonight we have another subject for you, Jackie. Yes, I tell you that we all continue to evolve and all continue to go forward. I acknowledge your happiness for us in regards to our evolution. I am not going away from you, though I know you are so happy for me and the others that you would not ask us to stay with you if it was time for us to go. You miss some of the guides that you have worked with in the past, but understand they have many to assist. Ego is not interfering here, you see. Ego does not have control of you completely. Ego goes away when you see that your ego is taking hold. Not everything is about you.

You on the Earth have your own paths to walk, and you all need assistance. You, Jackie, are here to assist in specific areas by showing others the way. We tell you that you are a teacher. Take responsibility for yourself and follow through with your agreement to your Higher Self and all others. *We are One!*

Picture Shows and Healing Energy

Quem: Sarah and Clare have insisted I tell you the rest of what is going on. As you know, you are working on what we will call "picture shows." You haven't received anything of significance as of yet. We are practicing and doing the pictures in steps.

Tonight you asked if you could receive the pictures another way besides laying down to rest. We tell you while you are in the area of Mt. Zion and in the company of your husband, the only way for you to receive the pictures would be to lie down to take a "nap," or find a quiet secluded place to meditate until we get back home.

I will go ahead and tell you that what you will receive concerns your future, but also the future for many others as well. This causes you a little anxiety, because doing this holds much responsibility.

The other piece of this that we are ready to reveal at this time is that we will be getting together, all of us, to help you write this all down in a book format to be published and distributed. This again concerns you, because much responsibility falls on you. We will guide your every step.

Reasons for the Energy

The Akasie: We will move on to another subject. In regards to the energy you receive from us, we are ready to explain more about what is happening to you. Currently, you are receiving energy many times throughout the day and night. Up to this point, you haven't fully understood why you are receiving this energy and exactly what it is doing to you and for you. You have asked for a more detailed explanation from us. I tell you, you receive energy for many purposes, and this giving and receiving of the energy takes much time. First, the energy is for healing on all levels of your being.

I must go back and give you a little teaching here. Your higher self is in total control of your entire being. We have spoken of this before; you have many parts, levels, and layers to your entire being. We are speaking of your ethereal and physical bodies. You are comprised of mind, spirit, body, and soul. You are in the process of healing on all levels, all layers, and also in other dimensions. Your higher self knows when it is time to work or heal certain pieces or aspects of yourself. Your higher self is in constant communication with us, your guides.

The higher self is a part of the mind and has many functions. The mind is divided, yet united. You have your higher self or higher consciousness. The higher consciousness is memory and knowledge and is not accessible to you on a lower awareness level until you are at the level of understanding and ready for this connection. We purposely are not explaining all there is to know about this subject. The mind is mysterious and vast. It would take many volumes to disclose all that the mind is capable of and still there would be more.

You also have your conscious mind, which is memory and knowledge that is accessible to you now. This is all for a good purpose.

Second, you receive energy from us because we love you, and we express our love by giving you energy created from this love. This is emotion that I speak of. We feel much love and we direct it to you. This love that we give you is beautiful energy.

Third, we are giving you a precious gift. We are attuning you to resonate with our energy in order to bring your vibration much higher. It takes time and patience for us all to do this. One example of what a higher vibration does is activates psychic abilities.

According to many spiritual men and women, you have little time to "remember" your true selves, yet you have all the time in the universe because there is no time. There is no space. You question this because here you sit in an area you call space and you look to your clock and say it keeps track of your time.

What we want to say at this moment is that it is time to release the toxins stored in your body. We are all working to cleanse your bodies, as your bodies must carry you through many years to come. You have much to do and much to accomplish in this lifetime. You are to be healthy! To carry out your agreement, please pay attention to what you ingest. Please, Jackie! We know you are conscious of healthy eating and would prefer to do better. Do so! We give this affirmation as gift for you to work with.

The Affirmation: I only desire the foods of the highest nutritional value. These foods make it possible for me to be at my optimal health at all times, which in turn enables me to have extremely high energy.

In addition, we say to you, food is not the only source of toxins that have come to reside in your body. You have spent many years in an environment unbecoming to healthy persons. Sarah and Clare are here to assist you in the release of toxins in particular areas.

You wonder why they do this when they are here to show you the picture shows. They are here to assist with several things concerning your health and spiritual growth. Do not be concerned. Believe only that you are in loving hands and loving care. We all love you truly and only have your best intentions at heart. *We are One!*

Sarah and Clare: We are not here for one purpose only. While we are here, we help the Akasie with all to be accomplished. Angels assist wherever they are needed. We all are united; we are all One. We reside in the now. Also, we are multidimensional beings. Jackie we tell you now to go about your business, and think about what we have told you. *We are One!*

June 25, 2009
Suntans

While I was cleaning up in the kitchen, Colér showed up quite unexpectedly. I don't "see" her, but I hear her words in my mind, and if she chooses, she can speak through me. I was really glad to hear from her. Colér said, "I have been out getting a suntan." She went on to say that, "The sun is beautiful here."

I laughed because she is a light being. How can a light being get a suntan? They do make jokes and have such a good sense of humor. I love that about them. I love them! She insisted, saying, "Yes, I got myself a suntan! I can't wait to get home to show everyone!"

I am still chuckling about this! Colér said that the light beings turn a nice golden color. What I saw in my mind's eye stopped me in my tracks! She wasn't like you or I with a dense physical body. She had an ethereal body of the most beautiful, pure golden light. Such a beautiful sight!

Just then, I was asked to lie down. The Akasie then said they were ready to show themselves to me. When we get home, they would do this. I responded with, "You have already shown yourselves to me by allowing me to hear you." They said, "Yes, you are astute. Will you keep going forward?"

June 25, 2009
Time in Zion

As we were working our way back through Utah to Las Vegas, we stopped at a newer looking ranch-resort on the east side of Mt. Zion and rented a log cabin. One of the unique draws of the resort is a large herd of bison residing right on the property.

We would be staying on the east side of the property among approximately twenty log cabins nestled on the hillside with a thick backdrop of pine trees. The cabins were really nice with huge showers and a modern kitchenette. Everything was of a high quality. Scott especially liked the flat screen TV and stereo system. Me? I loved the bed! They had decorated the place in rich hues of greens, rusts, creams, and browns. From our front porch, we had a panoramic view of the entire area. The layout was impressive, and I could see that the owners had put much thought into their dream to have created such a beautiful retreat.

A half-mile gravel road connected the cabins to the building that housed the office, gift store, and restaurant. It was no surprise to me that the restaurant's menu included buffalo burgers, meatloaf, and steak.

Each log cabin sat on a very small sandy lot. What I noticed first about our new front "yard" was that there wasn't a single blade of grass to be seen anywhere. Our lawn appeared to be nothing more than a bunch of scraggly weeds. Taking a closer look, I saw that those scraggly weeds were in fact many beautiful varieties of wildflowers.

After traveling all day, we were excited to finally have arrived at our destination, so we quickly carried our luggage inside. We were both hungry and ready to try out their diner, but we wanted to clean up first. I headed for the shower first, which was a totally enjoyable experience; there were two shower heads in there!

While I waited for Scott, I headed for the front porch swing. I sat for a few moments enjoying the sunset, and then I decided to try counting the different wildflowers in bloom. I came up with fifteen species before I began to lose track of the different varieties.

The gravel road that I mentioned earlier that connects the cabins and the office also serves to divide the north side of the property from the south side. The north side has a large fenced in area with a tack room, a corral, and a grazing area for the horses. On the south side of the property sits one thousand acres of fenced in pasture and wooded area where the bison have free reign. As we drove over to the restaurant for our evening meal, I noticed there were some men on horses on the south side of the property where the bison were. I wondered what they were doing.

At the restaurant, we were greeted by a young man who had a heavy accent. I wondered where he was from and what had brought him to this part of the country. The diner was small and had a family-like atmosphere. The young man seated us beside a large picture window that looked out toward the southeast. I noted another well executed plan in the layout of the retreat. From that window, we had a spectacular view of bison and the ranchers.

What we were seeing could have been taken straight out of a western movie. My first impression was that they were rounding up a few bison to slaughter. They did serve buffalo meat! I asked the server what the ranchers were doing, and he said, "They are working to separate the herd, so tonight the customers are getting free entertainment along with dinner!" (We were told later that this was the first attempt at dividing the herd.)

There before us was about a hundred head of bison including two dominant bulls (that looked to be very angry), several cows with their calves, three ranchers, two Australian shepherds, and one mutt. We were glued to the scene before us. The bulls were frantic and made countless attempts to run the men off. As a group, the bison were determined to stay put. As I looked on, I could feel my adrenaline build. From where I sat, I could see the crazed look in the bulls' eyes. Their stance clearly indicated their determination or was it their fear?

Both bulls used the same tactic, repeatedly digging in the loose earth with their hooves to warn the ranchers that they meant business! The ranchers held their ground. The bulls actually would act like they had lost interest in their adversaries by turning their backs on them and walking away. Then unexpectedly with an explosion of angry energy, the two bulls would each suddenly turn toward their selected target with heads lowered, and charge, running full speed to give the full impact of their bulk and horns. The bull's aim was to bring down either the horse or the man. There were many close calls and a few actual physical hits. I noticed that my body was stiff with anxiety and worked to relax.

The entire time, the dogs were barking fiercely as they ran toward the bison to drive them toward the fence. Over and over, the massive creatures attempted this same technique, and it was like a tug of war, only we are talking about a two-thousand pound beast with horns versus a two-hundred pound man with nothing but his horse, a hat, and a rope! The bison would gain a little ground and then suddenly the ranchers would take it back.

I sat there on the edge of my seat, watching and feeling the anxiety mount. It was obvious that if those men were distracted for a single instant, these bulls could and would do some serious damage to them.

After a good while, the herd was divided into two smaller herds. This lasted for about fifteen minutes. Some of the herd was directed to the north side of the road where the corral was located, while the rest stayed behind on the south side. The men seemed to know what they were doing by successfully driving the smaller part of the herd to the area with a large gate. They then were able to drive the bison across the gravel road to the area with the corral. Thankfully, no one had been hurt and none of the bison had escaped. We kept watching to see what exactly these guys were going to do with all of these bison. Being a mother, I felt more concern for the cows that were being separated from their calves before it was time.

My mind drifted back in time when we had first moved into our home in the country. Our house was located beside a pasture that was home for a few cows and their calves. One night I heard the most pitiful sound from these cows. They kept mooing and wouldn't stop. I was truly concerned for them. The next day I called my neighbors up and said, "Hey, what is wrong with your cows?" Their response was, "Oh, the cows were separated from their calves last night. They were just bawling." I will never forget that mournful cry.

Suddenly, with unfathomed force, the bulls stormed the fence and broke it down. The herd regrouped. The bison had always been together; they were family.

As I sit here and contemplate this situation, what we were watching at first appeared to be nothing more than a show, but what we were really seeing was man at his finest ... or was it his worst? First, the bison were captive on one thousand acres. We can argue that the animals were well cared for, and they were! In reality, however, those animals were there for two reasons: 1) as food; 2) for entertainment for the tourists. Add this up and it equals money.

Second, we were witnessing creatures being forced from their "natural" habitat and from family. Isn't this what it was like in times of war? I am specifically thinking of WWII, when the Jews were marched to trains, not knowing their fate. They were separated from family members not knowing what to do, how to feel, or who or what to believe.

The will to live is mighty strong. Furthermore, so is the desire to protect loved ones. When one's life, or the sanctity of family, is threatened, survival instinct comes into play. Anything can happen depending on how strong this instinct is. I think back on how some people will allow themselves to be herded off without so much as a single whisper, while others fight back with a mighty vengeance knowing full well they may die in the process. There is fear in both scenarios, and I wonder what I would do if I were faced with a similar situation. My thoughts again shifted back to the herd; some of the bison fought while the others were passive and willing to go wherever they were directed.

How deeply do these animals feel? What I saw in their eyes was fear, confusion, and anger. If they are capable of becoming angry, then can they hate? Do they have the ability to love each other? Did the bison feel protective of their family members, or were they just reacting because they sensed danger? Was it pure survival instinct that we witnessed?

Today the bison took control; they used pure strength to overpower the men. There will be another day. Who will persevere then?

Yesterday, as we were hiking in the middle of the desert, I found the only water hole around and slipped into it. Somehow, in the process, I managed to drop our digital camera in the water! Scott has a very even temperament, but even so, I was nervous that he would be angry. After all, this was our only camera. It wasn't like we had a spare in our car! He worked to lighten the mood by teasing me and saying that he had wanted a new camera anyway. Even so, several hours were spent with much effort on Scott's part to get the camera working again.

Today we explored a few interesting areas before I looked for a secluded spot to commune with the Creator. Before we even began this trip, my intention had been to find a beautiful spot to sit, pray, and be one with all of creation. We will be heading home in a few days, and I was running out of opportunities to take advantage of this beautiful country. I saw a promising place and directed Scott to pull over at the next spot available.

Getting out of the car, I commented on the fact that the temperature had risen a few degrees. Immediately my skin began to burn. We began to assess the situation. What I saw before me was this single, solitary rock that was really a gigantic stone mountain. Which direction would be best to climb? With much apprehension, I began to grasp the size of this undertaking; the ascent was much steeper than I had previously thought. The surface of the stone mountain was smooth and barren. Thank goodness, I had remembered to wear my tennis shoes, but I wondered if they would provide enough traction. From my vantage point, I could not see a single tree to steady myself as I climbed up the mountain, and certainly not anything to hold onto as I came down. If I should slip and fall, there were no bushes to cushion me. The logical side of me said, "Jackie, you aren't safe." A part of me said, "Don't be stupid! Just say you have changed your mind!" I kept thinking that I could very easily slip because I had nothing to grab onto to prevent me from falling. To put it plain and simple, I was afraid to do this, but the other side of me, the part of me that wants to create experiences and feel the beauty, wanted to spend this time with the Creator from a place like this. Zion is a holy place; I could feel the energy so beautiful and peaceful.

If I backed down and let fear overtake me, I knew I would be extremely disappointed in myself. I was torn right down the middle. Would I allow my fear to control me? I can go up okay; the problem is the coming down. I just froze in my footsteps! I could feel the momentum building. This giant rock was growing before my eyes, and so was my fear. In my mind, I continued to talk through and access my situation. I decided I just couldn't do it. So, I began to argue with myself and plead with

Scott; I began to whimper like a little child. Scott coached me saying, "Yes, you can do this. Just don't look down."

Inside, I was laughing at the absurdity of his words, because where else was I going to look when I did come back down? He continued to coax me, telling me to watch where I stepped as we climbed higher.

All thoughts of my descent to the car were deliberately pushed aside. I forced myself to focus only on each step and my ultimate goal. I was here to feel the love and gratitude for all of creation!

Finally, I saw a dwarfed pine tree on a fairly level place that looked safe. I knew that this was the place. Scott quietly walked away, leaving me alone with my thoughts. Carefully, I sat down and began to center myself.

While I sat atop this glorious giant of a stone mountain, I did receive a teaching. The angels spoke about all of the beauty that surrounded us and how it was created.

I asked the Akasie, "Do we, the people, manifest all of Mother Earth's features, plant life, and animal life? Do we somehow manifest what we look like, how our bodies evolve physically, mentally, emotionally, and spiritually?" The Akasie replied by saying, "Your question is a separate subject. We will speak about it at another time." Instead, this is what I received:

The Akasie: Mother Earth is an individual entity, although she is very connected to all that is. She is a highly evolved spirit. Mother Earth is a living, breathing being.

You notice that we call her Mother. We have much reverence for all that she is and does. She expands, contracts, shifts, and heaves in the birthing process of creation as it is constantly unfolding. Mother wants to always care for her children, as she loves all her children equally and loves them all unconditionally. She desires all her children to thrive. However, children sometimes have ways of not staying where they are put. Sometimes they endanger themselves and others. We are talking about all her children, not just the human children.

Mother Earth's human children sometimes are rebellious in nature, as they have free will. They will most always push boundaries, sometimes not thinking of the consequences they impart. This is of course what is intended. This is creation in the making. Boundaries must be pushed and crossed for creation to expand and evolve.

All creation is intended to become greater, more beauteous, more technologically advanced, higher evolved spiritually (not necessarily in this order), and to always be in harmony and in balance with all of creation. This is not always so, however, as you are not always in balance and harmony. There are times when your desires are not for the highest good for all of creation.

We will focus on being in balance and harmony with others, the peoples of the Earth now. What this means is to always allow the other to learn at his or her own pace without any judgment from you. You may feel he or she is making an error, that his or her thinking is incorrect, and that his or her judgment is most certainly askew. In your view, his or her priorities seem to be erroneous, but in reality, what he or she is experiencing is the physical manifestation of his or her evolution on all levels.

I always feel humbled after I receive a teaching. Thank you. After the Akasie had finished with their teaching, I called out to Scott who was just over the ridge. He said he had found some petroglyphs! How exciting! Immediately, I wanted to jump up and go see, but remembered where I was. Instead I thought it was better if moved slowly and deliberately to make certain that I had a sure footing. Just as I stood up straight, Scott came into view. As he walked toward me, he told me that apparently whoever left the message was an ancient Indian named Dale who loved an Indian maiden named Alisha. How sweet!

The Akasie: Jackie, we think this is the appropriate time to express our gratitude for being able to have this time with you here. We had a wonderful vacation with you and Scott.

We look forward to being at home, though, where there is peace, love, and harmony. We know you question this, but your home is a sacred space for all. Not just you, but for us also.

June 26, 2009
The Law of Attraction

The Akasie: We speak on the universal law of attraction now. By giving thanks to Creator for food and all things necessary for survival, you are manifesting the continual security of like matter. You give thanks in the present tense or the now always.

This is the example we give you this day: You have not received even one drop of rainfall this entire month. You are beginning to be a little anxious about this. You have seen the tiny cracks in the Earth's crust grow to large crevices. Even so, we instruct you to always give thanks for the rain you receive. Envision the rains coming gently and abundantly, quenching the thirst of all living creatures. Give thanks for this of which you receive. Believe these affirmations to be true with all of your heart!

The same goes for your physical health. Every day affirm with gratitude that you are healthy and strong. Thank your higher self for your outstanding health! Know what you are saying to be the absolute truth!

Your mind is in control of all that you are. Your higher level of awareness is always listening to what you think and say! If you are constantly saying, "I feel bad," you will continue to feel bad.

As we were working our way through security at the Las Vegas airport to come home, I was observing a mother and her two young children. I was watching how far ahead the mother walked in front of the children. She did not look back to check on these two, and my concern was mounting for these young children! I felt it would be far too easy for her to lose these children. The little boy was close to three years of age.

Quem: Jackie, what you were doing is creating negative emotion through your thoughts. You felt the turmoil in your body as you watched these young ones venture through the airport basically unattended. These thoughts were creating much emotion. Your thoughts concerning this particular case are dangerous to all children. We know that you were concerned for their over-all safety. As you watched, your mind was inventing different scenarios of their demise!

These thoughts that you were creating join like thought forms, making the probability stronger that all children are susceptible to being snatched by someone of an undesirable nature.

In the future, as you realize what you are thinking, place your thoughts to loving the children. Instead of focusing on how easy it would have been for someone to grab these young children, know that these children, as well as all other children, are perfectly safe! Shift your thoughts to the love you feel for all children. Create joyous thoughts of innocence and beauty. Acknowledge the love you feel for the children—all children. If your thoughts begin to wonder as how they are cared for, focus on the mother. Affirm that she is doing a wonderful job with the children. Look to all the things you see that prove this thought, such as how clean and well behaved the children are. Acknowledge that they are able to go on a trip. Look at how easily the children smile.

As you watched, you possibly sensed that the family was having an off day. Taking two young children on a trip can be an extremely stressful time for anyone! Understand that she must arrive at her destination on time with her two young ones in tow! Send the family positive energy and a blessing for a safe and happy journey. Imagine them on a good day at the park or someplace where children are mesmerized or enthralled. Imagine the joy the children feel as they experience a new adventure! Envision these types of scenarios, as these are positive thoughts. Enjoy yourself when you see the young ones. They are beautiful. They are filled with the newness of creation. They are innocent and know nothing of the dangers before them. If everyone had a child's way of thinking, *there would not be any danger.* Everyone would be safe and full of love!

While we were waiting for our flight, Esse showed up. I was so glad to hear from her. She says she doesn't work with me any longer, but will visit every so often.

Esse: Jackie, I bring news! A great stirring is upon us! We rejoice with this great stirring. The great shifts, they are at last here! With these great shifts, we rejoice! New energy is being created. We are not only speaking of where energy is born, but also we are speaking of "The Force," the angelic presence that has much fortitude, thought, and precision. We are here in great numbers to assist the masses of star beings in physical form at this time.

Many are aware of the energies now. We are upon the horizon, and it is such an exciting time! The advancement of technology brings forth information at lightning speed to your minds. This advancement coincides with many of you who are looking deep within for the meaning of life. We are grateful to be part of this transition to a higher level of consciousness. We are One. I love you and will be back.

June 27, 2009
Spiritual Teachings Are for the Highest Good of All Concerned

Quem: When you ask for certain information that has nothing to do with spiritual awareness or evolution for self or others, we refrain from answering.

Two days ago, you asked about the well-being of Michael Jackson. He has been in the media much lately and they have raked him over the coals. You are becoming more aware of how the media works. For you, the compassion grows for those who seemingly have no privacy. But still you are curious so you asked how he was. You also asked if the rumors about his sexuality were true. We told you he was fine. He was with his family and doing well.

A day later, you found out Michael had passed from his earthly body, and that this passing had occurred prior to your questions. You wonder why we did not speak to you of his transition. We tell you first that your questions were answered correctly. Michael was fine and with his family! Second, Michael has very little to do with you.

I fail to agree with you on this. He probably touched everyone in the US, at least in some way or another with his artistic ability.

Quem: Yes, Michael is a great energy mover, and through his successes, trials, and traumas, he has given many something to ponder. A great teacher he was. Always remember this about the one we speak of. However, I do not wish to discuss him at this time. What I want to tell you concerns your questions specifically about what type of questions are appropriate to ask.

The Akasie are here with you at this time to assist in many ways, but first, for your conscious self to focus on self. Presently, this is the number one reason we are here to work with you. We do not concern ourselves with the well-being of others who are not directly connected to you in the physical realm. You do not understand completely yet because your questions about this particular individual came from concern, and you felt compassion toward this being because of extreme hardship he had endured. Jackie, you feel that your questions were valid.

All that is required from you is that you feel love toward all other beings. Just send your love to others who move the energy. There is no need to ask about them. If you are meant to know anything, you will find out by the way of the physical. Do you understand this?

What I have to say concerns the harmony and balance of all the peoples of the New Earth. I tell you that the peoples of the New Age of Aquarius have their work cut out for them, but at the same time, this period in our history is the most magnificent experience yet. These emotions that I feel bring tears to my eyes when I think of this transition that is taking place.

We are at the dawning of this great new age! My breath catches when I think of the results of what we have been working on for such a long time. Evolution is a slow and tedious process. When we see before our very eyes the grand results of what we have been creating, we feel the excitement and the gratitude build, because we have been given this opportunity to play a part and to bear witness to this new energy that is here at last!

We work with you, Jackie, in deliberate fashion to accomplish all we can. We feel you are committed and grounded in this endeavor, yes?

Every day is a precious gift. The enthusiasm I have about spiritual matters keeps me going and will continue to do so always and everywhere. I am remembering myself, and it is a beautiful time to experience this. I am not sure how all of this happened, but I am most grateful to have come to this place in this level of understanding. I pledge my sincerity and my commitment to always seek the truth and the love, going higher in my power and wisdom.

Quem: It is time you have your name given back to you. You have made a great commitment today. It is important that you receive.

I do not speak these words lightly. You are Akasie; you have always been. You were born with many others in a cluster or group. We call these clusters soul groups. Because you have little memory of your existence before this life on the Earth plane, I am here to lead your way and to teach you. I am here to give credence to all that you are. You are not just a wife and mother in this present lifetime. Long ago, you were born to me! Your mother is Sarah. Your name, your heavenly name, the name I gave to you, is Cathryn.

The emotion I feel is totally pure love. I know instinctively that what Quem says is true. To have Quem reveal this to me makes me doubly happy. I can't even begin to describe how I feel, except to say that I know in my heart that this is true.

The feelings I have for Quem, who is my father, my Pleiadian father, are different than I have for any of the other guides. There is this bond there. I love him dearly. My feelings for Sarah are not like how I feel for you; I don't feel this bond with her.

Why is this? She is my mother. I want to feel this love for her. Why doesn't she work with me like you do?

Quem: First, I am your father. I always have been. From this day forward, I ask you to call me "Father" when you call upon me.

Honey, your mother Sarah works with many. We have many to watch over and to guide here on the Earth plane and in other dimensions as well. Your mother will come to visit you soon. She has offered to be of assistance in a more profound way, but I have told her it would be best for you to take little steps, get used to this idea, and integrate this knowing on your lower level of awareness. She will be active in your life at a later time.

The Akasie are like a five-pointed star, ever turning, brilliant and pure in nature. I am Quem, the point at the very top. (We go in clockwise rotation here.) Olim, she is the next point of the star. She is my right hand. Jithury is next. She is the bottom right point. Jithury is my right foot. Colér is the bottom left point of this beautiful star, and she is my left foot. Essemotial (Esse) is the upper left point of this beautiful star, and she is my left hand. Together we are almost complete. Jackie, you are the center. We protect you and guide you. We form the perfect union.

Time and time again, you come here to physically give birth to ensure another generation. Like Mother Earth, you are a creator. This is what you do.

Earlier this morning, I went to do some grocery shopping, and while driving home I suddenly began to think of how the angels are the best kept secret, hidden in plain view. I thought of how many people don't believe, and how they have closed themselves off, forming a protective shell around themselves and around their hearts. I began to weep as I do now.

June 28, 2009
Divine Energy

The Akasie: Jackie, we want to tell you that last night we worked with you energetically. You received healing energy from the Creator. We facilitate healing by allowing the divine energy to flow through us. We call upon our Creator with love and gratitude in our hearts, and the divine energy flows like the pure waters that pour forth effortlessly down a pristine mountain stream.

We tell you that each one of you on the Earth plane are spiritual beings and also have the ability to allow this divine energy to flow through you.

If you were working with an individual on your healing table, you would be the vessel or the giver for the energy to pass through to the other who is receiving. What we are speaking of is energy healing. There are many names and modalities for energy healing just as there are many names and modalities for creating.

When a person is ready to be healed in some area, he will be divinely connected to a healer. We wish to give you a teaching on manifesting here.

Consider that a person is only aware of the medical doctors who give the pills to ease the symptoms or possibly do the surgeries to correct some affliction. When a person is in discomfort and that discomfort has grown to the point that there is much pain and suffering, the person wants relief! He goes to his medical doctor for the remedy because this is what he knows to do; this is his level of understanding.

After you evolve and begin to understand that there is more than the physical to heal and also more than one way of healing, you will begin to look to other places and other healers for assistance.

Jackie, in this time of your conscious awareness, you have been shown that you, as a people, are manifesting these illnesses and these diseases by way of negative thoughts and emotions. We are specifically speaking of how you treat your body. It is time to begin anew and to teach the people a healthier way of living. For many of you, it is time to look at different modalities of healing.

After a time (and this is not always the case), you will find that after a healing you are still suffering somewhat. Your body has many levels, and the structure of the body is multifaceted. To acquire true healing, you must understand how the illness was born in the first place. You must understand that on some level you have created this discomfort, this disease, by the way you think and feel. What we tell you is not absolute, meaning that there is not one simple answer for all. That is certainly not the case. The human body is complex, and when the energies of the body are enmeshed with the mind, soul, and spirit, it grows even more complex.

You must understand, however, that with true spiritual healing comes an understanding on a conscious level that you are spirit in the human form. There comes a deep understanding that you are perfect, unique, and balanced with all of creation. You are God/Goddess, and you are complete. All creation is in divine balance with you. You will transcend to a higher level of awareness—a higher level of consciousness—when all is in alignment to do so. This is the perfect and divine plan of the Creator, you see.

June 29, 2009
To Love Self

Quem: I was traveling about during your sleep time when I was reminded of something I feel may be of interest to you. I give this information to you. Please look at it closely and feel with your heart. Ultimately, what you do with the information depends on how you feel about it.

Remember, we are all unique and have a different purpose here; different lessons, different roles to play out, and different ways to contribute to the oneness of all creation.

The information is to love yourself. Your body is the holy temple of God/Goddess. You have agreed to the responsibility of taking care of this temple. God's spirit resides inside this temple, which is your physical body.

God wishes to partake in a communion ceremony. The ceremony must take place in nature in the presence of Father Sky. Father Sun must be present also. To welcome the participation of mankind in the form of an energetic embrace would be most pleasing. The presence of all who wish to come is encouraged. Welcome all with love from the heart. Great love! The time of the ceremony will be disclosed at a later date.

This ceremony is to welcome all into the oneness of all creation as a reminder to be grateful for all. We speak of Mother Earth, Father Sky, Father Sun, all that comprises the cosmos and the ethers, all angelic hosts, those from the various star nations, nature spirits, elementals, and devas, all in the animal, plant, and mineral kingdoms, and all in the bodies of water great and small. This ceremony will be a time to acknowledge those who have gone on before you, those of you who share this existence with you, and those who will come after you. To be grateful for all beings that are of service to you in all ways imaginable and unimaginable is most pleasing, for there is much that is unknown and unseen to you at this time. We will get back to you later on this. *We are One!*

July 3, 2009
Emotional Release

I have felt so emotional today! It seems like every time I turn around I burst into tears. I didn't do anything, and no one has done or said anything to me to upset me. I really don't understand why I feel like a total wreck!

The Akasie: We would like to explain your sudden emotional outpouring. You are extra sensitive and emotions are on the surface waiting to break free, because you had a major emotional release last night. This, in combination with your travels that have left you with not enough rest, is a good recipe for emotions to be on the surface.

When you are experiencing much growth in spirit, you will have times such as these. In order to make room for the emotions of love and gratitude, you must first release the negative emotions like sadness. You have harbored these negative emotions for such a long while. This comes as a surprise to release such a vast amount of negative energy that you seemingly have not created. Be assured that you have created it, and thus it must be released! Recently, you have noticed the emotions of love and gratitude has been easier to access. This is simply because you have released much of the pent-up negative emotional blocks.

You feel more relaxed and at peace. The very things that bothered you yesterday now seem insignificant in comparison to today. What you feel is on a much deeper level. This is a teaching and a gift for you at this time. If it doesn't feel right to you, do not do it or allow it to be done to you!

July 4, 2009
To Allow

The Akasie: Today we danced with you. For all of us, the dance is always such a beautiful expression of love. This is the first time you have allowed this total guidance in body movements. What a joyous occasion!

This dance we share with you is two-fold. While this dancing brings you higher into a state of complete oneness and in the now, you are also able to work out most of your physical kinks this way. This is very good for you, yes?

July 4, 2009
To Trust

The Akasie: The three of us—Quem, Olim, and Colér—are with you now. We love you completely, as we do with all of our children. We have many children, you see. We are all united in spirit.

Jackie, you are floating effortlessly down the river. You are quite aware that the current is quite strong and could very easily sweep you away. You are not at all concerned about the swift moving waters, however. Large stones and boulders are scattered all around you, yet you float smoothly down the river, moving easily around every stone and every boulder as if it didn't exist. You are not in the least bit disturbed that there are dangerous obstacles all about you. It is as if the stones are to add beauty on your journey. You are in complete harmony with what is happening and where you are going.

Looking back at your journey, you see all that you have passed on your way that has brought you to this very spot. You wonder how you could possibly have gotten to where you stand now without a single scratch or a single bruise.

We tell you how, Jackie—with complete trust. You have been divinely guided all this time. We love you as we do all of our children and all of creation. *We are One!*

July 5, 2009
In Your Heart

Quem: You have asked me many times where I am. Understand now that I am in your heart, so beautiful is the energy. I tell you, I am always near. With your physical eyes, you have not seen me yet, but I am here with you always.

After a time, however, you will occasionally notice energy about you. This energy is something that maybe you just feel with your physical body. Maybe your vision is a little distorted. This is a presence of some sort. It might not be me, as another spirit could possibly be with you.

As you approach the fifth dimension, your chakras become more balanced with your entire being. As your conscious awareness evolves, you find yourself mastering the ability to see the different and unique energies. There are many levels of your being and numerous aspects to yourself that have balanced and are in harmony with self. You are working in the now more and more.

Yes, we take you to the fifth dimension. You question this statement, but at the same time, you feel excitement and expectation. You totally want this. We know it is possible, probable, and inevitable! We do this. *We are One!*

July 6, 2009
The Body Listens to You

The Akasie: Again, you have questioned us about the energy you receive. You have experienced heat with the energy we give to you. Sometimes the energy is manifested as a vibration that is felt throughout your entire body, or perhaps in one particular area, or possibly several areas simultaneously.

Now, you wonder about cold. Can we give you an energy that is cold? We say that, yes, we have done this a few times with you already. You are beginning to put this together on a conscious level now. We go further with this teaching on heat and cold that is manifested in the physical body. Cooling the body with your mind is possible, as heating the body with the mind is also possible. Your mind controls your temperature.

You as humans have gotten yourselves into many boxes, one being your present belief that your body must be hot when you are in weather that you believe to be hot. That is a relative statement, because hot to one may not be hot to another. The same is true with cold. Your mind tells your body what to do and how to feel at all times. Your body has been programmed by what you think.

The reason I keep asking about the energy I am receiving and the heat is because I have these hot flashes. I am just at that age. I know part of what I am experiencing is my hormonal imbalance. How does this tie into what you are saying?

The Akasie: We are not discussing hormonal difficulties at the moment. We are discussing how the body listens to you. We give you this example. You go outside in the sun and say,

"Oh, it is hot out here." The body naturally thinks that it is also hot.

It is time to take command of the body and to get out of those boxes that have been preventing you from moving forward up until this point.

We tell you the truth, the body responds according to how you think. Take an illness, for example. One way illness is manifested is by being fearful of becoming ill. Disease is manifested in this same manner. The same is true with your internal thermostat. All of what we have mentioned is controlled by your belief system.

July 7, 2009
The Ascended Masters

Jackie, we are here. The four of us are here with you now. We feel your energy, your apprehension, and your excitement. Yes, you hear well. We are here for the specific reason of finding out how you may help us. We have many projects going on at this time. Your father Quem tells us what you are involved in. You like energy, do you? We are pleased to find another as you.

We will be observing you for a few days, perhaps a few weeks. Then, we will decide how to approach the subject. We know you do not understand, but not knowing is fine with you for the time being. We will keep communication open for now, yes?

We tell you at the present time to continue to follow your guidance in all areas. You know what we are saying. We leave you for now.

Today was a complete surprise. I have been visited by many Akasie members and as I understand it, I have been visited by others who are not of the Akasie group, but related somehow. I feel apprehensive about all of these different beings coming and talking to me. It all seems a little much.

July 8, 2009
If It Doesn't Feel Good, Don't Accept!

Quem: Jackie, you ask about the energy you receive at night that makes you short of breath and feel sick. I tell you that it is an energy that we are giving you that is for a specific purpose. You are not used to it and it makes you extremely uncomfortable and agitated. The reason for this energy is for you to become more aware to ask for help. It doesn't feel good to you. If it doesn't feel good, don't accept it. This is the case. Also, learning to breathe through pain, discomfort, agitation, heat, cold, stress, and all sorts of uncomfortable situations is beneficial for you. Breathe to relax.

I am confused here. Every few days I receive different guides. It seems I am constantly being introduced to someone new. I have difficulty getting the names, so the guides will spell the names out for me. Why am I getting all of these different guides? Is this really necessary?

Also, someone is giving me energy that makes me feel sick and then telling me that if I don't feel comfortable, I should not accept it. How do I not accept it?

Quem: First, I will address the names. It is like everything else we do. Our teachings are multifaceted. We spell the names out for many purposes. You, Miss, are blocking our communications because you grow fearful every time someone "new" to you comes to the forefront. You will learn to relax and receive the names with practice. Just know for now that this is part of our teachings. Relax and allow.

Now, I will address your concerns about the energy you receive. We are teaching you to focus on what you are receiving. More specifically, we are giving you opportunities to feel different levels of energy from different beings. Some of these energies are so powerful that they overtake you. There are infinite energies.

Take into consideration the fact that each being holds his or her own unique vibration, simultaneously he or she is creating thoughts and emotions. In addition, these beings are coming to you for some purpose. So you see you are interacting with all of these energies all at once. We began this teaching the day you first begin to hear our words.

When I told you "do not accept," I wanted you to question my words. You have the logical side of you, and it is for your own good to not only question everything you experience, but to *feel* what you experience!

Many go about their day just thinking through the situations at hand and forgo feeling with the heart. I am teaching you to integrate the two and to know why you feel certain things. Your feelings are there to guide you. Trust them! You are to feel first. Trust your instincts and think later.

When you work to logically understand certain things, it doesn't work because sometimes there isn't a logical explanation. We will work on this later, but what we are doing is teaching you to identify your emotions and follow your instincts. You are going to the fifth dimension. In this dimension, you work with your higher knowing, your guidance. You must learn to trust these aspects of yourself.

July 9, 2009
Over Extended

The Suthers: Jackie, we would like to introduce ourselves to you at this time. We are united as sisters and brothers in one cause. This cause is to relieve humanity of the pain, the fear, and the hate they are entrenched in. This is our cause, Jackie. We see that you have awakened. Like a new babe, you are just beginning to walk. You have much to remember and much to learn.

We see you learning and feeling much love and gratitude because of what you are experiencing. We are happy for you! Your time brings us all back to when we felt the way you do now.

We hear you say you wish to know our names. We also see that you do not receive names easily. We will spell the name of our group for you. Our group's name is A–P–U–R–S–E.

I could hear the guide laughing and wondered what this was all about. Apurse? Oh, I get it. A purse. Oh, brother.

Our names are Hanal, Bejamen, Chereece, and Stephanó. We are the Suthers.

Jackie, we have decided to tell you something. Listen closely. Write this down. You are a writer and you study under Quem, yes? We tell you to listen closely to what the Akasie teaches you. For now, this is your way. We will come back later to see how you are doing. Right now, you are into too many other projects. We have spoken to your masters. They tell us about the complexity of your life right now. Simplify and we will come again. We wish to work with you regarding a particular endeavor, you see.

Will you please share what the project is with me?

The Suthers: We tell you that our wishes are for you to assist us in a little leg work. Make friendships, a network of like people who work with us knowingly. You would be on the move.

I don't know how I can do this plus write.

The Suthers: Exactly, that is why we consult with the Akasie. Right now timing is not cohesive with ours. We look for another to assist. We will keep apprised of your advancement. *We are One!*

July 10, 2009
Loving Your Self

Quem: We intend on keeping our word. We teach by the way of segments. When you have completed one step, we continue onto the next step. Each step consists of many segments. At the present time, we are working on the step of *loving yourself.* You will continue to learn to nurture yourself. You have been making steps toward more awareness of how you treat yourself in accordance with how others perceive you and what they desire of your time.

To be more specific here, it is your perception that you must do what other people expect you to do. Up until this time, when someone has requested your help in a particular matter, you have felt obligated to oblige. In the past, when you have turned someone down, you allowed your being to be flooded with guilt. You felt you weren't pleasing them or living up to their expectations. In other words, you felt you were letting them down. You think you are the only one to assist the other? I tell you that your ego is involved here. Look closely and examine this for yourself.

You must realize that you do always have a choice in what you do. It is a matter of whether you allow yourself to relax and do what you'd like, or whether you suck up and do what the others would like you to do. Look at when you do something for another when you really do not want to. Do you think you possibly felt resentful because you gave in and did what you perceived to be the correct thing?

You also have the choice to feel guilty about the decision or you can choose to be grateful that you have a choice at all and rejoice in this freedom! You have freedom in all areas of life, Jackie. You have the freedom to live anywhere, go anywhere, or do anything. You have broad freedoms.

People sometimes will journey into a box, which is a confining belief and think "this" is all there is. Not so! Live your life to the fullest by experiencing all you can imagine ... or not. It is your desires that make up your physical experience, but don't limit yourself because of little imagination or the perception of this being all there is or that something is what you *must* do. These are misconceptions. Enjoy yourself!

You saw how you were in a box concerning Las Vegas. You thought you didn't ever want to visit this city because of the reputation that you had preconceived about it. You didn't think it was possible that this place could or would bring to you anything other than discomfort or anxiety. Your box was very confining. Now this box is forever gone. Boxes are burdens of thinking, belief, and choice. You do not confine yourself concerning this belief any longer. We are pleased at your progress.

This lesson is on how you treat yourself and others. When all is agreeable and you are living in the now, there is never tension or stress. It is easy for all to get along and do what is necessary to survive, have a good time, or whatever the case may be.

Whenever there is a bump in the road, however, you have either traveled with your thoughts too far into the past or too far into the future. You are worrying about things that cannot be changed in the past and fearful of what is in store for you in the future. If you entertain these thoughts, they will bring you much concern. Life becomes more difficult because you are adding unwarranted stress and tension to the mix.

I am moving the subject forward to show one of the ways people release tension. People in general tend to copulate when all is in turmoil. This is done because of tension and frustration. Sexual activity is used (and is meant to be used) for release of stress of all kinds.

However, people in general have forgotten this reason for copulation. Many use the practice of copulation for other reasons. One is to get off on self. You do not understand what we mean by this statement. I'll explain this to you.

What we mean by "get off" is that a person (not persons; this is singular) has the desire that is focused on having possession of or being in control of the other. This is what they do to please themselves! Where is the love in this case? Nowhere is love to be found! They use this act so they may control the other person, not to please the other person.

Control is a symptom of *fear*. What is it you are afraid of? I tell you it is the fear of the unknown. This person (or perhaps both people) who is engaged in copulation is unaware of his or her fear or need to control. He or she is only aware of the desire to have.

The bond of sexual energy is meant for a far greater purpose. I tell you this is a sacred union for raising the love vibration of self. In order to raise this vibration, you love the other, please the other, and connect with the other; you take the other up to feel complete uninhibited sexual pleasure and release the pent-up sexual tension.

Sexual tension is the result of encounters with the opposite sex (or the same sex). The encounter is an exchange of energy that many times goes undetected by the people involved.

The encounter is like a dance, an emotional dance. There is an underlying appreciation (on some level), and love (on some level), and attraction (on some level) for the other person. It is a dance. One must be very aware of the emotions to detect the exchange of the energy of this dance. This dance is called foreplay in your language. Notice this dance, this exchange, with the other, Jackie. As you have noticed so far, all teachings from us concern you personally. The Akasie are currently assisting you in realizing and releasing your blocks.

These blocks that we speak of are capable of creating a hemorrhage of sorts in the body. The blood seeps or flows uncontrollably in an area and forms a pool of unwanted substance, which causes much discomfort and stress to the body. If left unchecked, this stress will cause illness and ultimately result in the death of the body.

Old belief patterns that do not serve you any longer cause negative emotion or stress to settle in different parts of the body. It depends on what those old beliefs are and how tightly you hold onto them as to where and when they manifest in the physical body. These beliefs cause discomfort because they are not in harmony with spirit. The discomfort is there to tell you that something is amiss and to look at your life closely. Listen to your heart to prevent any hemorrhage.

When you are beginning this process, you must pay much attention to your thoughts and emotions. What is it that causes you to feel angry, depressed, or any other negative emotion? First, you must identify what is causing you stress and discomfort. We tell you that this stress will settle in the tissues of your body, the temple of God/Goddess. This stress will destroy mercilessly without any concern whatsoever for the host, the body. Thank the Creator for the realization that you can now identify that you are angry or depressed. This is the first step toward healing. Be grateful!

In the deep recesses of your mind, which we call the higher self or your higher awareness, you are always aware of your growth in all areas, and you are constantly working with all levels of self by the way of dreams and fleeting thoughts. There are also other ways that your higher awareness communicates with you. We will only speak of these two ways at this writing, however.

Dreams are a way of working through your challenges. As you know, dreams are elusive, as they are easily forgotten or perhaps you aren't even aware that you are having them. You must remember your dreams until morning unless you are willing to rouse yourself from sleep to journal your dreams. Getting up in the middle of the night to record dreams is not convenient nor is it desirable. There is much value placed on a good night's rest. Dreams will be discussed another time.

Now, your thoughts are right there in front of you. You just have to catch them. We use this analogy because thoughts come at such a rapid speed, so fast in fact that some of you are barely aware you have had a particular thought before you have created another one.

I wish to move forward with this line of thinking. When people become too busy, too involved and too controlling, their thoughts speed up. I tell you this in itself causes much stress. Are you one who has trouble turning off the mind to rest at night? Do you feel that you could use a vacation? Are you one who thinks that you would like to walk out a particular door and never return? Perhaps you entertain thoughts of wishing you had another life or just ending it all. These thoughts are clear indicators that your life has become a bit too stressful. It would benefit you greatly to begin to make the appropriate changes that will bring you into balance and harmony with self and all of creation.

For the so-called responsible person (we say *controlled person* in this axample), a thought like, "I want to walk out the door and never return" might seem unreasonable or even preposterous. You know that to run away would most certainly seem impossible; you have too many responsibilities to even consider a break!

We tell you, dear ones, that it is all about choices. We advise you to examine these thoughts closely, as they are most important! These thoughts and others similar to these are far more than mere clues that something is amiss. Please pay attention to what you are thinking!

I remembered this happened to me back when I worked outside of the home. After a long day of being on my feet, I felt utterly exhausted. As I was driving home to begin my second job, I was thinking of how dead-tired I was. It seemed that I was always working. I had yet to pick up the kids from daycare, cook dinner for the family, do laundry, and the cleaning; you know, that stuff you have to do. I was driving on the highway and there was a split in the road. One way went north and the other went south. I had a crazy thought to head the opposite direction of home, but the thought didn't end there! I went on to imagine myself beginning a new and totally different life, starting from scratch with nothing and no one but myself.

I considered my resources; I looked at all the different ways I could get my hands on money to see me through, the clothes I was wearing, and how long it might take me to secure a job. There was this longing to start over all by myself at the same time I knew logically I would never abandon my family like that.

Quem: Yes, this is what we are talking about.

The conscious self is the part of you that gets you through your day, this life. The conscious self holds the memories that connect you to all things that enable you to do things like your job, relate to friends and family, and remember what you have on your grocery list. You are connected to your conscious mind, but what about what your heart is telling you?

Much of the time, instead of being aware that you would like to go outside and drink in the fresh air, you feel anxious or irritable. Sometimes you are not even aware that you feel anxious or irritable! I assure you that the people around you are most aware! We are here to teach you to become aware and to listen so you can begin to make the necessary adjustments in your lifestyle. We would like you to live a long, comfortable life with much happiness.

To ease any discomfort and ultimately prevent disease, listen to your body. Your negative emotions are a tool and a gift from your higher consciousness to your conscious awareness that something that you are thinking, feeling, or doing isn't in alignment with spirit; you are not on your path.

Your mind communicates with you by the way of emotions. When you feel negative emotion, it will manifest with physical discomfort like a stomachache, headache, and so on. Your body tells you that something isn't right through discomfort and illness. After a time, your body will no longer tolerate the stress and become diseased. Unfortunately, there are many times when people have ignored the communication for so long that the disease is too far advanced, making it very difficult or maybe impossible for your medical doctors to assist you in physical healing.

We, the Akasie, say that when a person has descended to the level of manifesting physical disease, the negative thoughts and emotions have become very ingrained in his daily habit. Physical healing sometimes is seemingly out of reach, but we tell you nothing is impossible. Know this, for what we say is truth! Yes, you may seek your doctors and they may ease your discomfort for a time, but listen here! We tell you that you must heal on the spiritual level to receive true healing on the physical level. You must remember who you are! You are spiritual beings, gods and goddesses who are most powerful! You have the full potential to love self and all of creation unconditionally. When you have realized that love for self, you have ascended higher.

Although physical disease manifests itself because of many reasons, they all lead back to the cause of not knowing your true self, not listening to your emotions, and not being in alignment with spirit. Emotion is a language. To learn and fully understand how to use this language is to gain much knowledge and much power.

You have heard us say to you that you must listen to your heart. What we mean about listening to your heart is that you are listening to your love and recognizing it when you feel that love; feel that energy emanate from your heart.

The emotions are there to let you know when you feel good (positive) and when you are in alignment with your soul and spirit. When you feel discomfort (negative), you are not in alignment with your soul and spirit. To be healthy you should listen, interpret your emotions correctly, and then follow the guidance they give you.

August 1, 2009
There Are No Real Goodbyes

A few months ago, my great Aunt Vina passed away. She was the last of that generation and an awesome woman; the love in her heart went out to everyone. Aunt Vina has been instrumental in my life by supporting me with my writing, filling in the many blanks concerning our family genealogy, and by gifting me with her autobiography that was added into the family historical records.

In the roaring twenties, straight out of school herself, she had gone on to teach others. Until the day she passed, she was a huge presence; she was the glue that held our family together. At the age of ninety years, Aunt Vina decided she would move into an assisted living facility. For the next twelve years, she lived in a tiny apartment sharing most of her meals with those who were nearing the end of their lives. Each time she would befriend another, she wondered who would be going home first. To me that took a great amount of courage.

Her main passions were connecting to people any way she could and helping them. She often spoke of the many people that she corresponded with. When I went to see her in her later years and she depended on others to drive her places, she would request a trip to the local restaurant to get her "fix" of fried chicken and biscuits.

Each year at the assisted living facility, her daughters would give her a huge birthday party complete with birthday cake and punch; the place would be packed. We always asked Aunt

Vina if she would play a tune on the piano. Her reply was to laugh and smile as she made her way through the crowd to play her favorite hymns. Because I have spent years taking piano lessons myself, I was especially amazed that she was able to play any tune without the assistance of sheet music. She told me that she played by "ear."

On Aunt Vina's 100th birthday, her daughters created a time line out of craft paper. They taped the paper to the walls. They began with the year she was born marking down every major event, like inventions, wars, each elected president, all of her accomplishments that included the births and marriages of all of her children, grandchildren, great grandchildren and great, great grandchildren! The paper easily covered fifty feet. She had all of these people in her life and yet she continued to give to each one in any way she could. She left me the legacy of love.

Over the years, we exchanged hundreds of letters. In almost every letter toward the end of her life, she would say, "God must have forgotten me." And then go on to talk about how much she loved everyone. She was so ready to go home, yet she lingered; her mind still intact as her body continued to waste away.

Why must people endure such pain? None of it seems fair to me. A part of me didn't want her to leave because she was so important to me, but even so, I prayed to God that he would please take her so she wouldn't hurt any longer. When she finally did pass, I hoped that she would come to me in a vision or to talk to me, but she has not.

The Akasie: We say unto you, Jackie, you have had another great opportunity for learning, and a multifaceted learning at that! Please know that we, like you, grieve for many things that happen that are seemingly unjust.

When you lose someone, you miss them; you miss his or her smile and laughter. When he or she is gone, you miss the many aspects of that person. Please remember they are not gone forever. They are just on a short journey back home to visit other family and to do other things. You will see them again, just as you will see Esse and Jithury again. Keep moving forward toward your goals.

August 3, 2009
Manipulation

The Akasie: Tonight while doing your meditation, we took you down into a deep relaxed state. We did a manipulation on you that was two-fold. This was an intense time for you. You experienced no movement in the body except for what we did for you. You did no breathing except for what we did for you. Do you remember not breathing? You had no desire to breathe. This was to let you feel what it will be like when it is your time to pass from your body. What you experienced is what it is like to have an assisted peaceful passing, or a transition to the other side. We will assist you when the time comes.

In addition, the procedure we preformed was to enhance your memory. Writers require a great vocabulary and a great memory. We are assisting you to acquire a great bank of words that you can put in a safe place and retrieve when they are needed.

How do you do this stuff? I mean, how do you manipulate my body, brain, and mind like you do? I am in total awe. During the "procedure," I felt like I was in my body but at the same time, not. The whole experience was pleasant but rather peculiar! I remember being aware that I was paralyzed, but I didn't care.

And the not breathing? I had no desire to breathe whatsoever! On a conscious level, I knew that I wasn't breathing myself. It seemed like minutes passed before another breathe came. In between each breath, I was totally calm. I felt no fear at all.

There have been many times in my life that I have gone into a complete state of panic if for some reason my breathing was interrupted. This experience was the exact opposite for me; I felt like if I didn't ever take another breath again, I would be perfectly fine with it. I felt a separation from my physical self almost as if I was an observer, but I couldn't see myself. You know, I have always been fearful of how I would die and if I would physically suffer during the process. To know that you will assist me when the time comes for me to leave this world is a huge relief! We are One!

August 4, 2009

New Teachers: The Harbañaro Brothers

The Harbañaro Brothers: We begin by saying that you are a gracious hostess by welcoming us into your home. We feel very comfortable here, although the couch is a little short for the four of us.

I heard the guide speaking chuckle. All sorts of thoughts began to fly through my mind. Who are these guys? I felt apprehensive, like, what now? I tried to relax and let them continue with their words. So many guides and they all have a different style, a unique personality. I feel like all of my senses are on high alert.

Today we have a different sort of teaching that will enable you to move forward. Remember good humor through this. You'll need it.

Again, he laughed and I began to feel more comfortable.

As we were saying, today is a bit different. We use a variety of unique techniques for guiding people such as you.

I am feeling a whole lot of anxiety here. You come here and introduce yourselves as the Harbañaro Brothers? What kind of name is Harbañaro? Isn't a harbañaro some sort of pepper? Is this another one of your jokes? I wanted to satisfy my curiosity so I got up to get my dictionary. Okay, the word is habañera and it is a pepper that is extremely hot. Who exactly are you, and why are you here? I really don't want to be rude to you. It is just that I keep getting different guides (I guess you are guides), and I feel like this is just too strange. I wish someone would explain all of this to me.

The Harbañaro Brothers: We are sorry you feel apprehensive. We work to relax you by giving you words of assurance. We do this by showing you that we have a sense of humor; we are not so stiff. We give you smiles and work to make you feel at ease and comfortable with our presence. The energy of fear emanates from your being. We wish you to put your feet up and enjoy our visit. We are pleased to be here in your company!

For a long while, we have watched you in your climb up. We have waited for you to reach the point where we could communicate with one another.

You have made agreements with many to receive teachings while in your Earth body. These teachings manifest themselves in a way for you to go through the rest of your Earth life and teach others. You are to guide others who do not hear the words from their guides. This is with the belief that those you teach have come to a place when their hearts are full of love and gratitude.

The reason for today's meeting is we are here to teach you. We will be with you for a long while to teach you many things. Yes, you'll have time to write and fulfill your many physical responsibilities and care for your family, and do your artistic endeavors, such as creating with your tiny colored beads, too! Always remember your love, as this is what makes your heart sing and this love is what will always guide you on your path into the Light.

What we will be working with you on is simple, yet seems complex. Remember as we begin this journey that it would be best if you were relaxed and allowed things to unfold. You will learn faster and more efficiently when you are in a relaxed state. For the subject matter, we begin with this lesson. You are to manifest a group.

From out of nowhere I said, "I already did! You're here aren't you?"

The Harbañaro Brothers: Done! You already passed the first lesson. We move on ... the jokes are finished for now, onto the real lesson.

We tell you that our name is the "Suthers." Remember we came to you a while back? It is good for you to examine your feelings when you encounter anyone, even your guides. Miss, you are to venture out of your comfort zone. There are many guides other than the Akasie who wish to work with you. It is time for you to understand that you will work with many over the coming years.

As we stated before our "dance," we are ready to begin teaching as agreed before your physical life began this time. What we have for you is a series of lessons beginning with how to maneuver through the energies. It sounds like a matter that cannot be discerned, but we tell you this is the first teaching.

As your vibration climbs or increases, you will become increasingly sensitive to the energies by knowing the feelings, even the thoughts of those around you. You will find yourself in situations that you'll find disheartening. Other situations you'll find love embracing you totally. This all comes with the territory. When you reach the fifth dimension, you will traverse through and around energies, allowing them to be. There is no desire or need to manipulate them. The energies are as they are. Your objective is to feel love and gratitude in totality, at all times and everywhere.

You will begin by purposely putting yourself in situations like listening to beautiful music to lift your spirit. Play your music as often as possible. Be in nature, go outdoors. Talk to the plant life and love them. Treat them like people. You go about pinching and pruning the plants and trees as if they are nothing! You would not dare cut a person's arm off or even trim his or her hair without discussion first! The plants are alive. Treat them as such! You'll be rewarded countless times by doing these things. *We are One!*

August 5, 2009

Moving Forward

The Akasie: This writing is to discuss with you changes in the book, When Angels Speak. After rereading the beginning of the book and listening to your constructive criticism, this is what we think. You are correct that the first chapter is dry and boring. We need examples from real people and stories to make this book not only educational, but something that will draw the reader in and for the reader to relate to personally.

We have decided to venture to a subject that you feel the reader may benefit more from. In addition, we have decided to look at a subject dearer to the hearts of those who seek a higher understanding of the spiritual nature.

We continually monitor your feelings and listen to your comments concerning the books that we have presented to you. We know the order of books. We know how they should be presented. We feel at this time you should be more open, willing, and patient to see what materializes with the writings; let the writing evolve.

Quem: I am doing the writing, Jackie. I am telling you what to type. All writers must edit and rearrange their work. The words will change and the ideas will grow. You see, I do not have a written manuscript before me. We will continue as planned. Will you be patient with me, please?

August 5, 2009
Sensory Input

Clare and Sarah: Good evening. We hear you have been reading some of Drunvalo Melchizedek's work and have found some additional information on the Internet. You are very excited! Get all the material by him you can and read all of it thoroughly! He has not been on Earth long. We are pleased to be working with him. He is here to show the others the way. We will speak to the Akasie about a project that we agreed to do. No, not the picture shows. We have additional projects to do.

I feel apprehensive for some reason.

Clare and Sarah: The project entails much prayer, enlightenment.

The Akasie: Jackie, Clare, and Sarah had intended to show you pictures today. Instead, because you were in the middle of transition to a higher vibration, they assisted in the adjustments of chemicals in the brain and releasing of toxins in organs of the body.

In the beginning, you did not use discernment on all that you were allowing to enter into your conscious mind. We are talking about all the different types of information that you constantly receive in the form of sensory input.

We will be working intensely with you on the input of what goes in your mind. All external stimuli will be monitored and dealt with. We are speaking of positive and negative energies in all forms.

We are moving you toward becoming more aware of all that you absorb through the senses. As you become more aware, you will be better able to discern which choices to make. One of the things we speak of concerns what you listen to as your choice of music. You will notice when you listen to certain types of music you are uplifted, and you are able to feel love and gratitude much easier. Everything you hear goes into your mind and has either a positive or negative effect. We remind you that you are connected to the mass consciousness, so on some level everything you experience affects all of creation!

You receive input from the five physical senses. Do you really pay attention to that input? Do you really appreciate all that you receive? We talk much of the sound of your music; how the tones uplift, relax, and energize. We also ask, "What is it that you set your eyes upon that gives you pleasure?" We tell you to always see the beauty in everything. Think about what is positive that you see, and notice the positive emotion swell up in your heart center.

Become aware of what you feel not only with your hands, but what you feel with all parts of your body! Take special interest in the textures and be grateful. May these feelings be pleasing to you always.

Smells and tastes also are of special significance. Particular smells and tastes may evoke sentimental memories of friends and family when you felt the exchange of much love. Also, certain foods bring a special pleasure that most of you partake in. What is it about this chocolate that you all seem to love so much? Is it the unique taste, the creamy texture, the chocolaty smell, or simply that you can indulge in such a treat?

We also bring up the aromas such as freshly baked bread or the delicate perfumes wafting in the breezes. These are gifts from the Creator intended to induce love and gratitude from all those who partake. As the saying goes, stop and smell the roses. Enjoy every moment, for each is a treasured gift.

August 6, 2009
The Ascended Masters

The Suthers: What we have here is a little bit of a paradox. You seem to think that you are not up there; you are not evolved enough, do not know enough, do not love enough, or perhaps do not have a high enough vibration to accomplish your task. You feel you must be an understudy for years to accomplish great things.

We tell you that your beliefs are inaccurate and untrue! You are ready now to do amazing things to assist the people who are near and dear to you. You go now and do what you feel you are meant to do and say to these people. There are times when you have the feeling that you should just listen to them and love them. Sometimes these people just want to be heard, and all that is necessary is for you to listen. Yes, we say this is your intuition and your heart giving you guidance. Your intuition is your higher consciousness communicating with you. Your heart is where you feel your positive emotion. Positive emotions are what let you know what is right for that moment. Pay attention to the feelings and do what your inner guidance tells you to do. Your angels are always near to assist you; just ask.

Tonight during my meditation, the Akasie were working at disturbing me, drawing my focus away from my third eye by making noises and talking. I was appalled! I asked them, "Why are you doing this?"

You must learn to go deep within yourself by not allowing any distraction of any kind to hinder your relaxed state. We will continue to practice this, because there will be times when you will require a practiced focus that is impenetrable. In case you have not noticed, we also create obstacles to strengthen you. How committed are you? No matter where you encounter obstacles, you are to push forward. This encourages you to become more determined, to have a stronger resolve.

On another note, today we are going to discuss our future. You like this idea? We say always live in the moment, but have an eye on your goal. Your goal is enlightenment and traversing to higher dimensions in the physical body. Although enlightenment and traversing the dimensions seem to be two separate enfoldments of the evolutionary process, it is similar to writing this book and receiving pictures; they are two separate works, but are both guiding you further home to the Light.

Jackie, you have much emotion and longing when we speak of home. When you go home, you will be leaving the Earth plane where there are no earthly restrictions or boundaries that the physical body entails. You are free of the weight the physical has set upon you. Being in the physical body is restricting as you are of the ethereal—spirit and to join with a physical body is rather unpleasant for many. You have a subconscious desire or memory to return to your natural state. We stay by your side always. This is the way. Nothing can touch you when we do this. You continue to wonder how we can do this *always*. Jackie, this is what we do and who we are. We live this way to assist those here on Mother Earth. We do this because we love all of creation.

As we assist those of you on the Earth plane, we ourselves evolve higher and become more divine in nature. Our love grows stronger, more powerful, and accordingly, we grow to be wiser in all that we do. These are all positive assets that are all relative. Even though our essence is of the positive nature, we continually strive to be greater in all that we are and do.

We affirm that all of creation goes toward being more positive always and everywhere. This is the goal—to have our hearts fixed on love only. At this time, there is much happiness and joy that you are unable to even begin to imagine.

August 7, 2009
Believing in Divine Guidance

The Akasie: Last night, we were in deep discussion about how people come to acquire their truths or form their beliefs. Your question was: "Why are people aware that there are angels, but do not believe they have divine guidance?"

Jackie, you think the reason that people do not believe is because as children they were not taught there were angels who were there to assist and guide them in all that they do. This is the truth, but still there are other reasons.

There is a vague notion of angels. Jackie, the previous statement is your truth, was your truth, and your experience. You knew of angels as a child. Did your parents ever discuss these beings with you? No, your parents did not incorporate this information into their teachings, nor did they teach you anything that would assist you with your spiritual steps. Know that there are many reasons people do not have that level of awareness.

Teaching of the angelic beings to people while they are still open to the esoteric is the wisest. We say to speak of us openly. Ah, we have a campaign! We write books for children. Yes!

Thinking this was a fantastic idea, I immediately began to brainstorm! We need to find an artist to draw beautiful pictures of the angels. In my mind's eye, I looked to the Akasie to write the books. I asked the Akasie: "Who is better than angels to know what the children need?"

One of the guides sent a picture that was absolute in its message. He stood there with his arms crossed, his expression very stern and determined like we were in a sparring match. I knew immediately that I wasn't going to win this one! We agreed that we would write the books together.

My mind raced ahead. As I turned the pages of this "book," I could clearly see the angels portrayed like beautiful people who were dressed in exquisite gowns and robes adorned in precious jewels with their majestic feathered wings extended wide. Their silky hair set perfectly in place that was complimented with headdresses decorated with precious metals and faceted gemstones and crystals.

The Akasie: Make no mistake, to portray us like you say is not required or even what we desire. Remember, this is a children's book. Angels are not of the physical realm like you are. We do not wear clothes of any sort. We are not of the flesh, although sometimes in extraordinary circumstances we do manifest ourselves in such a manner.

Wait! You are Pleiadians, right? You are a people who have lives and families, right?

The Akasie: What you have before you is a misnomer. Presently, you are working with different beings whom you know not the likes of. At this time, you are unable to see these beings, as their vibration is of a much higher frequency. There are many, and each species is distinctive in nature. Some of the Akasie still reside in the Pleiades star system. In addition, you have the ascended masters about you, some of which are also Pleiadian-born and of the Akasie linage. We surprise you now—you have archangels about. Look before you and know without a shadow of a doubt that there are thousands of different beings going to and fro.

August 8, 2009
Divine Beauty and Perfection Is in All of Creation

Quem: It is important to think, feel, and know in your heart that divine beauty and perfection is in all of creation. Everything and everyone has his or her purpose and his or her time. We give this message to you. Remember this and it will take you far.

August 8, 2009
More on Spiritual Rape

Earlier today, I was up into the city and had some spare time in between appointments to read a few pages in Drunvalo Melchizedek's book. What stood out was a particular passage describing a woman (his girlfriend at the time) experiencing a cosmic sexual union. The whole scene was far out, and I probably would have dismissed it as something that was totally fictional had I not had my own sexual experience with energy beings.

Again, I began to wonder about the "spiritual rape" that I had gone through. Maybe I didn't have the entire picture of what really happened or what their true intention was. The angels always tell me that the teachings are multifaceted. I questioned the Akasie about all of this. Their response was, "Wait until you get home and eat a bite before we get into a discussion."

Here I am at home and very calm. I am not sure I really care anymore what their reasons were. Even so there is undoubtedly, a teaching here somewhere, so I am here, ready to listen.

The Akasie: We tell you one thing for sure; you have come a long way from your endless questions to this point. You know now that all will be revealed at the correct time. You are learning to allow. Be grateful, Miss.

Yes, you feel different and more complete. You could sit there for hours completely relaxed, and maybe you should, except we have work to do young lady. So let's get to it. We tell you that, yes, you have experienced a major shift in your awareness. This is good for you to realize. You have affirmed that you are relaxed, balanced, and one with all of creation many times. All is working in your favor.

Olim: Jackie, let's talk about your sexual encounter with the other ones. The other ones came for many purposes. As you know, the experience, the teaching, was multifaceted like all teachings. We were working with you on many levels at that time. During this time, you were learning to focus on creating energies with your mind. In addition, we were assisting you in activating the third eye to also visualize the energies. We also were working with you to activate the *kundalini*. This particular energy stimulates the sexual apparatus. This stimulation was to show you many things about yourself. I say here that many women at this time do not allow themselves the sexual pleasure. Be it known, there are many men with this challenge also.

Your sexual dysfunction has been caused by a belief of yours that manifested into a physical block, thus preventing you from having a satisfying sexual relationship. This experience was also a gift to help you feel the raw sexual need for release and to free yourself from this self-imposed prison. Jackie, that encounter was allowed in order for you to have the experience.

You were allowed to believe the other ones who worked with you were earth-bound spirits out to use the females who are vulnerable and unsuspecting, when in reality, those beings came to help you open on all levels.

The stress of the energy you experienced leading up to, during, and directly after the encounter rewired some of your mental apparatus. The full result of this experience is yet to be realized.

Is this a good thing?

Olim: Miss, stress does unkind things to your physical apparatus and this includes your brain. With our assistance, you are healing in entirety. Relax. Be grateful for all that you receive.

It was spiritual rape because it was against your will, but at the same time, the teaching was paramount and allowed for these reasons:

- To realize the different energies in the universe

- For the experience

- To learn to ask for help from the angels

- To learn to protect yourself and use discernment

- To learn to speak about the ordeal with others

- To learn to ask for help and protection from your husband

- To realize the possible depth of sexual pleasure/obsession

- To learn self-control

- To understand how powerful energy is on a human sexual level

- To learn to be aware of how stuck you are in old belief patterns therefore engaging you to see a bigger picture

- To know your true strength

This was a period of initiation for you. Be grateful for the teachings you have received, as they are a rare gift.

August 9, 2009
Balancing the Masculine and Feminine Polarities

The Akasie: We like how you are thinking and feeling today. You are upbeat and full of happiness. You are looking for the beauty in all. Remember to do this always.

Many suffer from imbalance due to the masculine energy that has been dominant for approximately the last thirteen thousand years. Now is the time to come together to unite the male and female polarities so all women and men can know his or her true self.

It can come at no better time in conjunction with the coming of the fifth dimension, which is the time of harmony, balance, and union. It is time for love and peace.

The fifth dimension is a higher level of consciousness. To attain this higher level of awareness and to know your true power, you must go within and seek your divine nature. This is the time to understand who you truly are. You are special and unique, and you have a great purpose and a great gift to share with all of creation. You must know this divine gift in order to share with all, you see? *We are One!*

August 10, 2009
Expression of Emotions and
Growing Balanced Adults: Part One

The Akasie: We have a special purpose in our writing today. You are to go on your way to the great city and be with another woman whom you had clashed with before. The energy of the other one is strong and brazen. She has much pain inside that she carries. When the pain bubbles up and spills forth, it is manifested through her verbal and body language. This way of negative expression causes others anxiety and discomfort. On some level, she realizes this, and because of this, she continues to push down the pain. Unfortunately, these feelings of anxiety and anger manifest at seemingly inappropriate times. This is why you have felt uncomfortable when you were with her in the past.

Sometimes people do not want to show their feelings or insecurities. Often people perceive this exposure as a sign of weakness. This is the ego in control here.

How many times have you heard someone sternly tell a child to stop crying? The child is crying for a reason. The child is unhappy. The reason for the crying should be explored. Maybe he is hurt physically or emotionally or perhaps the child seeks attention on another level. What does this tell you? The child desires interaction of some sort, but instead the child receives a reprimand.

This is where it begins for some in their childhoods. Some children are taught from day one that crying is not to be tolerated, so they learn very early on to deny their feelings, burying them deep inside. As they grow older, they become more entrenched in this behavior of not being able to express themselves properly; to allow the tears to flow is simply considered an unacceptable behavior. We see this especially with the young boys, but the little girls get this type of chastisement also. Tears are of great value and necessary for the release of both positive and negative emotions.

We'd like to point out the different reasons why this is occurring in your social structures:

- The crying is annoying and gets on the nerves of the caregiver.

- If in public when the child cries, the parents can be ashamed or embarrassed by the child's behavior.

- The caregiver does not take the time to help the child work through what he is feeling and why he is feeling it.

- The caregiver simply doesn't appear to care, but in all actuality, the caregiver doesn't have the level of awareness to understand the importance of this self-expression.

By the time this child has grown into an adult, it is quite possible that he is no longer in touch with his true feelings.

We have explained that expressing any emotion is of great importance. To feel and express the negative emotion tells you a story of what is happening to the individual.

Now, we tell you that the same is true for expressing positive emotions. Self-expression comes naturally. To smile, to laugh, and to cry are all natural and quite healthy for you to release positive emotions, such as joy, happiness, love, and compassion. To not allow yourself to express these feelings through the physical release of a smile, laughter, or tears is what we render as stuffing your feelings. We feel a good example would be the giving of a son or daughter in marriage. You rarely see the father express his emotions with tears of joy, happiness, and love for his child.

The same thing happens when you see a good "tear jerker" movie. Some viewers rarely shed tears, because for some reason they are not emotionally "connecting" to the message in the movie. Others try their best not to let the tears spill because they do not want others to know how deeply they truly feel. Are you considered weak or out of control to cry during a movie? To cry is a form of self-expression; if you feel it, then express it!

There are many other reasons people do not express themselves. The circumstance may have been such that it wasn't an appropriate time for the expression. Maybe there was a traumatic event or a sudden flurry of activity. Anything can happen that can be perceived as good or bad (positive or negative) that prevent people from this self-expression. In other words, there may seemingly be no time for this expression! We advise you to revisit those moments and go through whatever happened step by step, because on some level, the feelings were there, but you didn't express them or allow them to blossom. For some reason your emotions weren't allowed to come out, but at some point they must and they will.

Another scenario is perhaps your emotional expression is perceived as unacceptable on some level. Possibly the feelings are considered inappropriate. People have many reasons they choose to not reveal their feelings. Take the time to understand what it is you feel, examine everything closely, and deal with it all in a positive manner.

What does holding back the physical manifestation of those emotions do to you? When you stuff emotions, you create an imbalance within your being on all levels. We will discuss this more later.

You know, when I watch a movie that really gets my emotions rolling, if someone is in the same room as me, I will do my darnedest to control myself by choking down the tears, and I feel this pressure that actually becomes painful. I mean honestly, for some reason I do not want people to see me cry.

You have been programmed this way. As a child you were instructed to not cry because this display of emotions was not how adults behave.

August 10, 2009
Expression of Emotions and Growing Balanced Adults: Part Two

The Akasie: In the previous part, we explained how people have come to the place of being experts at stuffing emotions. Now we wish to assist you in knowing how to raise emotionally healthy children by giving positive feedback, or what we call "giving strokes."

When you are teaching the young ones, look for something that they are doing well and praise them, even if the praise is only for their effort! Praise them when they accomplish something positive. Let them know in no uncertain terms that what they did was the correct thing! We tell you when they do or say something that isn't correct, if possible, refrain from a verbal reprimand. Instead, show them the correct way. When they follow your example, again give them praise. As they grow older this type of praise is not needed so often.

Stroking children with praise instills a knowing in them that they are worthy and loved as individuals. Touch your children often and tell them that you love them because they are beautiful, unique, and have love in their hearts. You know this because you have seen them express kindness, generosity, and love to others in their own unique way. This ability to give unselfishly to others is a beautiful gift that the Creator has instilled in them. You are pleased that they have the strength that allows them to reveal their true essence of love.

Children have amazing capabilities for quickly learning anything and everything. What they see and hear, they mimic. The children are preparing themselves for adulthood. It is like they are rehearsing for a play. The parents are the directors showing the children the way to interact with all of creation. The children are following their caregiver's examples and do this with incredible accuracy! They drink this information in and absorb it in their thirsty minds with unbelievable speed like a dry sponge soaking up a much-desired liquid. The challenge here is that the children take in *everything*. There is no discernment. They haven't learned this yet!

You must know that these little ones arrive here with a clean slate. Their conscious memories have been wiped out.

For new parents, the child's ability to assimilate huge amounts of information so quickly may be a huge detriment. Sometimes young parents haven't yet gained the maturity to determine what is best for the children to observe. It is quite possible that they have not yet realized how quickly these children pick up new information and assimilate it into their conscious minds. Between the ages of one to three, the momentum for learning is at the highest possible rate.

We say that ignorance in this case can cause much upset, much unnecessary upheaval. It would be very wise for the parents to educate themselves on the psychology of children before they embark into parenthood. There is much on the subject that would be beneficial to all.

August 11, 2009
A Precious Gift

During the night, I awoke from a dream. I was extremely sleepy and ready to go back to sleep, but the Akasie had other plans.

The Akasie: We wish to explain in detail what happened to you last night. We woke you up at the precise moment of sleep so you would be in a deeper state of consciousness. You remained in this state for two hours.

Your higher consciousness has instructed us to go to the next step. We did some very deep cleansing and some manipulations in your cranial cavity. We told you that you would be uncomfortable during the procedure. Do you remember? Your body kept screaming to let it go to sleep, but we would not allow it. The procedure had to be finished.

Colér was playing the part of the concerned mother, looking after your welfare and giving you much comfort during the entire process. Quem and Olim encouraged you by telling you this was for your highest good and insisted that all continue the procedure. We had to finish! The release of toxins in the body has to be complete before we may continue, so we move forward.

Jackie, do you remember that we laid out a grid of many different crystals? We extracted the essence out of each crystal that was for the highest good for you and put the combined essences in your heart. This was a special gift for you. We know you do not understand this, but we assure you that what your higher consciousness has instructed us to do is for your highest benefit on all levels of your being. Please trust us. *We are One!*

August 12, 2009
The Archangel Jacob

I went outside to check my plants. By this time of the day, they are usually ready for a nice cool drink. The weather was so beautiful that I decided to stay outside, sit, and meditate.

I sat down, shut my eyes, and proceeded to visualize and bring up my energy, but instead my attention was drawn to the beauty of the trees, the sky, and all of my surroundings. My heart opened wide and the love for the beauty poured out. The Akasie encouraged me walk out to the tree that stood directly before me. They said, "Go lay your hands on this tree and feel its vibrant energy." I did and I felt a strong presence of masculine energy emanating from the tree. The space between my hands and the tree grew tingly and warm. The tree seemed to have a personality. A connection was made between us, a bond if you will. The experience was beautiful.

Later, I went indoors into my studio to sit down to relax on my navy blue recliner. I made myself comfortable and began to listen to some peaceful music. Quem was talking to me while he was giving me the beautiful love energy. He suddenly stated, "My Cathryn, you have a visitor."

I asked who it was, but he didn't answer me. Quem acted like he didn't even hear me! Nice. In my mind, I went over the possibilities for what his motives could be for disregarding my question. I knew without a doubt that he had heard me. Our guides hear everything! Not answering my questions isn't a new tactic, although I don't have it happen often. Sometimes I get adamant and say, "Hey! What's up?"

Perhaps it isn't the correct time for me to know. When this happens, I go into gratitude and acknowledge that I am asking, allowing, and accepting the guidance from the angels and I also affirm that what I receive is for my highest benefit and for the highest benefit for all of creation. Instead of answering my question, my father, Quem directed me to lie down on the floor.

Without any other communication, a fragrance permeated the air. The smell was familiar, but I couldn't quite place it other than realizing it was sweet like some sort of flower. This visitor told me to continue to do as Quem directed. He then identified himself, saying that he was an archangel and was waiting for the time for me to sit with pencil and paper ready for his words. He would wait.

I received more help with the releasing of the toxins and instruction on my breathing. Quem coached me saying, "You must breathe deeply to get more oxygen into your blood stream, thus moving the blood faster and cleansing the organs of any and all impurities."

After a while, I became very tired and began to cry uncontrollably. Here I was with an archangel waiting on me and I was bawling like a big baby! I felt embarrassed, out of control, and even angry that I would behave like this in the presence of an archangel! Then it dawned on me that maybe this "release" was all part of the process and was supposed to happen. After a while, I stated that I thought they were trying to break me down, to see how far they could go to test me, to see how much love I have in my heart. With much emotion, I went on to declare that even after Bradley left, I never hated

God. I never blamed God. I would always love. With that, they said, "We are finished for now."

Jackie, I have come here to assist in your care. I love all. You require assistance with your releases, not just the release of toxins in your physical body, but your emotional releases as well. The tears you shed were an emotional outlet. Since the very first communications (the words that you heard with your inner ear) from your guides you have been concerned about many things. One of the main concerns that you have had since your opening is what exactly your guides' intentions are. I know that you have not completely trusted them. It is time to identify your emotions and release them. They must come out. I see you deeply love our Creator and all of creation. Please be grateful for this time we share together, as we work as one for the highest good for all.

Jackie, I am an archangel. I am high up on the totem pole. You asked who I am. My name is Jezebel.

I vaguely remembered the story of a Jezebel from my Sunday school days. Jezebel is a woman who encouraged idolatry. I thought to myself, "This ought to be real good ... an archangel named Jezebel." I knew instantly that everything was fine. I have heard the totem pole joke before and know that yes, he is high-up, but he is not in the least pretentious.

I lightened the mood for you just then. My name is Jacob.

The energy that Jacob emanated was pure love and joy. No matter what he had to say, I felt a huge weight had been lifted from my shoulders; everything was okay.

Archangel Jacob: I will be with you throughout this process, which is much like having an overdue baby. It is painful, but many are assisting you through the birthing process to ensure you live through it! We all assure you that you'll live. Afterward you'll be so amazed and grateful for having this period in your life completed, enabling you to move forward to your next step.

After the jokes, I began to feel my anxiety lift. Laughing felt really good, even though his jokes were corny. As I began to process Jacob's words, I blurted out, "But I thought people continued to release all of their lives."

Archangel Jacob: Yes, this is true, and you will continue to do so. This particular process is to purify your body of toxins so you may move on and continue to heal on the physical level.

What on earth am I going to be doing that I need to have my body purified for? I know it is best that my body is cleansed, but it seems like there is this big rush to release the toxins out of my body. I have had these suckers for a long time now. I do not want to seem ungrateful here! On the contrary, I am very grateful, but I just feel put on the spot! Does this have to happen right now?

Archangel Jacob: I think you protest much. Know that this is your time to move forward. We have come to you to work with you for the ascension of Self; to move you higher and enable your vibration to rise so that you may transcend to the fifth dimension.

You have noticed the increase in energy, a deeper, more expanded love and gratitude haven't you? Yes, lately you feel more emotion and more appreciation for all of creation. Your moods have stabilized immensely; you have realized that you must allow others to live their lives without your physical or emotional entanglement. There are many other positive "symptoms" of ascension of Self.

You have made many changes on many levels with great success. Many walls have been knocked down, yes? I will return when I feel it is necessary to do so. Your guides have my instructions and my phone number. They will contact me.

His phone number? Before Jacob left, I heard the sound of his deep, rich laughter.

August 13, 2009
My Guides Tell Me That They Are Leaving Soon

Quem, Olim, and Colér: We regret to inform you that we are stepping aside for others to take over our teachings. Our work with you is almost complete. You have assimilated most of all that our group came to teach you.

Jackie, *When Angels Speak* is an integral part of our teachings. We are not finished with this. You do not understand, but we will explain ourselves. We will return from time to time to give you words. The book is important for many reasons. As the book progresses, you will continue to be guided.

You have made a tremendous shift in your conscious thinking by allowing yourself to feel with your heart more often. Yes, you have more work to do. Who doesn't? It is all right; you'll get there! Now you are able to adapt this teaching of feeling with your heart into your physical experience. We are pleased for you. We joke about having a party complete with margaritas, but seriously, it is time for celebration, yes?

Remember these words: Always stand firm in what you believe. *If it doesn't feel right, or if you are in doubt, stop; don't allow!* Follow my counsel, even if your guides are the ones initiating what you question. Remember this is your inner guidance (your emotions) communicating to you that something isn't harmonious with that particular situation. Listen to yourself! Honor yourself!

Always listen to yourself and others with your heart. Words don't always convey truth. There will be times when you are with another and the words he or she speaks are not his or her truths. The truth is almost always conveyed by the emotion expressed. When you listen for the emotion, you will understand their truth even if they don't.

In many situations, your work will be to listen for signs to guide you to facilitate healing for others. You will begin to make a practice of carefully examining what people say and how they say it. Many times, you will know intuitively that you should help someone "hear" what it is they are feeling. Many times, you will find a person to be angry and he or she will not realize it, or possibly not realize the depth of his or her anger. You will help this person hear what he or she is feeling by rephrasing what it is he or she has said.

I will give you this example: You are visiting with your friend, Ann. Ann is speaking of her duties as a wife and mother. She begins by complaining that she has too much to do and her husband doesn't seem to notice that she could use some help around the house. (Ann and her husband, Tom, have several children together, so there are always many tasks that keep Ann on the go.) She continues with the story of what her husband, Tom, does each and every evening. When he gets home from work, he leaves a trail through the home. Tom must walk directly through the kitchen and past her to get to the living room, so he should be able to clearly see that she is preparing their evening meal. He goes a few feet, kicks his shoes off right where anyone can stumble over them, throws his jacket over a chair, and then tosses his papers on the kitchen table.

Ann feels overwhelmed by all that she must do to care for her family and her home and is working to sort out her feelings. Ann tries to justify Tom's actions more to herself than you, by stating that Tom is understandably stressed after his day and that maybe she expects too much from him.

She continues her one-sided dialogue, and begins to wonder aloud why Tom isn't seeing that she is getting ready to set the table for dinner and that by throwing papers on the table he is causing her more work. She mentions again, with more venom this time that he throws his papers right on the kitchen table! Then Tom proceeds to plop down in his recliner, grab the remote, and glue himself to the news or the sports channel on TV.

At this point Ann is on a tirade that her husband leaves messes all throughout the house and never picks up after himself! She wonders aloud if her husband is truly blind or just an expert at being grossly inconsiderate to her efforts.

You hear her words, but what you hear more clearly is the tension and anger in her voice. You can see the tension building in her body as she sums up her daily injustices.

Understandably, Ann's negative emotions are like a pot of simmering water that has been left unattended on the stove top for a very long time. Every time she thinks of Tom's insensitivity, the heat under the pot is turned up. The water is beginning to boil and will overflow soon unless she is able to remedy the situation.

You then ask her if she has talked to Tom about any of this. She reluctantly admits that she hasn't verbally expressed her feelings regarding this situation. You can sense her embarrassment by her confession.

What you can then say to her is, "Ann, I hear your frustration and anger regarding this situation. Furthermore, I sense that you are beginning to feel some resentment toward Tom, because he doesn't seem to appreciate how much work you do. Is this correct?"

Ann takes a deep breath and says, "Yes, I am feeling a little angry!" You can in turn ask her what it is she can do to alleviate the situation. After she has thought about it for a few minutes, you suggest to her that perhaps it would be a good idea to sit down with Tom and express her feelings to him. Perhaps together, they can brainstorm on ways to alleviate some of the stress she feels.

By asking this simple question and then following it up with a suggestion will get her to examine her possibilities and formulate a way to solve her problem instead of reliving her anger again and again.

Often just reviewing what emotions are being expressed and asking what it is that they think they can do or say to facilitate changes is enough to initiate the healing process.

When you rephrased to Ann what you were hearing her say in addition to asking for confirmation to that understanding, you were validating her feelings. With this validation, she will likely be more able to examine the entire situation in a new light. This is a new beginning for them.

August 14, 2009

Your Emotions Cause the Akasie Concern

The Overseers: Jackie, we were contacted by the Akasie. The emotion you are creating causes them concern.

You are aware of changes coming in guardianship. Your understanding is that a transition is coming and that Quem and his assistants will be leaving you soon. We feel your energies regarding the writings of *When Angels Speak*. We all are here to assure you that the book will be completed. Your present guides asked to finish the book with you, but we as overseers of your progress say that is not possible and will not happen. You have new guides arriving shortly. Please brighten yourself; emanate the love we know that is in your heart.

We will introduce ourselves. We are six in number. We will not tell you each of our names at this time, but soon we will return and spend more moments with you. You will be more receptive then. We are angels from the Most High. We come from the same place as you, Pleiades. We are your overseers. We have looked after you for many lifetimes. Our name is many, but you may call us Comterous.

Today, I danced my last dance with who is left of the original group: Quem, Olim, and Colér. My tears flowed like a river. I guess I have grown attached to the one I now call my father and those who I feel to be my sisters. Our time together grows short. I understand that Quem will stay a while longer, but I know he will ultimately leave also. Because of that, I grieve. At the same time, I am happy knowing that they will soon be free to experience a new and grand adventure.

August 15, 2009

Energizing Food

Quem: Miss, you have asked many times if you must continue to keep energizing your food. Is it that you tire of the practice?

I do get tired of stopping to give thanks before I eat. Each time before I eat, I must remember to stop and center myself and focus on how I feel. There are also times when I am tired, and I just want to eat my food and go. I have noticed there is a big difference in my energy level according to what time of the day it is. (To be more specific for the reader, when I talk about my energy level I am referring to the feeling I get when spirit flows through me.) It is a vibration, and sometimes the energy flows easily while at other times it takes more time for this flow of energy to move. I do get frustrated at times.

Quem: The question of energizing food is to be answered at this moment. Yes, you will continue this practice, as you are what you eat. Eat healthy, nutritious foods with the highest vibration possible and your vibration will continue to steadily rise.

August 16, 2009
Perceptions

Quem: For some time you have had some of your friends wonder about your new gift. They wonder if it is real. They wonder about the possibility that you may be talking to yourself. Some are absolutely sure that is exactly what you are doing! We have repeatedly assured you that all is fine. You are to allow them their perceptions and their own truths. Do not try to get them to believe that what you have is real. They are in their own place of understanding. You will come to know that with this gift, many of your friends will go on their way. At the same time, you will join in with many others who share in the same type of gifts and beliefs.

We understand it is difficult for you to have some of your friends question what it is you do. To change your beliefs is to change your identity. When you change your identity, you become a different person in many ways. You look in the mirror and see the same face, but you know in your heart that what you feel has totally and unequivocally changed.

The relationships you have had in the past were formed while you held different beliefs. You have evolved and grown. You are different now. While many of your friends and family love you no matter what you believe, there are still those who pull away. You must move on and forge new relationships.

What has happened to you, this psychic opening, will initiate and provoke many questions from those you converse with. You will undoubtedly say things that will raise their eyebrows, so to speak. We understand that these statements, if said to certain people, will cause quite a stir! At the same time, we hope that they will go on to question their perceptions of this world they live in and then re-examine their beliefs.

At the present time, we know that you have not completely adjusted to the changes that you have gone through. We are telling you to look at this opening of yours in a different light. Yes, you are causing everyone you know (that you chose to speak to about your gift) discomfort. You yourself are in discomfort! With this discomfort comes a new and glorious opportunity that perhaps what you share with others will cause them to go within and examine all possibilities and become more accepting to other ways of life. We speak of other realms that are unseen by many at this time. What we are saying is that this is one of the many ways to bring about change and to grow as a spiritual being.

We are from Pleiades; that is who we are and who we guide. You have a soul group. What do you suppose this entails? We tell you. Your soul group is Pleiadian-born by cosmic origin. We care for each other. We also work with all star beings. We love all. *We are One!*

Last night, I woke up several times. Most of the time I felt like I was burning up! I could have been on fire and it would not have surprised me. What I was feeling was not the typical hot flash. At one point, I remember waking up with both hands numb. The numbness has been going on for some time. The medical doctors call it carpal tunnel syndrome, which is a work related issue. For many years, I framed artwork. Because there are many repetitive movements in this line of work, over time, there can be damage to the tendons in the wrists, and the flow of energy is restricted so your hands become tingly and numb.

When I awoke, I knew immediately that I was receiving healing energy from the angels; I felt the vibration. The Akasie worked on my hands, giving me very intense deep healing energy. What I felt was a much deeper healing energy than I have ever experienced before. Yesterday, the guides had mentioned that it was time for them to work with me to release more toxins. I didn't know they were going to work on my hands also! Wow!

Last night it rained, and I also had the pleasure of hearing the great Thunder Being speak. He was evidently on a big mission. He worked long and hard to cleanse the area. I was grateful to be able to sleep in this morning.

Quem: I wish to speak on the behalf of the Akasie. Because of some circumstances surrounding your psychic awakening that continue to disturb you, we wish to explain further.

The energy you received upon your psychic awakening was given to you for reason of activation and alignment of what many call the *kundalini*, the serpent, or the fire within. This is energy of an extremely sexual nature. It was an intense period of time for you. We were assisting you in visualizing the energy moving in this pattern of the "serpent" coiling around, up and down your spine. From this time, you have moved forward spiritually. Your flower is blooming.

It was a time of initiation for you, a ceremony, and a time of rejoicing, except you didn't understand. Why would you? You were not informed of the importance or validity of the experience. To understand this now is very important for you on many levels. Because of the movement of the energy and the vibration that you felt on a physical level, you felt sexually simulated, more so than ever before in your present lifetime. This simulation introduced you to the primal urge, the raw need. This primitive need is what has kept the human race going in terms of reproduction as long as you have been in the Earth bodies. This need ensures that you will return to this great planet Earth generation after generation. You must have the physical bodies to continue your evolutionary steps to a higher level of consciousness.

There were many reasons for this exercise and this initiation. The basic reason is that you must heal in all areas, all levels, to ascend. There are many beliefs that you hold at this time that do not serve you for your highest good, and they have kept you imprisoned. You have imprisoned yourself! Each belief corresponds to an individual chakra, and in order to clear and balance each chakra, you must free yourself of this self-made prison.

At this time, we begin the healing process with the root chakra and work up from there. The root chakra is the chakra associated with being grounded and the survival instinct. We feel this plan will work for all to the highest good. You now ask about the spleen chakra, but we are not finished with the root chakra yet.

This whole thing really blows my mind! There are so many facets of understanding here. I just know that I am not getting the entire picture. Why did I have to go through that experience? I was scared to the point of being almost out of my mind! I didn't know what to do to save myself. Things are better now, but I still feel unsure of what is happening.

Quem: Jackie, when you were first opening up, none of your people understood the validity of your experience. There was not one person who could help you. Your experience was frightening to say the least. We tell you we know, we understand. We comforted you as best we could.

During my meditation last night, the angels told me to lie down. I told them "No" three times. In response, they told me three times, "Listen to your heart." I felt like I wanted to lie down, but logically I questioned all of it! It seemed that to take me from my meditation time was invasive, and that this might be a test of some sort. My meditation time is very important for my growth, and to have that time disrupted seemed wrong in the logical sense!

Even though I felt very conflicted, I went ahead and did as they asked. They wanted me to receive, and a tremendous heat overtook me. I could not move. I realized without a doubt that this was happening. At the same time, I knew logically I should care about what was happening, but I just didn't.

Over and over, the angels asked me what I saw in my third eye. Almost always, I saw nothing. Sometimes I thought I felt something was there, but I was unable to see anything. Evidently, nothing was there at all. Finally, the heat left, and the angels said that I needed a spirit doctor, that they were unqualified to fix the glitch. WHAT? Now they want to explain further.

August 17, 2009
Listen to Your Emotions

The Akasie: Jackie, we just gave you the symbol for the Akasie group. You are upset with us because we took you from your meditation and then told you that you needed a spirit doctor. You felt that we were toying with you. Your knowledge is limited, and understandably, you are frustrated and perhaps a little angry. We are here with you. You were unaware that we stayed last night; you thought you were alone. We saw you cry like a child, Jackie. We stayed with you until we saw that you were calm and we knew you were all right. We stayed until you breathed easily; we did not leave until we were sure.

Jackie, we apologize for this. You felt abandoned. This was done to teach you to get the name of the group first and find out what they teach. You must also examine what you *feel* in your heart and work through the situation with your mind as well.

There have been many times when I didn't understand what was expected of me. In the beginning when I received a teaching from the Akasie, I would only look at the teaching with my logical self; I would not see the whole picture. I understand that part of this is to get me to listen with my heart—specifically with my emotions—but honestly, sometimes I am just so mixed up that I don't know what I am feeling. Right now, I do know in my heart I will not give up. This is my chosen path. This is who I am.

This is Quem, your father. We go by many names depending on the situation. I tell you that I am securing a new group to teach you. This is another step for you. At this present moment, there are those who are assisting me. Know that I stand firm in my duties to assist, to teach, to protect, to give the healing energy, and yes, to love you, Miss. I always love. Know this. I have not relinquished my duties as of yet, but we will leave shortly as explained earlier.

Right now, I am feeling some confusion. There have been so many different angels who have come to me. Some just stay for a short time while others stay to teach me. Why do I require so many different teachers? I have been told that I am on a need-to-know basis. At the same time, the angels don't always give me a complete teaching. I get bits and pieces, and it may be months before I figure out the entire picture. Even then, I am not always sure that I have gotten it all! This is where having patience really is imperative!

The Akasie: You must understand that our teachings may be viewed by some people as unorthodox. We do not fit neatly into one of your many boxes. We are unique and we have unlimited teaching strategies; we monitor your reactions in all situations and use them to our advantage to teach you for your highest good.

August 18, 2009
Law of Attraction: Manifesting All That Is

The Akasie: There are many Akasie members. We are the ancient ones from Pleiades. We come here to serve you. You come here to this Earth plane to serve all creation. You are a creator. You have come to Earth to grow spiritually. You are a person, a soul. As you grow, you go up higher in vibration and in consciousness.

When you pray, the thoughts, words, and emotions all have specific vibrations. Everything in nature has a specific vibration. More specifically, each vibration is a tone. You direct your prayers to the Creator in hopes that those prayers will be answered! When you pray, the energy rises toward the heavens. All "feel" this frequency that you have put forth. This is how the others receive your requests and your positive thoughts.

What you must understand is that *all* of your thoughts, not just your prayers, go to the heavens to the Creator. What you express goes to the Creator no matter what. This is one of the universal laws: the law of attraction.

Your culture—and we speak of the worldwide culture, here—is at a zenith. You have reached an apex. What we are telling you is that you must change the way you create. It has not always been this way, but at the present time, the collective creates by default due to ignorance. We are here to teach you that you are co-creators, and that you manifest what it is you put your thoughts on. If you continue on this path of thinking destructive thoughts, you will continue to receive destructive outcomes.

Creation in your planetary system means both one thing and many things. We want to discuss the prospect of how each of us is a creator and how we all contribute to the universal cause by thinking positive thoughts, negative thoughts, and even neutral thoughts.

First, however, what we want to touch on is your specific creation. Each of you on the Earth plane is responsible for your particular creations. We speak of what you are doing in your evolutionary process that brings you closer to the Christ Consciousness and to the fifth dimension in the human body, or what the Christians call the resurrection. What we speak of is all esoteric.

You are all creators whether you wish to be or not! This is who you are, dear ones! You have chosen to come to this Earth at this time to remember that you are divine beings of the Light. Your purpose is to always fill yourselves with love and gratitude. The more love and gratitude you fill up with, the higher your vibration will rise. This is the ascension and the resurrection!

The fifth dimension that you are approaching is but one level of consciousness. You as a human species are always evolving, as with all of creation; all continue to go forward toward the Light.

Your planetary progress has come to an apex. You are nearing the end of this chapter in your evolution. For those who do not evolve alongside of those seeking illumination, the awakening, they will return from whence they came. *We are One!*

August 19, 2009
The Holy Spirit

The Akasie: You ask us, "What is the Holy Spirit?" You have spirit, but not an individual spirit. All creation is connected, like an enormous spider web that is woven with one strand of silk. So when you talk about your personal "spiritual growth," this statement is both correct and incorrect. One Great Spirit connects us all! You are all growing and evolving as individuals and also as a collective. The two go hand in hand.

Spirit is positive energy and the life force. When you feel love, gratitude, or any other positive emotion deeply, this is the energy of the Holy Spirit moving that connects us all. This energy is what gives life to all!

This Holy Spirit is the energy that I feel flow through me when my love and gratitude is high?

The Akasie: Yes. This is the energy that takes you high.

Oh, if only all could hear this, they would remember!

The Akasie: Jackie, they all remember in their hearts, they just have to listen. *We are One!*

August 20, 2009

Leaning on Others Instead of Listening to Self

One of my good friends, Linda, who is gifted psychically, has told me that she has been concerned about me since the beginning of my psychic opening. Repeatedly, she has stated to me that my guides do not have the frequencies that are in alignment with me. It seems to me like she talks in code. I did not understand the meaning of her words, and I found this statement to be very unsettling. I felt like I was attacked or judged somehow, like I wasn't doing the correct thing. Ultimately, I became defensive and angry.

Quem: Tonight your energy was very low. Tell us how you feel.

I feel sad, let down, used, angry, resentful, and depressed. I know that I have created many negative thoughts and felt many negative emotions. I am sorry. God, please forgive me.

I experience things on a different level, because I am in the physical form. At this time, I feel it is wise not to obsess about anything concerning the angels, more specifically the Akasie. I have decided to allow myself to learn in my own time and to stop being so judgmental about everything. I wish to accept what the Akasie have to offer for the betterment of myself. In other words, I will try not to be such a control freak!

Quem: We have deliberately and elaborately staged this situation with your friend Linda to give you the opportunity to learn about ego, specifically yours. This is all a way to teach you how your species has a tendency to puff up with ego and create negative energy like anger and resentment. This is a good lesson to ponder.

It doesn't matter what the situation was or what happened. What you should have done was allow Linda her own opinion. In other words, you should not react to the words of another. What Linda told you was her perception, her truth. The very best thing you could have done was to talk out your concerns with her. If that was not possible at the time, it would have benefited you greatly had you gone out and hugged a tree, done some physical activity, or possibly talked about your feelings with someone, perhaps with us instead. Remember, we are here at this time, full of love and understanding. We always take your words without judgment. We use these opportunities to teach you. We ask you to allow us this.

Now let's get down to business. Your friend Linda has said that we are not in alignment with you. This is quite the case, as your friend is very astute. We are not human, and therefore we are not in alignment with you. Still, you should call her and find out what she means exactly. Do not concern yourself any longer until she explains herself.

You say that we told you there was something else, another reason our frequencies are out of alignment. Yes, this is so. We will explain this now. We are highly evolved light beings. No, Jackie, we do not have the physical form anywhere. If you could see us, our appearance is an orb, a sphere, a globe of light. You could say we are "spheritual." This is a new word for you to learn. We would like this word that so accurately describes us to be added to that dictionary that Mr. Webster has so meticulously written.

We each have a mind, yes, but we do not have organs as you do. There is no need for us to eat, drink, sleep, exercise, or eliminate. We are multidimensional beings, which means we exist on more than one dimension—this dimension and others. We go back and forth. We are not here with you always, but we can be here in a fraction of a second. You are not aware of the traversing about that we do. We leave you often with you unaware. Nevertheless, be it known that you are *never* left unattended.

You have questioned us many times about our energy and about what we look like. You have a tremendous desire to see us, and someday you will, as this is the plan.

There were photographs taken during several spiritual ceremonies that you have participated in. In those photographs, there were orbs present. The orbs were us, Miss Jackie; spiritual beings, light energies.

You have noticed that these spheres of light were different sizes. The reasons for the difference in the spheres are quite the same as why you on the Earth plane are different. Our energy pattern is distinctive by size, color, density, and above all, vibration. You will find no two to be exact duplicates.

I finally decided to go ahead and send an e-mail to my friend concerning this alignment business between myself and my guides. Linda simply said, "Jackie, you are focusing too much on your guides."

I feel this could be true, but I am receiving so many teachings that are so beneficial and totally awesome! I realize that I have not balanced my time, my energy, and ultimately my life. I have put most of my focus on my communications with you!

I don't feel good about what Linda said, but at the same time, that is how she feels. Linda, like everyone else, has her own truth. Linda has also said a couple of times that there is a window of time in life; that if I am not living my path and if I do not get it together, I will not make it. I do not know what this means. I am happy and feel like I am doing what makes my heart sing.

Quem: Now, we are going to talk a little bit about this. Do you have strength, backbone? Is your ego in check?

I heard him laugh, and knew he was working to soften his teaching; this is his way to help me to relax.

Quem: Remember we do not judge, but we are happy to tell you how we see it. Call it constructive criticism. Put a smile on your face please!

You know that time as you know it is accelerating greatly. There is a threshold, so to speak. The polarities are shifting from the masculine to the feminine, and soon this shift will be complete. In addition, you are nearing the apex of another cosmic cycle. The magnetic poles will be realigning. A new era is beginning. This means that you have less time to accomplish what you are here to do. You are to find your place and have your feet well planted. For you personally it would be best to have your heart connection well established at this time.

Now is the time to remember how to listen to your heart. It is the time of the feminine, of love. If you are not feeling and listening with your heart when the shift occurs, it will be like swimming upstream against the current. The water is icy cold and the currents are extremely swift! All is foreign to you.

Everything is changing. Shifts are occurring in the physical, on the Earth plane, and in the outer realms, which result in incredible releases on all levels. All of creation is feeling the upheaval in one way or another. The people are feeling more emotional, which is a release in itself.

This is a time of great triumph, and you should express much gratitude for the birthing of the new energies and a new age! Do you not celebrate a new birth? Are you not full of love and gratitude when a new one takes her first breath? You do not know what this new one will bring to your lives, but you see the beauty and rejoice at the possibilities!

Linda is saying that it would be best if you were in alignment with the energies during the shifts, and most definitely when the shifts are complete. She wishes you, as well as all of her spiritual brothers and sisters, to be comfortable, well balanced, and in harmony with yourselves and with all of creation. To follow your heart's desire at this time is more important than ever. This is to be in alignment with spirit.

You misunderstood Linda's intentions and harbored a little resentment, maybe even a little anger, yes?

We are sorry that you were not able to allow the other one's perception. You created a bit of negative energy, because at the time you had not learned this lesson in its entirety. This is okay. You are getting it now.

We will tell you a little about your friend, Linda. She is on a higher level of awareness. Where is your ego now? This is fine that she is on a higher level of awareness. You can only go one step at a time, and you are on this step. She desires you to see the bigger picture, the one she sees.

Linda warns you that you may fall. Maybe you will. Sometimes people do fall; Jackie, they all fall at one time or another, do they not? This one tells you it is best to know your heart, to stand strong, and not to depend on another (us) to tell you how to do things.

When you ask for another's opinion, you never know what it is that you will receive. Remember, ego sometimes comes out when least expected. Keeping an eye on ego will benefit you greatly. Know where this one resides at all times.

The fall she speaks of is your relying too heavily on others instead of yourself. When we, the Akasie go, will the bottom fall out? She may possibly feel that you won't be able to function on your own because you have not learned to listen to your heart. Instead, you are listening to us. This is the time to listen to your inner self, your heart. This way guides you in all.

Our view is that, yes, you are heavily dependent on us. We try different techniques to get you to see this. You are the one to make changes, you see. You must make your own decisions. This is your learning opportunity. You must set your limits and boundaries. You must feel what is right for you to do at all times. This is your responsibility. We wait until you figure it out.

You are doing better, yes. Do not think you are not. We are much pleased with your progress. Your friend does not understand our techniques, and this is okay. She doesn't know everything. She isn't supposed to! We are here for you, not her. She has her own guides. Linda has made agreements of her own. You are different and unique individuals, both going to the same place, okay?

I received this message in meditation: It just doesn't matter what others think or think they know about me. That is their perception. They may be correct, but this is my life. I am not going to worry anymore about what they think. I am free to go forward at my own pace. When I am ready, I will make the clicks. Pushing myself to learn too quickly will ultimately slow down the process. I am to just allow myself to grow at my own pace.

August 21, 2009
Reincarnation, Souls, Heaven, and Hell

The Akasie: The following writing contains special information that we are pleased to give you. It seems that a few of you are confused about where you come from before this life time on the Earth plane, and where you go from here when the Earth body grows weary and dies.

Listen closely. It matters not where exactly you have come from. What matters is that you remember who you are—your true essence.

Again, we say that the temple of God/Goddess is your physical body. Your physical body is very important. Your body is the vehicle that allows you, a spiritual being, to evolve in the physical on the Earth plane. This experience, the physical is of great importance.

This is the zenith of your evolution to come to the Earth to experience the dense energies. Each lifetime you come to the Mother Earth intending to awaken, knowing full well that your chances are very slim. You have great faith and great hope when you are on the other side of the veil, which many of you call heaven. This is the time you are in between incarnations. To the best of your abilities, you plan into the long hours of the night for the time when you once again are to return to the third dimension, to traverse through the dense energies in search of the connection to your higher self.

Many scholarly books have been written on this very subject of reincarnation. Even your beloved Bible presents a kernel of truth about reincarnation. You may read the words, but until you are open to receiving the knowledge you will not understand, as the true meaning of the words is hidden, encoded until the time when your heart opens. Pray for divine guidance to open your heart and reveal the mysteries of the universe so you may glean the true secrets of the esoteric that have been bestowed upon the many and diverse peoples of the planet Earth.

To awaken and remember your true spiritual self is one of the greatest gifts that you will receive while on the Earth plane. You are intentionally using these dense energies to make it difficult to go within and awaken. To awaken while in the dense energies is a fantastic accomplishment. The planet and her peoples have been under the influence of the masculine energy for such a long time. The logical has reigned. Now, the energy shifts to the feminine, the heart, and to pure love. Yes, coming to the Earth to awaken has been such a huge challenge. For the most part, the peoples have listened to their logical minds and not with their hearts. To open your hearts, you must first begin to listen with your hearts by feeling love and gratitude for all of creation. This is to come into alignment with spirit and to go into the Light.

Your physical body is the modality that you have chosen for learning purposes this go-around. You have been given the gift of the physical body to traverse about anywhere you desire on the physical plane.

We go further with this discussion. For now, we use the term "Creator" synonymously with God. The Creator is all that is. You look out your window. What do you see? God. God, the Creator, is all encompassing, omnipresent. The Creator is in all things. We say this because all things are alive with energy and are part of creation.

There are multitude of diverse energies on the Earth plane, and there is a hierarchy beginning from the highest intelligence, which is you, to the tiniest particle of energy that can't be detected with the naked eye.

The Creator is the combined energies composed of all thoughts, emotions, things said, and things done by all beings in the entire universe and beyond. Everything you have here on the Earth plane has been set forth by a compilation of all that you do as a collective.

We see you're lost, so we back up a bit here. Every creature has the ability to think and to feel. Every creature has intelligence. Every creature, no matter how small or how large, is connected at some level to the great mind, the higher consciousness. All creatures can and do communicate with their own species, but they also venture outward and communicate with creatures other than their own kind. All are connected to the web of life and the higher consciousness. Every creature has a soul just as you do. After they shed their Earth bodies, their soul reincarnates in a new physical form.

We see that you're confused. Up until this point you have believed that the creatures about you do not think and feel. You have taken it on yourself to dispose of the tiny creatures as you see fit when they are a bother. We know your thoughts and your feelings. You question the concept that we have just presented to you. Yet, you see the possibilities. If what we say is true that all creatures have souls and reincarnate, then what is it you have been doing? Are you not taking the life of another, such as a fly or even your aging cat? You are struggling with this idea that you have possibly murdered another being. It's difficult for you to comprehend that a tiny creature like an ant might have a soul and that that soul will reincarnate again and again!

A soul is merely the particular type of energy that you are, who you are. A soul is an individual person or creature. All creatures have intelligence and the ability to communicate in some manner. This is the ability to think and feel. This ability to think and feel is creation. We are all in this together, you see.

You are a light being who has evolved from a certain type of energy long ago. You began as a tiny speck of atomic energy and evolved to a being fully capable of creating absolutely anything from thought! You have evolved this far!

In this planetary system in which you reside there are numerous hierarchies. At this time in creation, we speak specifically about nature; all has a purpose. All must have food, energy, to be able to survive in their specific habitat. All is energy. There is a constant exchange of energy to keep you alive in the physical; a constant coming and going of this energy. This energy that we lovingly speak of is Spirit.

You have been given the power and choice to co-create life, to give birth in the physical to another. Also, you have the capability to give up your life in the physical for another in order for them to survive. This is the inherent order of the nature of creation. This is witnessed in many life forms in your world.

Fortunately, for you in the human body, you're at the top of the food chain (most of the time.) As a human, you have been given dominion over all of the beasts on this great Earth plane that you, at the present moment, call home. Be grateful for this gift.

All is in perfect harmony and perfect balance. This is the way the Creator designed creation. All live on to evolve, to go to the higher realms of creation. It is your desire when you come to the Earth plane to remember your true essence of love.

Spirit is the part of you that yearns to keep moving forward toward a higher level of love. At the same time, you live in a world of duality— the negative and the positive. This is the way with the entire universe! You must experience both negative and positive things to move forward. There is but one Spirit that connects us all.

You see, the Creator is of the highest intelligence. The Creator is comprised of all levels of consciousness or light. When you speak of heaven, you are speaking of the higher state of consciousness. When you have attained this level of awareness, you are free of your own perceived limitations. When you go into the Light, you know there is no longer a need for the ego. The Great Mind is vast. There are no boxes; there are no constraints. All things are possible with love.

We move on to the subject, a place, of hell. When you hear the word hell, many of you envision a fiery pit deep within the bowels of the Earth. There stands the ruthless devil sporting thick horns and cloven hooves. To complete your vision, you see this dominating monster threatening those who lag at their post with his legendary pitchfork. What I have described to you are symbols of a soul being tortured.

The hell that many of you perceive at this time is a particular place of the physical making, like Chicago perhaps. Chicago is a city that you know exists because you have heard about this place, you have seen its mark on the map, or you may have possibly even visited this city. Ah, perhaps you reside there at this time! For these reasons, you know that this place, Chicago, exists.

Many scholars have written about hell as a physical place. We are here to help you open your awareness just a bit. Hell is indeed a place, but is it a place that one physically goes to? We tell you that, yes, it is a place, but a place in one's own consciousness. Hell is a state of mind. When a person is severely depressed, he or she sometimes says that he or she is truly in hell, experiencing what feels like eternal damnation. We tell you again that your thoughts and emotions manifest your physical realities. When a person sinks this low, he or she is unable to escape this torture to get relief or find peace. Sometimes a person will *attempt* to escape this hell by ending his or her physical life.

When you make the choice to end your life, yes, you leave the physical body, but your level of consciousness or awareness remains. It matters not what this person thought; he was desperate to flee from his current state of mind. In his desperation, he made a pivotal choice that he hoped and prayed would take away his pain, but we tell you this action does not resolve anything. It only makes matters more complex.

When you pass from the physical body, you continue to create the same thoughts and emotions. This is where you are in your level of understanding.

Know that if you wish, you will be assisted in all ways throughout your journey by those who love you unconditionally.

It is obvious that I just don't understand certain things. So my son, Bradley, was in hell before he took his life and afterwards. He was volatile in his behavior most of the time, so much so, that for no apparent reason, he would lash out at his brother and sister. His mood affected all of us. We were in a constant state of anxiety. I guess we were all in a hell of our own making. There are a lot of questions I have regarding my son. I still worry about him.

Honey, there is much to this subject of when a person ends their life. Know that we will address all of it when the time is correct—when you are ready. We have before us many teachings that will assist you in your ascent. Please trust that we have your best interests at heart. We love you as we love all of creation. *We are One!*

August 23, 2009
Society's Dependency on Electricity

I was in a deep sleep when I was abruptly wakened by a loud noise. Still groggy, I saw that it was still dark outside, but there was this flashing light around the window. Was that noise a car crash? Maybe someone's house exploded. What time is it, and what on earth was that noise? I took a look at my clock; it read 5:08 a.m. I was a bit frightened by the sudden boom, and the thought crossed my mind to grab my gun as I got out of bed, but instead I went directly to the window. The only thing I could see was a flashing light. Finding my robe, I walked to the front of the house. Oh, nice! Right in front of my house, all lined up in an orderly fashion, were three cherry picker trucks. Okay, do I have electricity? Nope.

Nearly two hours later and four more explosions, I knew there would be no chance of getting any more sleep. My electricity was off and it appeared that it would be some time before it would be restored. Even though I looked like hell, I decide to venture out to the road to find out what was going on. Before I uttered one word, an electrical worker offered, "Transformer exploded. We are working from this point back to your home to see where exactly the problem is. That is why there have been four explosions." I went back inside.

Olim says, "Look at this as a gift, a teaching. Get your pencil and paper."

Olim: Jackie, I say this to you; yes, this is a great gift for those who recognize it. Learn from this. Your society is greatly dependent on this current form of power. Much of what you do during your day depends on this energy.

Each morning, we see you have your herbal tea, dry your hair, listen to your soothing music, and eat your breakfast. The activities of which I speak of are all dependent on electricity. You also have your lights. How would you go about your days and nights without your electrical lighting systems?

The gift, the teaching that I speak of is to remind you to look for the positive in every situation. This experience is to show you, to remind you of your dependent habits. We will teach you how to manage your lives without being solely dependent on man-made energies.

We advise you to begin to ease off of electrical appliances, such as your coffee maker, clocks, stereo, and microwave. Just make a few adjustments to begin with. Use the kind of tools that do not require this type of energy instead. I tell you that it would be for your highest benefit to *not* be dependent on any one source of energy. You say that you cannot make coffee without a coffee maker. I ask you to go back and remember how coffee was made before the electric coffee maker was invented. Coffee was brewed on the stove top the old fashioned way with wood or gas. We say it tastes better this way!

Uh, I am not of that generation.

Olim: No matter; you are a fast learner, are you not?

I go on. Clocks are easy to eliminate, as you still have the windup clocks available. Your stereo may be a little more difficult to let go of, but to let go of this device will be much more rewarding in the long run. Make your own music by listening to nature or perhaps singing your own tunes. Make your own music with what is available. Keep that piano of yours, Jackie. Yes, it is necessary for all to hear the tones and feel the vibrations created from song and the musical instruments.

I say this recognition and elimination of your dependence on electricity will help you to go forward, but I hear you balk. You state you feel that to give up these great modern conveniences is surely to go backward. No, Jackie; you are going forward by being less dependent on others for your everyday living.

Jackie, what have you been doing since you haven't had your electrical power? You struggle to find something to busy yourself with. You have been at a loss as you wander about your home looking for something you could do that does not require the use of your electricity. You are finding this to be quite the challenge. You partook in cold cereal that you found less than enjoyable while you worried about the foodstuffs in your refrigerator spoiling. I remind you to be grateful for all, Miss.

The majority of you are not well versed on how to care for yourselves without the assistance of your electricity. This reliance has grown so massive that during a power outage, the population is unable to sustain themselves as they are accustomed to. Is this a good thing? I am sure you know the answer to this one. We tell you that to survive you must know how. You must attain the skills necessary to survive! How many of you could comfortably carry on for more than a few days without electricity? You would become unkempt, cold, hungry, and very short on patience.

We chuckle at the insolent nature of humans, yet we grieve at the stupidity. You have all grown too big for your britches.

We ask you to stop and assess your lifestyles. We look to you for a steady influx of change that will ultimately take everything in different ways that are beneficial to you independence.

Some of you look to a lifestyle of community living with others of like minds. In those communities, each of you would have particular attributes and skills that would benefit the entire group; everyone would gladly pitch in where needed. Within these small farm-like communities, there is an energy like a common thread that unites all together in a common but great cause.

When choosing those to unite to in a community setting, listen to your heart; know the energy of those who you seek. Does the love emanate from within? This must be the number one priory in choosing those individuals to come together to form a community.

We joke that you are of the turtle clan because you are slow at making changes. We love you even for this. Some things are best given in a slow methodical pace. Even so, you must be the turtle who wins the race. By this statement, we mean you must not only survive, but thrive. You are here to go forward, are you not? To go forward you must change your lifestyle. To cease your dependence on others is to change everything. You will begin to go back to nature for your needs. Nature provides all. Know where to look and you will see that you are well provided for without doing physical harm to yourself or others.

Electricity is harmful and even deadly when not respected or used in the correct manner. When there is a concentrated amount of electricity in a particular area, you bring about imbalance in nature and imbalance in the physical body. Look at cancer, how it has run amok in your world. High voltages of electricity are only a small contributor to the cancers that grow rampant in the Earth bodies of this day. You humans have created a world that is in total imbalance, not harmonious with body, spirit, and mind.

Electricity is but one of the many causes for imbalance in your world, but we chose to educate you in this one area to begin with.

How harmful the effects of electricity are on the physical body has been more than well documented. The majority of the world, however, has become soft and compliant. They no longer have fight in them. They go with the flow even though they know society is no longer cohesive, not having the individual's best interests at heart. You know as a collective society you are no longer in balance with nature, with the Mother Earth.

When you have disharmony in nature, this causes fear, disease, and ultimately death. Live in harmony with the Mother, the Great Earth. She knows what is best for you.

August 24, 2009
Have You Given Your Power Away?

Quem: Just to let you know, your power is intact. You are a student who is very eager to learn. The information that we give to you is specifically suited to your energy and your level of awareness.

Today was a good day for you to learn many teachings. You spoke to one of your good friends about the energy you have been receiving from your guides. I know that you have continued to be concerned about this energy. She warns you about giving your power away. You have free will always. You must know what is in your heart. This is how you know when you are in alignment with Spirit. You are a powerful being; remember this. You decide whatever it is that you desire to do and then do it! This is to have your power intact, Jackie. Fear does not play a part in this unless you let it.

How you feel when we say or do a certain thing is an indication of your allowing yourself to be controlled by another. There have been many times when you sensed that we have overstepped our boundaries. Perhaps it wasn't our place to tell you to do certain things, but at the time you felt it was such a good idea and it all made sense, so you agreed. You realized that you could have come up with that thought yourself, but didn't. You feel maybe we are overstepping some sort of boundary again.

We say no, we are not crossing your boundaries. You have not yet established your boundaries! We are guiding you to care for yourself in a healthier and more productive manner. Up to this moment, we have been guiding you in your daily segments (planning ahead in chunks of time) and advising you on your choice of foods and drink. We tell you to drink more water, eat healthier food, and organize your day. We know at this time you have the perception that you have too many responsibilities with little time to see it all through. It is fine that we help out in this way if you allow us to do so.

August 25, 2009
Life Goes On

Quem: We have told you that this segment, or cycle, in your evolutionary process is a great opportunity for all of you who have chosen the physical experience.

Some of you have become fearful because there are no more days on Mayan calendar after 2012. Much fear has been unleashed, so to speak, because a few of you feel you must have your days marked in stone before those days can become a reality. Your days will continue to come regardless of the Mayan calendar.

In addition, some of you are in a tizzy concerning these shifts in the energies from the masculine to the feminine. I assure you that these cycles have been in place for millions of years. Do not fear what is given to you as a precious gift. These gifts are to continue the evolutionary process, to go forward and to ascend!

Evolution will continue on my dear ones, no matter where you stand. Many of you dig in your heels screaming that you do not understand what it is you are to do with your lives. Others look upon the masses in judgment and contention. You look about murmuring that all you want is to be happy. True happiness is a state of mind. When you no longer create a need or even a desire to control the outcome of any given experience, you will have allowed yourself to relax and live in the moment. We have been teaching you with the words and through your own personal experiences to be in the now. To feel regret and guilt is to look too far into the past. To fret and worry is to look too far into the future. Be grateful for this moment and enjoy this moment to the fullest. This moment is the beautiful expression of the I AM.

You have been told by your friend, Linda, that you must get yourself in tow concerning the heart connection, or you will lose the opportunity that has presented itself through the shifts in the energies. Linda didn't disclose all that she knew. This time of the great energy shift is a grand opportunity for all to go forward. The energies are such that most if not all will feel discomfort on some level. For some of you this discomfort will be immense.

For others, you will align yourselves with the ebb and flow of the ever-changing energies, joining yourselves together with these beautiful energies in a most wondrous dance. Linda wishes the transition to be a comfortable one for all. Also, she has an intense desire that all the peoples of the Earth be in alignment with Spirit and for you to ascend to your highest capabilities, because the energies that promote this growth are being created at this moment.

Yes, I tell you to be at the level of awareness where you intellectually understand and purposefully work with the great movement of energies is a great advantage. No matter what your level of awareness is, however, the evolutionary process continues always and everywhere!

We remind you to be in a state of *Oneness*, to be in the *Now*. When you are being bombarded with energies that are of a higher frequency, naturally you are not going to be comfortable. These energies challenge you, bringing out the negative emotions that are fear based, such as anxiety, anger, and depression, but these higher frequencies can also take you to great heights of bliss. Remember Bliss Land, dear ones? These shifts in the energies are a great gift to you! Use these energies wisely, as they are meant for your highest good.

You wonder why we say a challenge that can cause you to feel negative emotions is a great gift? It is a great gift because through these negative emotions, these upsets that we speak of, you are being motivated to look at your life and figure out what you can do to make it more pleasurable, satisfying, and truly full of love. Just as important, we look to these great energy shifts for cleansing and healing, not only for those in the physical form, but for all of creation. It is a time for great renewal and celebration!

The shifts in the energies are a way for you to learn to communicate with yourself and others, knowing where you should change in order for you to go forward and to be in alignment with Spirit. Do you recognize where you should make adjustments in your life?

You are light beings, star beings much like us! You have chosen to come to this great planet Earth to work toward achieving the Oneness that I speak of in the physical form. At some point, all will remember that they are spiritual beings and begin to consciously make the steps forward. Make no mistake here, you all are going forward to a higher level of consciousness.

Your higher self is always working with your lower self to guide you so that you may receive the information that resonates with you. You are here in order to learn what your higher self already knows. You are on the Earth plane to connect to your higher self to achieve Oneness. All continue to make the steps to know and feel their truths by working with their emotions.

Many are awakening at this time in evolution. The peoples are hungry for the knowing and the love. Many have come to a place in their understanding that they no longer want to feel angry, depressed, or intolerant of others. They are ready to be shown the way. That is why we, together, have chosen to write the books!

Even if there are some who don't remember who they are this go-around, they will have another opportunity. They will incarnate again and have another chance to remember their true essence, which is love.

August 26, 2009
Telepathic Communication

The Akasie: Jackie, a couple of weeks ago we communicated with you on a different level. We transmitted the communication with the same vibration as a particular word in your English language. In other words, we sent you a vibration instead of the word. You received the vibration on an energetic level and knew exactly what we told you, and it was beautiful.

Last night we went a little further by exposing you to a deeper level of understanding concerning this type of communication. Call it telepathic communication if you wish. We sent you an entire message without the use of the words. We sent you our thoughts with our emotions. There is always emotion attached when you communicate with thought. We chose to use thoughts and emotions that you could recognize quickly. You received the thought and the emotion and just knew what we were communicating to you.

At this time, we are giving this teaching to you to further your understanding of these types of communications. It is time for you to learn to focus your thoughts and emotions to begin this type of communication with others on the Earth plane.

Jackie, we have heard you speak with many of your friends in reference to this communication. Although, when you spoke of this you did not realize that this was a type of communication. You thought when you had someone on your mind that was the extent of it. There is much more to the story, however. Remember, thoughts and emotions go to where they are directed. If you do not direct them, they just connect with like thoughts in the cosmos. To some degree, all of you on the Earth plane have been communicating in this way since your physical birth, but until now, many of you did not realize what you were doing.

We wish to teach you this way of communication so you will understand how we communicate with you. As you continue on your way to the fifth dimension, more and more of you will harness this ability to communicate not only with those who are on the Earth plane, but with others in different dimensions as well!

To intentionally send a telepathic message, first know what you want to say. Then focus your attention on the person while you send the message. It would be most beneficial for you to notice the level of your emotions while you are sending the communication.

In order for someone to receive your message, he or she must be aware and open to this type of communication on his or her lower level of awareness in the first place, and he or she must listen to receive.

Anyone can become extremely skilled at this type of communication and have the ability to converse with anyone in this world and beyond. Know this. At this moment, the way of communication between the peoples of the Earth is mainly by electronic devices. As a culture, you have become quite attached to these ways of conversing with others and is quite the rage! Your telephones will soon become obsolete, however. We laugh because we realize that this information may astonish more than just a few of you. We assure you that this transition will come about with ease.

When you have someone on your mind, say your mother, take notice. Who is it that originated the thought form? Is your mother thinking of you, or is it you that is thinking of her? Perhaps when you are first thinking of your mother, you pick up the phone and ask if she was thinking of you. Pay attention and realize what is happening. How strong is the thought? Go further and see if you can pick up any emotions behind the thought.

Each thought and emotion is a vibration, but don't place yourself in a box here. Each emotion has many levels of strength. You are familiar with the Richter scale that measures the magnitude of energy movement in a particular area of the earth. This energy that is measured shows how strong the force is.

Imagine a grand measuring device that has the capability of determining not only the emotion itself but the level or strength of that emotion. When you create a thought and feel an emotion there is strength to it. We will explain it like this: When you play a musical instrument like the piano, you push down a key. This key has a particular tone. If you wish to put more or less emphasis on the tone, then you will push the key down with lesser or greater force accordingly. The tone will be the same but will be louder or softer depending on how much force is behind it. This same concept applies to thoughts and emotions.

August 27, 2009
One Thought Leads to Another

The Akasie: All of a sudden, you stop and think, "How did I get here with this thought?" At one point or another all of you have had a thought and wondered about the pathway that brought you to that particular thought. One thought leads to another and then another. So you trace the thoughts back to the original and say, "Oh, yes, that is what started all of this!" We wish you to examine this, as thoughts are most powerful. Accordingly, be attentive to what you are thinking. Pay attention, because if you are not focused on what thoughts you are creating, you will inevitably create thoughts that are not for anyone's highest good.

Emotions follow thoughts and make the energy you are creating stronger and more focused.

Energy travels to where it is directed. Think about this for a moment. Think about some of the thoughts that you create. Are you focused now? Are you creating positive thoughts at this moment? Where are you directing your thoughts?

Thoughts are magnetic. Thoughts are created from energy. Every thought holds a specific frequency or magnetic field. Thoughts join with like thoughts.

Before we explain further, we will show you how thoughts build. You begin with one thought and off the mind goes to explore all possibilities. Questions and answers arise following the initial thought. This is our example to you and a teaching.

You see or hear something that triggers your memory concerning a TV program that you thoroughly enjoy. Because you have quite a bit of appreciation (positive emotion) attached to this show, you begin to work through the possibilities and plan so you will be assured of this interaction. Your thoughts take off.

What day is this? Friday. Okay, it's on tonight. I wonder if it will be a rerun. Let's see, it comes on channel 5 at 7:00 p.m.. Is there anything else that I have committed myself to for tonight? Oh, I told my son that I would watch his children tonight. I wasn't remembering my show when I talked to my son. Oh well, it will probably be a rerun, and if it isn't, then I can just watch it another time. Oh, but I really want to see it tonight! I'd like to just sit and relax. I wonder what time he'll bring the kids over. Ummmm ... he didn't say exactly when he would be coming. Maybe I can watch the program while the children are here. Oh, they will never be quiet long enough for me to enjoy my show; they are just too young and active. Maybe I can I come up with something for them to do while I watch my program. I should make sure that dinner is over with before my show comes on. What am I going to prepare? I wonder if they will have dinner before they come over. Just in case, what can I put together that won't be too much of a fuss? Should I call him and ask what he intends to do, or should I just prepare something? I do have that chicken salad in the refrigerator. Maybe I should make a pot of spaghetti just in case they are hungry when they get here. I bet my son would enjoy some spaghetti also. I would like the kids to have a good meal while they are here. Maybe I should bake some cookies? Those kids sure love peanut butter cookies. It is good to see them enjoy themselves. Oh, but the mess they make! I'll have to clean the entire house if I bake any cookies! They leave a trail everywhere they go. Oh, but the children are so sweet. I do want them to have some home baked cookies! Oh, do I have milk to go with the cookies? Oh darn, I'll have to run to the store and buy some milk. That really makes me have to rush! Oh, that reminds me, I volunteered to bake those three cakes for the bake sale at the end of this week. That is tomorrow! I have to get to the store today to pick up the ingredients. Oh, but first, I'll have to find the recipes and figure out what I need. What was I thinking? I don't have time to do all of this! Why do I keep saying I'll do all of this stuff?

I just read your example again and the emotion I created just reading the passage makes me feel rushed, out of sync, and just plain stressed! I was oscillating from negative to positive thoughts and emotions. There is a lot of negative energy there. The sad thing is I know I do this and I do it often! The thoughts just get going and take off!

The Akasie: You see how one thought led to another, and some of those thoughts weren't for your highest good? Some of your thoughts had the implication that you were being put upon, inconvenienced. Once you create a thought like this, it is easy to build on those thoughts and make the feelings of resentment and discomfort stronger and stronger. Notice how your body feels when you think such thoughts.

It would be beneficial for you to know that the purpose of any negative energy is many sided. When you first hear the word "negative," you may immediately associate it with something bad, but this isn't necessarily so.

Negative energy is for many purposes. We will look at negative energy as a teaching in this example. This may surprise many of you, but we call negative energy a gift. Negative energy causes upheaval and discomfort and is for a great purpose— to bring about change! The purpose of the negative thought is to show you that you have many choices before you. You are intellectually sizing up your choices. With those thoughts that you are creating comes emotion. Those emotions are the communication telling you what the best choice is for you at this particular time. You always manifest a physical feeling according to what is for your higher good. Discomfort directs you to know that what you are thinking isn't for your highest good. When you feel comfortable about something, this is for your highest good.

Take the previous scenario: The children are to come to Grandma's for a visit. Place yourself in this situation. Is the time you spend with the grandchildren more valuable than the time you spend watching a TV program? Does the pleasure you receive watching your grandchildren enjoying eating peanut butter cookies outweigh the extra cleaning? Remember the smiles on those faces. Hear the laughter in their voices. You are creating memories that are positive for the grandchildren and yourself! Decide what you want to do. What is for the highest good for all concerned? Please remember this when you think of their visits.

Focus in on the positive and you will feel the love and gratitude in a grand way. Focus in on the negative and you will feel resentment and discomfort. Enjoy yourself! Live in the present moment. If you were to leave the Earth plane today, which memory would you like to take with you, the memory of watching your grandchildren sitting around the kitchen table with a plate of warm peanut butter cookies and a glass of cold milk, or the memory of watching your favorite TV program that, incidentally, is probably a repeat?

We wish you to look closely at your creation of thoughts. I ask you this: Do you imagine all the pleasant things that may come out of a given situation, or do you imagine the situation as how it may be of an inconvenience to you?

Ah, but there is another side to this. We tell you often, you are to balance yourself by remembering to take care of the temple of God/ Goddess. The body must rest. So when you are making your decisions, remember to assess how you feel and choose what is for the highest good of all concerned. This means to take into consideration what is good for the body also.

August 28, 2009
What We Believe to Be True

Today, my good friend Beth and I had our day up in the city. Every month or so, we take a day to get our hair cut and styled, do some shopping, and have a good meal that someone else prepares! It is a good time for us both.

Both, Beth and our hairstylist, Kay, are very knowledgeable in the metaphysical field. When the three of us are together, we seem to always have interesting conversations. While we were getting our hair done, we talked about how our beliefs affect particular outcomes. We as a society are being told by experts that our foods no longer have the level of nutrients in them to maintain a healthy, strong body. For that reason, we have been conditioned to believe that we would undoubtedly be healthier if we would supplement our diets with vitamins and minerals. In addition, we receive information from other sources that there are toxins in pretty much everything that we eat and drink! Okay, so we are told that we would be healthier if we took supplements, but there are most definitely toxins in those supplements. The conversation, for me, raised a lot of questions. What is really the best for us to do here?

The Akasie: The three of you had a most stimulating conversation. We say that gathering in groups and talking of such things is highly beneficial. All of you had the experience to go forth and explore new possibilities and to expand your thought processes. Your thoughts and beliefs are most persuasive. You as a collective society are told many things. Many of you take in what you are told without any question whatsoever. You take what you receive, no matter the source, as gospel, making it your own truth! We are referring to the many boxes you have created that do not serve you. Remember, there is no judgment and all is for a purpose. We are most pleased to say that you as a collective society are becoming more vigilant and wiser as you are learning to discern information before you integrate it into your own belief system. No longer will you blindly accept information given as truth before you examine it from all angles.

First, we will address your statement: You say that experts tell you that your foods no longer have the level of nutrients in them to maintain a balanced body. Yes, we agree with this information. You'll remember we discussed this subject previously. Some of you depend on prepackaged foods and fast foods to see you through your days. Most of you are very aware that these foods are not for your highest benefit. However, the convenience is great. Yes, these foods are handy, but to ingest foods that are laced with chemicals and void of nutrition is damaging to your entire being. When the physical body is thrown off balance for any reason, this imbalance affects all levels of your being.

For these reasons, there are those who are willing to do the extra work by taking on the task of growing their own foods instead of depending on other resources for their food supply. They are choosing to forgo the use of pesticides, herbicides, and fertilizers. Even so, we say to take into consideration the water sources and the quality of the soil, as there may be chemical run off from other locations that will greatly affect your produce.

Also, consider the fact that in municipalities the water supply has been treated with chemicals; the water is not pure! Furthermore, many vital minerals have been leached out of much of the Earth's top soil. For many years, the farmers have planted the same crops on the same parcel of land while using many chemicals with the intent to control every aspect of the growth cycle. You can see quite clearly that the molecular structures of most of the foods you have available to you have most undoubtedly been compromised. This is all for a purpose. We see you as a collective becoming wiser in this area also. Many of you are adopting methods to grow your foods organically. We wish to see more of you turning to these basic methods that are for the highest benefit for all of creation.

Next, we will address the subject of supplements. Again, we say supplements are beneficial, and yes, many of the brands have toxins in them; they are impure. In addition, many of the supplements marketed also contain fillers in them that are not for your highest good.

We see you in a state of confusion on this subject; you do not know what you should do. I hear you question how your beliefs play into all of this. We have coached you on the matter of manifesting your reality, and perhaps this is the part that trips you up. You have been taught to affirm that you are grateful for all you have and to believe that you are eating highly nutritious foods and your body receives all that it requires. We tell you every day to acknowledge with gratitude that your food has the highest nutrition possible!

One purpose for this affirmation is to manifest it into your reality. Your affirmations are energy, my dear. Those thoughts and emotions rise and join with other like thoughts and emotions. The more energy created for this purpose, the faster the mass consciousness comes to the realization that you as a collective must go forward and change the way you are growing and processing your foods in order to be balanced individuals.

You have had the knowledge for some time that there are currently small pockets of groups forming for the purpose to farm organically. More and more people will continue to recognize the advantages of growing their food themselves until the majority are moving forward with the realization that growing foods organically is the better way.

First, you begin to realize that the foods that you are eating are not for your highest good and there has to be a better way. Second, you begin to talk about these views with others, making the thoughts and emotions stronger, motivating you to search for information that will help you go forward in this endeavor. Third, you begin to integrate your teachings into your lives—changing old habits and creating new ones; you are on your way to growing foods that are nutritious and even delicious. (Many of you do not remember how food tastes when it is full of the life force.) Fourth and lastly, you as a culture have made the transition and are now successfully growing organic food.

The second purpose for affirming that you are grateful for your highly nutritious food is to work with your level of gratitude and love. The more you feel these grand emotions, the higher your vibration will rise. As a result, you are opening your heart chakra that allows the divine energies to flow through both your physical and ethereal bodies.

Okay, I understand what you are saying about manifesting healthy food, but at the same time, you have been working with me on reprogramming the body. Can't we program our bodies to take what we eat at any given moment and work with that nutrition? If we believe with our entire beings that what we are eating is the very best possible food for us, won't that be true?

The Akasie: You can program your body to do anything. The mind is vast and its capabilities are limitless. We tell you there are no limits as to what the mind can do! There are individuals on the Earth plane who presently do program their bodies for this exact purpose.

Up to this point in your current lifetime, however, you have not had the level of understanding to make this belief your reality. You see, you have never truly believed that what you eat is for your highest good!

So it is possible that I can program my body to work with the foods I now eat and be totally healthy and balanced?

The Akasie: Oh, yes! We tell you that what you seek you will find. We will take you through the steps to accomplish this if you like. Please continue to be grateful for all you have and know in your heart that what you have is for the highest good of all. Please continue to move the energy so the many peoples of the Earth plane will come to the realization that the present practices in the production of food must evolve for the higher good for not only the people but for the Mother Earth.

We wish all to heal. We wish to continue tomorrow with this line of thinking. There is more to the story of why growing your own food free of chemicals is for the highest good of all mankind.

August 29, 2009

Benefits and Methods of Energizing Our Food and Drink

I have really been thinking about what the actual benefits are for me to energize my food and drink. More specifically, I am examining the method I use to energize my food and drink. I have gotten bits and pieces of information from other sources that do not seem complete. Will you explain all of this in one complete teaching?

My understanding of how you teach is to get me to look at the information, process that information, and then formulate new questions to take me further. I am not sure if my observation is correct with this particular case, however. You want me to think and feel what is correct for me and get out of my boxes that I have created concerning many issues. We as a society have become placid and allowed others to think for us! I also understand from your past teachings that there are numerous ways to achieve any one thing.

Over the past few years, I have come across a few books that have mentioned energizing food. What I have learned so far seems to be obscure, as nothing I have read is clear cut. Maybe it is my analytical mind, my perceived need to know exactly what I am accomplishing and what method works best that keeps me reassessing all the different angles of this practice. I seem to be kind of hung up with this subject. Knowing me, I am making this way more difficult than it really is. I would really like it if you would oblige me and clearly explain this to me once and for all so I can get on with my life!

Quem: Yes, we all have seen you struggle with this concept for some time. You have pondered the many scenarios in your mind. Not only do you wonder what you are accomplishing when you send the energy to the food and drink, but you wonder if you are doing this practice effectively and efficiently.

First, we would like to explain what this energy is that we are discussing. We have previously discussed the matter that your food does not possess the highest nutritional value. Much of the food is dead. What we are speaking of is not only the vitamins and minerals that the body requires but also we speak of the life force. Until this moment, you have thought that the nutritional quality and the life force were two distinct and separate things. However, we tell you that you are incorrect. We laugh because we take a long pause here. We like drama in some cases! You are correct also; the two go hand in hand. You require the two to make your food to be the highest nutritional value, alive, complete, and whole. You receive nutrition from the food itself, but for the food to have high nutrition, it must have been grown in the correct conditions. We have spoken of this previously, but the subject is of utmost importance and we wish to reiterate our words. We speak here of the four elements: earth, fire, water, and air. To grow wholesome foods, the foods must receive the correct ingredients; the food must grow in the correct conditions.

It is here that we say that the peoples of the Earth have compromised all four of your vital elements to sustain life. Chemicals have been used in the soil, the air, and the water. All must be in alignment to benefit to the highest degree. What you do to and on the Mother Earth affects all. We speak of the interactions between the earth and all that encompasses the universe. We specifically speak of your sun. Your sun's rays are compromised because of your activities on and around (in the air) the Mother. What you do with or to one element affects all the rest.

Pesticides are intended to kill "harmful" insects. We will not discuss the devastation from the chemicals to the animal kingdom in this writing. We are speaking of the residual affects the pesticides have on the soil, the air, and the water. All of this is common knowledge, yet the poisons continue to be produced and used.

Herbicides are used to kill unwanted plant material. Again, these chemicals affect all. Chemicals are accepted and even encouraged by the agricultural communities to promote fast growth. "What is the harm in encouraging the plants to grow quickly?" you may ask. These chemicals are unwarranted and even dangerous. You notice what we are saying is of the negative nature. Do you wish us to speak only of the positive outcome here? We are referring to the positive affirmations. Honey, yes, we affirm that the soil is healthy and all that you do is for the highest good for all of creation. At the same time, we have come here to teach you how to go forward. You, Jackie, have asked every day for us to assist you and teach you for your highest good, and this is what we are doing at this very moment. We are teaching you to look at the positive in all. We are here to educate you so you will open your eyes and see what is before you. You must learn to see the error of your ways. There is purpose in all that we say and do.

If you look at the above passages closely, you will see that when we speak of the herbicides, pesticides, and other chemicals, we are painting a picture so you may see more clearly that your efforts to do things quickly and efficiently is for the aim to cut down on labor. Ah, your society wishes to accomplish these endeavors quickly and with precision, and make a large profit at the same time! Are you looking for the highest good of all when you make your choices? You are ones who wish to accomplish much in little time. Sometimes your choices are not for the highest good, but all is for a great purpose. Perhaps you realize the error in what you do when you receive the full measure of your actions.

Oh, heck, I thought my questions were simple. I didn't know we were going to get into all of this!

Quem: I speak now! Yes, what has come about is most complex, but in order to answer your questions once and for all, we must go back a ways. I am your teacher, Miss, and through my teachings that I give to you, you are to give to all.

I wish also to address your tone. You seem to be a bit impatient today. I ask you to work on this, please.

The Akasie: We continue, yes?

Yes.

The Akasie: Everything you do has an effect or consequence on something else. What you do sets something else into motion. We wish you to look at your actions carefully with respect to the outcomes. We wish you to do what is for the highest good of all concerned, as *we are One.*

Now, we will get to your original questions. Do you even remember what your questions were? That was a rhetorical question there, Miss. We go on. You wanted to know what the benefits were of energizing your food and drink and how to do this practice efficiently and effectively.

This is what I hear you asking: Am I actually doing anything that will really benefit me when I work to energize my food and drink? If I am doing something that will benefit me, what method can I use that will work best and that will be the fastest?

Oh geez! I sound just like some of these other people who are trying to cut down on labor and make things work more efficiently.

The Akasie: What you say is true, but you are seeing something here that you didn't see before. This is how you as a person, a society, and the mass consciousness evolve.

Let's go back to the teaching. Many of you have allowed yourselves to live in the fast lane. You are in a big rush to get here and there and to do this and that. Do you have the time to be grateful? We tell you here that energizing your food is multifaceted. Hang on here, as this is another teaching.

First, we teach you to stop and feel the love and gratitude for your food. Thank the Creator for all you have. This energy that you are sending to your food is the life source, love, or Spirit that we spoke of earlier. This action of energizing your food has many purposes:

- When you are grateful for what you have, you manifest more of the same.

- When you slow down, you can enjoy what you have before you.

- You are raising your own vibration by being grateful and allowing the life force to flow through you.

- As Spirit flows through you, you are receiving healing energy on all levels of your physical and spiritual being.

- By directing this energy to another, you are sending healing energy to them (in this case your food).

- By giving this energy to your food, you are raising the vibration of the food, making it healthier for you to consume. It is alive with the same energy that resonates with your body.

- To eat food of a lower vibration is not beneficial for you on any level of your being.

- To consume foods of a lower quality demands more from the physical body, as the body strives also to maintain numerous functions throughout itself and to also facilitate healing.

In short, when you consume food that is low or lacking in the life force, you are allowing energy to enter your body that is incompatible to yours. To consume energy of a lower vibration will keep you from reaching your goal. The goal that we refer to is to ascend to the fifth dimension. This is why we urge you to eat fresh foods prepared with love at home or in fine restaurants. Consequently, this is why we continue to prompt you to bring up your love vibration and send it to your food every time you partake in nourishment.

We are working diligently to cleanse and purify your body. This must be done in order for you to raise the level of your vibration. We ask you to work with us by being conscious of what you eat. Now you see the importance of being mindful of what you eat, yes?

When you create fifth dimensional energies (love and gratitude), you are healing on many levels. This is true also when you allow the fifth dimensional energies to flow through you to energize your food and drink.

We wish to get back on track here and talk about the methods or techniques of energizing your food and drink, but before we do, we would like to comment on something that has been entertaining your mind recently.

The size of your energy field at any given moment is the result of the emotions you are creating or feeling. Imagine a larger invisible body encompassing your physical body. The energy field greatly expands when you feel the love and gratitude. You have begun to wonder if your energy field in itself has an effect on your food. The answer is yes, your energy field does have an effect on all that it comes into contact with. The energy we are teaching you about at this moment, however, is the healing energy that flows through you, coming down from the Creator through your crown out through the palms of your hands.

You are comprised of Spirit, as all of creation is. When you call upon the Creator with love and gratitude, it is much like turning on a light switch. The power comes forth, flowing freely through your body as you allow it. You are the vehicle and you control the level of the power by the level of love and gratitude you feel. You are giving this energy direction, purpose, and also a level of intensity.

The exact technique is this: You hold your hands approximately one inch over your food or drink. Your hands can be flat or a little curved; this matters not. The thumbs are to be about one inch apart.

You are remembering when one of your friends told you that he stuck a finger in his water and this brought up the vibration. We tell you this does have an effect on the water, but to be of the highest benefit for you, we ask you to go through the steps to energize your food by being grateful and allowing the energy to come forth. There is much purpose in what we tell you.

What about knowing how long to give Reiki energy to my food and drink? Would you expand your teaching to cover that?

The Akasie: Miss, yes, we go further with our words. Since you have been attuned to this energy and have used this practice for some time, you are well aware of the subtle energies; you feel the energy build in the space in between the food and your hands. The energy feels like static electricity. Notice the strength of the energy that you feel. After the energy builds in strength the pressure becomes stronger, then you have accomplished your objective.

I have noticed that by saying a short prayer with the feelings of love and gratitude before I energize my food and drink the energy immediately begins to flow through my hands.

The Akasie: Jackie, when you set your intention upon your food with love and gratitude you reside in the now; and you have become one with your food. This was part of the reason we taught you to energize your food. When you create the feelings of love and gratitude in any circumstance, you are raising your vibration. To raise your vibration allows divine energy, the life force, to flow through you at higher levels promoting not only healing on all levels of your body, but healing for the food and drink.

Angels are with you always assisting in all ways. Just ask and you'll receive.

August 30, 2009
A Gift of Healing

Every night before I go to sleep, I spend a couple of hours reading, listening to music, and meditating. As I was reading and listening to some really nice soothing music, the Akasie told me that they had a gift for me and to go lay down on my bed. Usually before doing any energy work, the Akasie will instruct me to turn off the music. Instead, they directed me to leave my music on. As soon as I got comfortable, a very intense energy began to flow through me.

As I have mentioned before, I have experienced numbness in my hands and this really limits some of the things that I am able to do. I have asked the Akasie on several occasions to help me out with that.

The energy that I felt was extremely high and focused on my hands at this time. Colér took my right arm so it hung over the side of the bed. When she finished she gently picked up my arm and put my hand over my heart. The energy associated with the movement of my arm was very different, extremely loving. The beauty of that action was astounding. The compassion and love I felt from the Akasie was on a totally different level than I have ever experienced before. Colér says she used energy to move my arm; her mind directed the energy.

At this time the Akasie told me to focus on the music while they did an adjustment. I never know really what they are doing, but I usually feel some sort of tingling or pressure in my head. They have many times directed me to empty my mind when they are working with me energetically, so I wondered if they were using the tones of the music somehow to keep my mind from wandering. I had a focused sensation at my right temple, which was almost a piercing sensation; nothing they did hurt. Then they told me I'd receive a little electrical shock therapy. I was at that moment directed to turn off the music. I did feel some tremors. These tremors felt like something I'd received at another time. It didn't hurt, but felt weird.

The Akasie: Jackie, what we did was very simple. Healing work, yes! We worked on raising your vibration quite a bit.

That was what the music was for. Shock therapy was to stimulate damaged nerves in the body and to accelerate healing.

We have more information. Healing is being done on other levels now. Spirit is healing, blocks are being dismantled. The physical is healing in concession to healing on other levels. All the release of toxins is paying off. Thank you for doing your part.

August 31, 2009
Time for Change

I have been looking back at something you said. You spoke of our culture peaking. When you said this, did you mean in America our culture is peaking, or is this in certain countries or even worldwide? Did you mean that we are finished with our lives here on the Earth plane?

The Akasie: At this time, do not fill yourselves with fear. The culture we speak of is not to be revealed at this writing. You are to know, however, that you are to begin anew in certain areas of your lives. In order to balance you must go back to what makes your hearts sing. It is for your highest benefit to learn to relax and enjoy life once again and live in the *Now*.

What we speak of is a worldwide issue. You as a collective have misused your natural resources. You have abused the Mother to the point that she must go through the process of cleansing and healing on a grand scale. The natural way this is done is through great shifts and eruptions in the crust, climate changes, and the rotation of the plant life. Always, we encounter change of some kind on some level. The Mother needs time to purge herself of the many unfavorable, shall we say, transgressions. She must have time to rid herself of the many toxins that are choking her. She must have the time for her soil to take a rest and replenish.

There are many people who do not have the Mother's best interests at heart. There is no judgment from us, as this is their level of understanding at this time. In the coming days how those people will be dealt with will be for the highest benefit for all of creation. On a mass scale, the populations of the many countries will decrease to numbers that are more moderate. This will all come to be as the result of climate changes, floods, and many cataclysmic events that will ensue.

The Mother will not continue to feed this number of people. The Mother continually evolves; nothing stays the same. Your peoples expect her climates to be as they were decades ago. This is not to be. The climates change over time. Many of the people in your community have expressed their frustration when it comes to growing their gardens. The rainy season has grown much longer in the area in which you presently reside. If you wish to continue to grow produce, you are advised to choose plants that do not mind wet feet or create an area with better drainage. In addition, the plant life must be allowed to rotate to replenish the soil that is now lacking of particular vital minerals and nutrients. In order to survive and thrive, you must learn to adapt to the changes at hand.

We talk of this as the natural order to life. Many people have been and will continue to be displaced because of the happenings of Mother Nature. Many people will cease to exist on this Earth plane because of the various changes occurring on the Earth during the coming seasons.

Many societies depend on the mass production of foodstuffs. We have spoken of this before. When you mass produce anything, everything is thrown off balance. We speak of the portion of land mass that is used for one specific type of plant life. The animal kingdom alone is greatly affected by this unnatural way you coerce the plants to grow in certain areas. All require variety to maintain a healthy existence. When you are limited to one choice of food, you do not get a balanced diet. This is true with all species in the physical bodies.

You as a human require the interaction with your great Mother Earth. We talk of the importance of breathing in the fresh air and walking on the earth with your bare feet. To partake in the fresh breath is to continue life. To place your bare feet on soil is to release stagnant energy from your being. You as a spiritual being in a physical body require a continuous flow of the cosmic divine energy or life force energy. As we said before, when you are in a state of love and gratitude, you are allowing this energy that we speak of to flow through you at a higher level. All in your solar system plays a pivotal role in this flow of energy. We specifically speak of your sun, your moon, and your Earth, but we include all other planets in your solar system as well.

When was the last time you ventured outdoors, looked up to the heavens, and allowed the Sun's rays to warm your body? When was the last time you allowed yourself the pleasure of laying on the Mother's back to watch the clouds drift slowly across the sky? When you were a child, these exchanges were natural in their forthcoming. What has taken you from these joyful interludes between yourself, the Mother, and the Father?

All that we have spoken of is for the purpose of showing you, painting a picture for you, of the coming changes. Be most assured, they will come your way, as they always do. The changes that we speak of are for the higher good of all concerned. Maybe you question this because you see in your mind's eye that many people will suffer because of the earth changes. We ask you to understand in a relaxed manner that this is all part of evolution, and this has always been happening since the very beginning of thought. Souls continue to come and go for the purpose of spiritual evolution.

Someone I talked to recently used the term, "the protected ones" in reference to who would stay behind to begin again when the Earth changes happened. Are we going to begin again? Are these particular people going to be allowed to stay here on the earth because they know more or perhaps have special abilities or skills? Will you talk to me concerning this?

The Akasie: There are certain people who have been dubbed as "the protected ones." These protected ones are the ones that will carry on and rebuild on a more simplistic, primitive scale. The "protected ones" is a term that someone on the Earth plane has coined. More accurately, the ones who will carry on are the ones who have agreed to do this work. Those in the spirit form watch over all. We will continue to protect those who have agreed to this contract.

It is time for you all to change with the energy. We go forward with the feminine, the connection of the heart, which is true love for self and all creation. Also, we go forward with the thinning of the veil. Many changes on many levels are happening at this very moment.

One of the most significant purposes of the changes is to simplify; to go back to loving yourself and to loving all of creation. In order to do this you must balance yourselves by being out in your vast outdoors, to grow your own foods, and to care for all of creation with love and respect. In other words, go back to loving the Mother Earth and all of her children. *We are all One.*

The "protected ones" are those who know the heart language. You all have been introduced to this energy, this knowing, and this love. More and more of you are beginning to remember this language. It is a matter of you allowing this love to flow through you and become you.

Jackie, you have been given the opportunity to know about this heart connection. This is a big step and it is extremely important for you.

You must move forward, feel with your heart, and listen with your heart! When you practice this heart connection with the children, you will have a much easier and more enjoyable time with them. We are speaking to you specifically concerning your grandson. He is a tough cookie. He was brought to you for this purpose. It was his choice to come at this time. You have the knowledge to break the cycle of negative thoughts and emotions. We ask you to look to your heart when you are with this one.

Understand people and work with them on their own particular level. You are to listen with your heart, hear, and understand what they need. They must be given the opportunities to move forward in their steps no matter where they are in their growth process.

As we stated earlier, your planetary progress is at its peak. This chapter is ending. For those who do not evolve alongside of those seeking illumination—the awakening—they will return to whence they came.

You remind us of what we have said: all know in their hearts who they are, they just haven't remembered yet. At this very moment, all are in the process of remembering who they are.

The plan is not to leave out or forget those who have not remembered their true selves on a conscious level. They will come back in another lifetime in the physical body. They will have another time of growth. The fifth dimension arises anyway for those seeking higher consciousness, the Christ in you, The I AM. Evolution proceeds. We all move forward.

September 1, 2009
Meditation: Connection to the Higher Consciousness

The Akasie: You ask where your mind goes when you meditate. We tell you that you are connecting to a higher realm, your higher consciousness.

There are different levels of consciousness, and through meditation, you may access some of these levels of awareness that you seem to be unable to access otherwise. In essence, you are leaving the body and the physical world. We tell you that you may go so high in this connection with your higher self that you are no longer aware of the body, but you are always connected to the body. You wonder about the body; is it protected when you are no longer aware of this physical part of you? Yes, you are always protected. We always watch over you, but we also tell you that your higher consciousness is also aware of what goes on with the body. Do not fear this way of Oneness.

September 2, 2009
Healing Energy and Affirmations

The Akasie: Last night we worked with you on an energetic level. Spirit flowed through us. As you slept, we directed this energy to you for healing purposes. When you awoke, you noted that you were lying on your side and felt warmth that emanated from the middle of your back. You commented to us that the energy you received felt good and relaxing. We continued to allow the energy to flow through us unto you, and after a short period of time with our assistance, you drifted back into a deep, restful sleep. About ten minutes later, you woke up quite literally dripping with sweat. We tell you it was a big release you just had.

This was an intense cleansing and healing of the body. We did this because of your prayer before you descended into the sleep-state. You expressed your deep gratitude for what we have done with you and for you. You have remained true in your affirmations that you receive healing energy with the assistance of your guides and angels. We do this for you. We love you.

We tell you to continue to affirm that we always protect, teach, heal, and assist with anything that you require as long as it is for the highest benefit for all concerned. We do this for you.

You do not need to affirm that we love you. We love you always. We love all of creation always and forever. *We are One!*

September 3, 1009
Ways to Go Forward

My Dream

I woke up in a panic. I grabbed my journal, and as I write, I try to catch my breath. I am covered in sweat, my hands are shaking, and yes, I am crying. I am totally entrenched in fear.

The dream was vivid and felt so real! Right now, it is as if my emotions are alive and have taken over. Every emotion I feel is fear-based and extremely powerful.

In my dream, I lived in a quiet neighborhood much like my family did when my son, Bradley was still alive. I saw an aerial view of the entire layout of the neighborhood. We appeared to live in a well-kept subdivision. Each house was neat and orderly in addition to having nice-sized manicured lawns. Some of us had the chain-link fences around our back yards, but the neighborhood was mostly open. I saw a few dogs. The streets were curved so the houses would be located off to the side of the city and more secluded.

I had the awareness that I was raising my same children, only they were very young. Bradley was about three years old. He had been riding his Big Wheel tricycle, and suddenly I couldn't see him any longer. He had vanished! I remember being in a hyper-vigilant state and going to each house in the neighborhood, approaching each door and knocking. No one had any information that would help me find my son.

As I was trying to figure out what to do next, I suddenly remembered seeing this older man sitting on a Harley motorcycle that was parked in the street adjacent to our house. I remembered clearly seeing Bradley sitting on his Big Wheel talking with the biker with nothing but the chain-link fence separating the two. The biker was in our neighborhood at the same time Bradley had disappeared.

Judging from the biker's appearance, he was in his late fifties. He sported a scruffy beard and a ponytail. He wore torn, faded blue jeans, a red bandana around his head, and a black leather vest detailed with studs and fringe. He even wore those black, fingerless gloves and well-worn black boots. What was he doing in our neighborhood, and why was he talking to my son?

The biker was the epitome of what I would describe as a person who, if provoked, could easily cause trouble. He looked like the kind of person who might be an angry-drunk, suddenly exploding at the drop of a hat, and breaking beer bottles on the edge of the bar for a quick and deadly weapon.

My search for my son continued. No one had seen him. On the inside, I felt the anxiety build. On the outside, I appeared to be calm and focused on my search.

I instinctively knew that the biker had taken my son. At this realization, my breath caught, the fear turned into this deep compassion and anxiety all mixed into one big lump of raw emotion. I was aware that I didn't have any real proof that the biker was responsible; I just knew! I had no idea what to do next except to keep searching for any bit of information that would lead me to Bradley or the biker. I had looked everywhere and talked to everyone I could find in my neighborhood; my resources were exhausted. It was time to look beyond those perimeters.

There was a bridge that connected our neighborhood to the city. I went across the bridge, and I was suddenly at the scene of a horrible accident. Vehicles were crushed beyond identification. Torn metal and broken glass was strewn about. The remains of the wreckage smoldered, which signified that the worst was over. In the distance, I could hear the scream of sirens growing louder. Help would be here shortly.

As I continue to examine the dream and the realness of it, the feeling of helplessness grows stronger. Even though I know this is a dream and I am wide awake, I can't shake the feeling that it was real! The feelings of absolute agony and sorrow deepen. I am so worried about Bradley and know that he is in terrible trouble. Bradley is just a little boy. There is no one to protect him. I keep reminding myself that what I am remembering is just a dream and nothing more! I feel like I have somehow slipped out of my reality into another reality and I am unable to separate the two.

Terror and panic rise to the surface of my being with such power that the tears begin to flow freely once again. I put myself in Bradley's place and instinctively know that he must be feeling alone, frightened, and unprotected. I feel as if this is really happening. I feel the terror that Bradley must feel. I feel my own terror and my own instinctive need to find him and save him. On some obscure level, I know in my heart that this has actually happened, is happening, but logically I remember it is a dream. It does not matter to me if this dream is some sort of other reality or not. In my heart, I simply know there is absolutely nothing I can do from where I am. I am working to settle down, because I know logically that there isn't anything I can do to save him from where I am. Bradley is no longer here with me. Bradley is in another realm now. I feel like a piece of me has been unmercifully ripped out of my *heart and soul. Bradley has been gone from my life for fifteen years, but I am still his mother and I will always love him.*

Quem: This dream is very important, Miss, in that it is revealing of your true emotions that you are creating at this time. You are feeling very vulnerable. On your lower level of awareness, you feel that you are unable to reveal what is happening in your life to anyone, in particular to your husband. Also, I speak of the goings on between you and your guides. Some mighty unusual things are occurring during this time, and to speak candidly to your husband would surely raise his eyebrows at the least. You have been with your husband for thirty-four years now. For the most part, you have always been able to talk to him about almost any issue.

We do not speak the truth now, do we? There has been a schism between the two of you for many years, although the two of you get along very well in most situations and you appear to be the perfect couple.

Oh, Father, I really do not want to discuss my marriage in this book!

Quem: I wish you to consider this dream as a teaching for you as well as for others to learn from. That is one of the main purposes of this book.

You look at the dream and wonder how your relationship ties into the dream. I will get to it. First, I wish to talk about what is going on within your relationship with your husband.

You have had a major psychic opening, honey. You hear us talk to you! You channel our words through you. This is a major upheaval in your life and a major transition. Right now, you feel stress on every level of your being and your life. Making the necessary adjustments to feel comfortable with all that has occurred in your life will take some time. Please consider this and understand what we say. Give yourself the time needed to adjust to this new level of awareness.

Right now, I feel your frustration. Perhaps this is a good time for you talk about what you are feeling.

Well, I feel that if people knew about the weird stuff I am experiencing, they would think I was crazy as a loon. I receive information all the time from the angels. You talk through me. We dance together. I receive the energy, the love. You give me the movements.

Our family has already suffered so much. I just don't know how to handle this. Maybe everything will work out and I won't have to do or say anything to anyone, but at the same time, I know that I can't hide like this forever. This all has to come out, or I will go crazy!

I really need someone to talk to who will not look at me like I have a mental illness. I need and want someone who has the ability and desire to support me emotionally and who understands this sort of phenomenon. In order to have someone understand me, I need someone who is knowledgeable in this area. I feel like I need someone who can hold a conversation about the esoteric. I guess when it comes down to the nitty gritty, I am afraid that Scott will not accept me or even love me anymore if I reveal what I am experiencing, and he will think I should go to one of those places.

Yes, back in March, Scott was beside me when we did the release of the negative energy in the attic, but what he did was all show. He did his best to get through it, but I felt his extreme discomfort then. He truly doesn't know the half of what is going on with me, and quite honestly, I don't feel comfortable talking to him about any of it.

Quem: It is truly for your highest benefit to talk through what you are feeling. We will talk about the dream now. In the beginning of your dream, everything was fine; your children were safe. Your neighborhood symbolizes order, security, and peace.

In the first part of the dream, your son Bradley represented innocence and joy, specifically yours. He symbolizes the part of you that has no responsibilities, when you were innocent and joyful! Suddenly everything has changed and your son is gone. Your innocence and joy has vanished.

In your dream, on the outside (how you show yourself to others) you are in control of your manner, but on the inside you are terrified and in a panic. This is true in how you present yourself in your everyday life.

In an organized manner, you are traveling door to door in hopes of finding your son or at least some information so you may find your son. This signifies that, on a conscious level of awareness, you are systematically searching to once again find that carefree aspect of yourself.

You will notice that everything in your dream represents something. You have stereotyped bikers to be unruly characters. In your dream, this man in the very least represents someone who doesn't belong and in the very most could have the connotation for violence for you and your situation. He is someone totally out of character in your life who has come into your midst, your safe haven, and is someone you do not trust. This someone represents both yourself and Scott. You do not trust yourself or Scott to have the necessary conversation concerning your transition in order for you to go forward; you are fearful of the consequences.

Likewise, I will tell you that you are also fearful of what is occurring to you, because everything concerning the angels is unchartered territory. We do not fit nicely into your neighborhood. Equally, *what* you are experiencing doesn't fit nicely into your neighborhood either. Your search shows us that you are looking at different possibilities, because at the present time you do not have enough information that will help you to go forward concerning your life.

It is your responsibility to keep Bradley safe. Bradley symbolizes a part of you that has been taken, stolen. You feel you have been taken from your safe and orderly lifestyle. You are in turmoil, because quite suddenly that aspect of your life is gone; you do not understand what is happening. Our teachings confound you somewhat. At the moment, all is confusing and your thoughts are a jumbled mess. You fear for his safety the same as you fear for yours. You can no longer see where Bradley is just as you can no longer see where you are.

You look everywhere you know for your son. The neighborhood is comfortable for you; this is your comfort zone. You stay in this area until you have exhausted all possible leads. This part of the dream reveals that you are desperately looking for information to help you regain innocence, security, and order in your life. Consequently, in order for you to find what you are seeking, you must move out of your comfort zone.

Miss, you have been exposed to some extraordinary things in other realms that disturb you. They are out of the ordinary for you. You are scared and have no one on the physical plane to guide you. What we speak of is the unseen, the esoteric, and for many the unexplainable and even unbelievable! Understandably, you are frightened. You are looking for someone who can give words that will comfort you and help you to understand in a logical manner what has occurred. You haven't found anyone who can help you to ease your pain. You are looking for someone you can trust to give you information to make everything okay and happy again.

In a systematic fashion you have searched your neighborhood, which includes friends and family, and you have exhausted all possibilities to find your son who symbolizes your innocence. You must go across a bridge (out of the familiar and into the unknown) in order to expand your search. The bridge symbolizes going to another level of awareness. The bridge takes you to another place, the city, where you see the wreckage. To you the wreckage symbolizes violence, fear, and even death. You do cross the bridge, going beyond your comfort zone to find peace, but in searching for peace, instead you find yourself in chaos. Nothing is orderly; all is askew.

You, in the physical realm, are desperate to find someone who can help you to ease your mind, to comfort you, to let you know that everything is okay. You want to know that Bradley is in your sights and he is safe. You want to be safe yourself.

At this moment in your life, you feel turmoil; you feel as if your life is in total confusion and chaos. You perceive that you are witnessing a horrific wreck. The wreck is your life.

You hear the sirens in the distance. You know that there are those who are coming to help put things back in order. Is it too late?

At this moment, something doesn't feel right to me. Possibly the interpretation isn't complete. The biker represents violence, disruption, and disturbance. I can see that he is symbolizing what has happened to me. I perceive my "experience" with you to be violent in a way, because in my logical mind, what I have gone through makes no sense! I have had my sleep disrupted. I have felt much fear because I did not understand what, why, or how this was all happening. My home life has been disrupted, and I am most certainly concerned.

I feel like I have to talk to someone, preferably my spouse, but just thinking about talking to him scares me to the point of me feeling sick. I feel all tight and tense; my stomach is in revolt. I feel threatened, because I sense that he isn't going to understand this and he will regard me as crazy—I mean really, truly crazy.

Quem: What I am about to say isn't going to be pleasant, but I wish you to be open-minded and listen to my words. You know that there has been an underlying tension between you and your husband for some time. You know what I speak of. With the occurrence of your psychic opening, you have tipped the scale, so to speak. You were already feeling vulnerable with this one. You have not understood your feelings concerning him. You feel with the combination of this underlying tension—the loss of your son, and now this higher level of awareness—that if you do not somehow deal with your feelings, you will not be able to continue. Something must give.

Dreams are powerful tools and we are pleased that you are willing to work with this particular tool to help you to heal and move forward. This particular dream was given to you by your higher consciousness for you to fully understand your emotions concerning what is occurring with you on the physical level. This dream is a great gift and I ask you, I remind you to always be grateful for all you receive.

I give the following so you may clearly see what each symbol in your dream represents. Take notice that the meaning of these symbols may vary according to each person's beliefs. I speak of the biker, because for Jackie, a biker represents violence. To another a biker may represent freedom. When interpreting dreams, you also take into account what is happening with each symbol.

- Tidy neighborhood: security, order, comfort, peace

- Young son: innocence, love, purity, joy

- Myself: caregiver, protector, authority, love

- Three-wheeler: mobility, joy, freedom

- Biker: violence, threat, fear

- Chain link fence: division, safety; an attempt to keep in or to keep out, but at the same time to allow to see what is on the other side.

- Doors: to open or shut; beginnings or endings; opportunities

- Bridge: take to another place

- Wreckage: disorder, turmoil, chaos

- Sirens: emergency; help is on the way

Dreams often, if not always, are multifaceted. In this case, you have seen where the dream reveals your emotions concerning the changes in your life. You have angels that have disrupted your life and who *you* haven't yet learned to trust entirely. You find it more necessary to speak to your husband about all of this, but at the same time, you sense that conversation could take you into areas that are perceived as threatening. To talk about your experiences would place you in an extremely vulnerable spot and would reveal your true self. Are you strong enough to risk the repercussions of what you feel you must say?

There is another purpose to this dream. The boy in your dream is your son who has passed on. Jackie, even after all of these years, you still grieve for this one. Bradley has vanished seemingly into thin air. He was taken from you by a violent act. You can no longer see Bradley, and you do not know where he is. You are his mother and on some level, you still want to protect him and to love him. This is what mothers do. Jackie, you continue to search for this one and to find peace with what has occurred. There is another facet to this dream, however, this shall not be revealed at this time.

September 4, 2009
Why We Dream

The Akasie: Dreams are meant to be used as a tool to give you access to the deeper levels of your consciousness. By examining your experience, which includes the symbology of the dream and your emotions, you are further processing your life experiences on multiple levels. These levels may include the different facets of your relationships with yourself and others, a view of past lives (again to help you sort through emotions felt at that time), the ability to see into the future, and as a means to receive messages from others in different dimensions and other realms. So you see, dreams are multifaceted and can be of real value when working to understand yourself and your world.

We will examine one purpose of dreams at this time. Previously, the dreams that we have shared in this book reveal the emotions that you were feeling just prior to the creation of the dream. These types of dreams are given to you by your higher self to help you get a grip on what you are experiencing and to process it.

As spiritual beings in the physical reality, you are continually creating thoughts and emotions even in your sleep time. These emotions are a way of communication and self-expression between your lower level of awareness and your higher self. These emotions are for the purpose of directing you to make choices that are for your higher good.

Again, we tell you that when you create thoughts, you also create emotions and feel them in the physical body. We remind you to pay close attention to those feelings so you may learn how to make choices that will bring you to and keep you in harmony and balance with all of creation.

These dreams we speak of are gifts that are given to you by your higher self. At this time, we do not wish to get into the physiology of sleep patterns or the psychology of dreams. We wish to instruct you on a healthy way to access this gift to enable you to move forward. Dreams are a way to look at your feelings from another perspective.

To remember your dreams is the first step in this learning process. Jackie, we have been working with you in this area for some time. We wish to share this with those who read these words.

For some, dreams may be elusive, as they can slip easily out of your grasp. We have heard many of you say that you wake up in the middle of the night with a dream sharply fixed in the memory. You then felt that you would remember the dream in the morning with absolutely no difficulty, as at that moment you could see in your mind's eye every precise detail and feel the exact emotions as if you had actually had the experience when you were awake. Unfortunately, after your nights' sleep, most if not all of those memories have been forgotten.

We go back to the remembering of the dreams. We have heard some of you say that you do not dream. In other words, you have no memory of your dreams. While it is true that some of you do not dream, for the most part, most of you do. The challenge here is that you are not consciously aware of your dreams.

We wish to teach you to program yourself to remember your dreams so you may learn from them. Each night before you sleep, affirm that you are grateful that after a restful night's sleep you are able to access your peaceful dreams in vivid detail. What you access is for your highest good to remember. Also, affirm that you know in totality what they are meant to teach you. Also, we suggest that you feel much gratitude for this modality of communication and this gift.

To program yourself to remember your dreams upon waking is the desired goal. This programming may take a day or it may take months. If you are ready to begin to work with this modality of self-discovery and healing, it is important that you be patient. In the meantime, get yourself a journal. In this journey of self-discovery, the goal is to create and maintain a daily practice to thoroughly explore your feelings through your entries. This, in itself, may be very revealing. By examining your feelings in certain settings, you are better able to understand what triggers certain emotions. This is a great opportunity to go forward in your steps.

If you don't mind waking up in the middle of the night to get a few words on paper, have yourself a notepad and pencil handy or even an audio recorder. (Remember to be considerate of your partner.) It would be best to have a night light that will have a high enough illumination for you to write your notes from your dreams without waking you totally. A night light that is 20-30 watts is plenty. The goal here is to record a few main symbols and your emotions and then return quickly to a deep and restful sleep state.

We give you this example of how to record symbols of a dream during the night. You dreamt of being chased by a big black dog. The dog was threatening. You could see that he had his teeth bared. As you ran, you could feel that he was gaining speed. His barking was becoming louder and more terrifying. Your fear was escalating. You saw the calm ocean before you and wondered if the dog would continue to chase you if you entered the water. The emotion of fear woke you up.

Get your pad of paper and write down: "big black dog," "chasing me," "sacred," and "the calm ocean." In the morning, these words should be enough to jog your memory so as to record your dream in vivid detail. Remember to include what you felt physically (did you feel pain?), what you were thinking, and what you were feeling emotionally. Write down everything you can remember. Compare how you felt in your dream with what is going on in your life. When you make this a habit, you will begin to see patterns emerge, thus enabling you to make different choices during your day to bring you closer into alignment with Spirit.

September 5, 2009
Moving Up the Ladder to Positive Thinking

The Akasie: We wish you to listen carefully here, as this is an important segment to this writing. We speak of the spiritual at this time. When you have realized that there is much more to life than your physical existence, it is easier to consciously move up the ladder, so to speak. You will know when it is time to intentionally train yourself to think in a more positive manner, which is conducive to your spiritual growth.

There are plenty of books that you can familiarize yourself with that will help you to go forward in this area. Know that there are many tools available to you at this time that hold great value, such as positive affirmations and also asking for assistance from your guides. We take this time to remind you that all of those on the Earth plane have spiritual guidance available to them always. We are not too busy for you, dear ones. Assisting you on the Earth plane is what we wish to do and is also the promise that we made to you long ago. Always remember that we have plenty of time to assist all who are under our charge. You are worthy of our love and guidance. Know this, for it is truth. We honor the Spirit in you! *We are One!*

If you see ugliness in any part of creation—and we are speaking of anything: beings, creatures, nature, inanimate objects, and even cataclysmic events—you are not in harmony with self! All is for a higher purpose.

Yes, I realize that in order to be in harmony, I must be able to see the beauty in all things and at all times, but what about the upheaval of our Mother Earth, the earthquakes and such? When I hear of another disaster, I feel so much sadness and pain for the people who are suffering. I understand the purpose of the cleansing. I just wish there was another way; one where there wasn't trauma, illness, and death. All of the destruction seems like utter madness.

The Akasie: We have told you many times that there is a purpose to all. Our Mother Earth must cleanse her body of the negative energy, and through the seemingly chaotic upheavals she is able to accomplish this healing. Always look for the positive in all. Be in harmony with all. Love all!

The ego is the reason for disharmony, as ego is self-serving. If something on the surface causes you discomfort, then you immediately do not like it and you think it is bad and has no purpose. This is not so! Look at all sides of the situation.

Perhaps we give you an extremely simple example here: You are getting dressed and put on your favorite pair of jeans. Much to your disfavor, you find that the jeans are a little too tight. Because you have been forced to look at your actions by trying on your jeans, you have become consciously aware that you have become much too careless with the intake of your food. You could allow this realization to manifest into negative emotions, such as anger, disappointment, and depression because you are dissatisfied with the result of your actions, or you can use this situation to empower yourself!

Be grateful that you have been shown that if you want to continue to wear the same size of clothing, you should be more mindful with your habits. You now can look at your practices and change them just a bit as you have a better understanding of what to do to stay within your desired body weight. Despite your negative actions, at some point there will be a positive outcome. You look in the mirror and decide that in order to feel good about yourself, you must take action, be more diligent with your habits, and love yourself! There is positive in all! We ask you to be grateful that you have these opportunities to learn from.

When you are feeling the maximum amount of discomfort that you can handle, do you not say, "Enough!" Do you not look at the situation and proceed to make changes that will better your life? Look at this closely.

September 6, 2009
Unity Consciousness

We put our house on the market last month. Since the children moved to their own homes, we have found the house is much too large. It is time to make a change.

Today, I got the first call to show the house. The realtor wanted to show it in forty-five minutes! Egads! I had to really move quickly in order to get the house tidied up! I did make it, though. These days the realtors prefer that the home owner not be present when the house is shown. After I was satisfied with how the house looked, I decided to go gas up the car and then go to the park and just " be."

While I was out, I was shown the number 5-5-5. One of my guides told me that the next triple digit would reveal the new cycle I was in. 5-5-5 is the unity consciousness. This is the number given when the person has attained unity consciousness and they have mastered all levels of the mystery school. It is the highest number and the number of the Christ. I read the words, but to understand the meaning ... I am sorry, but WHAT?

The Akasie: We explain this to you. You completely understand basic concepts now. Everyone is united by the one consciousness and is connected by the unity consciousness grid. You understand the concepts of Creator, God, and Goddess. You understand how we manifest all. You have worked steadily to grasp all concepts and ideas. Well done. We are able to move on now.

September 7, 2009
Honor Self

Quem: Healing energy continues to come to you today. Remember to take care of yourself and listen to your heart! The heart tells you all. Feel the heart space and listen to it. What is it saying? Honor thy self!

September 8, 2009
Visual Techniques

During the night, I woke up with pictures in my mind's eye. The pictures were turning somehow, like I was looking at a TV screen but the screen was turning sideways. I would get the front view and then it would turn to the side. I watched with total fascination. After the picture took several turns, I decided to ask if the Akasie were doing something. I rarely know what is going on these days!

The Akasie: Yes, we were working with you on visual techniques, which will be useful later in training.

What we were doing was turning the image back and forth repeatedly. We did this because it is unusual and you have never experienced this before. Therefore, you would question this phenomenon. This is one way to show you that there are many different and unusual surprises coming your way. It is a technique that will help you further your visual skills and focus. Mostly, we do these visuals to get you used to experiencing different things. It is not good to bombard you with all at once.

Okay, I get what you are saying, but I see a conflict here. I need my sleep and you come to me in the middle of the night to show me images that are turning sideways? I think it is possible that you are not doing what is for my highest good here.

The Akasie: We chose to interrupt your sleep to show you the images for several reasons besides what we have already explained to you. Number one, at that time you are the most relaxed. You do not have anything distracting you. Because you have not learned to go deep within to receive, this is how we teach. Number two, we desire that you recognize that we did wake you up. We desire you to question if this is beneficial for you. Your body requires its sleep. We desire you to assess your boundaries. Number three, you are acquiring the skills at this time to be in control of the mind. By this we mean you are learning to not let the mind wander from one subject to another, and to simply shut the mind off to fall back to sleep instead.

September 9, 2009
Manifesting Physical Disease

The Akasie: At this time, we would like to put on the table a previous conversation that you had with your close friend, Beth. The two of you have a mutual friend, Joe, who has recently suffered a heart attack. It was this action that prompted the two of you to discuss the correlation of heart attacks and having your heart "broken." To prevent a misunderstanding, we will explain that a person may perceive he has a broken heart because he has had a significant relationship with another that has ended in a very painful manner. He may feel much hurt, pain, abandonment, and rejection. Of course, there may also be feelings of anger and even hate that will be directed at the particular situation, if not at a particular person. This person feels so much heaviness and pain that he feels as if his heart is actually broken.

Jackie, you have always been one who wants to know how certain actions manifest in the physical. You would like to put all causes and effects into nice little boxes so you may easily understand them. We tell you any provocation or end result of any thought and emotion is not so easily deciphered.

People on the Earth plane will suffer many stressors during their lifetimes. Without proper understanding and release of these stressors, people will undoubtedly manifest a physical disease. We wish the stressors would not be created in the first place, but at this time that is not to be. All is for a purpose.

We have spoken before on listening to your heart, and we can't emphasize enough the importance of this practice. When we say listen to your heart, we are saying listen to the emotions that manifest in the heart space. Those emotions are the direct communication for you to know what is best for you at all times.

There may be times when you receive this communication and are unable to interpret the meaning, as your mind may be telling you one thing and your emotions are telling you something entirely different.

There are many reasons for this confusion that you feel. You are put together, so to speak, having many facets, many sides, and many layers. You, as a spiritual being in a physical body, are to balance the two, living harmoniously. It is as if there are two of you joined to make the one. You must learn to live with one another. It is like a marriage, dear ones. You must learn how to listen to one another to live and enjoy life to the fullest.

What happened to the mental and the emotional bodies?

The Akasie: We wish to speak of the two for now. You must understand that you must work together to balance the total you.

When you look at your being in this manner, you get closer to seeing the truth of who you are. Look at it this way. You are spiritual beings, are you not? Spirit is energy. All living creatures have what we call Spirit. Spirit is the life force. Spirit is the energy that connects us all. We are all One in this universe, as all are united by Spirit. The energy that you feel is Spirit.

Your body is the vehicle or temple for you to use during each physical lifetime. The body is a gift given to you by the Creator to work with and through. Take care of and enjoy the body as you evolve alongside of your sisters and brothers going higher into the Light.

Another piece of this particular puzzle that we will discuss is the Creator. We laugh because to describe what the Creator is or does entails much. The Creator is the energy that comprises all things. You are a part of the Creator just as every other living creature is. We speak of the Holy Trinity here: Father, Son, and the Holy Spirit.

You wonder what the trinity has to do with the manifesting of physical disease? It is simple yet complex. You are here on the Earth plane at this time to learn to balance all that has been given to you. You are in the process of this learning.

This information that we share with you is crucial. You are here to live your own life by making your own choices, but there will be many times during your life when another will make a choice that you do not agree with. What should you do about decisions that another has made that affect you personally and seemingly in a detrimental way?

Let's go back to the original discussion concerning Joe who suffered the heart attack. Many years back, he had lost his entire family. This was the outcome of a not so pleasant divorce. His wife Judy took full custody of their three children even though Joe loved their children with all of his heart and was easily able to support them financially. This separation was not what he wished. At that time in your history, the mother was granted custody of the children in most cases, and the father would get the children every other weekend.

When we talk of divorce, there are many different scenarios, but we tell you that in custody cases there is always someone who loses at least part of his or her time, if not all it, with the children. This is a separation that wasn't wanted. In Joe's case, he fought hard to keep the family together, but because he wasn't able to, he saw himself as a failure. He was forced to let go of his family, and this letting go is often very painful and very difficult. Without direction of some sort, letting go often feels as if it is impossible.

The lesson here is that you cannot control what other people do, nor should you. Judy decided that she wanted to go on her way. We do not know the particulars and they aren't important. What is important is that this man had control issues, meaning that he tried his best to control what his wife did. We speak of the decisions that she made concerning their divorce. He created much negative energy by trying to control the outcome.

It is said that this is human nature, to want to keep things as they are and also have things your own way. The fact is change is occurring on all levels at all times and in all places. Change can't be stopped nor should it be stopped. The challenge is this: when change comes knocking at your door, can you gracefully allow and accept those changes to occur? Can you allow yourself these grand opportunities to learn from? What is for the highest benefit for all concerned?

People often fall into this trap of trying to control outcomes. We do not want to disregard Joe's feelings toward his wife and children. Joe loved them dearly and when you love someone, of course you wish to share your life with them. Joe felt like the most important pieces of him had been cruelly stolen from him; he felt like his life was over.

Did he look at this separation as a new beginning, a renewal, a time to learn, to go forward toward something possibly grand and never before experienced? No. Instead, he resented what had happened and he let the weight of that perceived wrongdoing take him down into the depths of despair. He felt alone, betrayed, and persecuted.

The ego is the culprit here. Because of his ego, Joe allowed his insecurities concerning this ordeal to take over. When you go through a period of anguish such as this, we say to reflect upon your life, take stock of what you have become, and examine your core beliefs.

So we have shown you that it is possible to look at a negative situation with a positive attitude and expect a positive outcome, an outcome that is for the highest good of all concerned.

Ah, I hear many of you firmly stating that what I have laid before you isn't so easy. I agree; for many of you, it is not so easy to allow the changes necessary for you to go forward in order to fulfill the agreements that you made before you arrived here on the Earth plane. As you gain a higher level of understanding, you will see that people must be allowed to make their own choices. You have all been given the gift of free will, have you not? Use these teachings to your advantage, learn from them, and allow yourself to attain a higher level of awareness.

When you find yourself going through any upheaval, we tell you to use this time as a gift and to use it as a tool to learn from. Accept this time to go within and find your true self worth.

When you have not been given this guidance, you are likely to find yourself in the same space as the man in this example. Joe allowed himself to react to what had happened, beginning the creation of much negative energy instead of looking to what wonderful opportunities lay before him. He continued to create these negative thoughts and feelings for many years. In fact, we say he is still creating them every time he thinks of his ex-wife, his children, and the home he once had. Joe wonders what he could have had or where he would have been if only his wife would have been happy. Joe has allowed these very thoughts to consume him.

Above, I have given you the example of how Joe dealt with his divorce. For many years, this has been his way of dealing with all situations that are not pleasing to him.

So you see, it is possible that there have been many times during Joe's life when he has endured unpleasant situations. Not only was his habit to ask the whys, what ifs, and the how comes, he was also growing an entire slew of negative emotions instead of asking himself what he was to learn from this situation.

Jackie, go back in your memory to a situation that concerned a family member. You know what I speak of. You felt this person was making choices that were detrimental to his or her financial security, and you would ultimately have to step in and fix what was in the making. You really had no control over this person's choice, however, you thought your way was the right way and the only way. I don't mind saying here that you tried several angles to get this person to see it your way. What I want you to look at here is how you felt physically when this was occurring.

At the time, I remember feeling tremendous anxiety, which for me results in a tightness in my stomach and in my chest. I was in turmoil— constantly going over every possible scenario. I felt very angry and resentful, because I felt that I was pushed into this situation that I had to fix.

The Akasie: What happens to your body when it is consumed with negative thoughts and emotions? You are constricting the organs, the muscles, and the flesh. You are restricting the flow of energy, the life force. This causes discomfort, illness, disease, and death of the physical body. What you experienced—the stomachache and heaviness in the chest—are classic symptoms.

Imagine feeling this way for a long period of time, so long in fact, that you didn't know any other way to feel. This restriction damages the heart. You are creating an excessive amount of negative emotion, which results in tightness, a pressure, or a constant restriction of the heart muscle.

This anxiety also affects other organs, but we speak of the heart muscle here. The heart is the center of life. When life is seemingly taken from you in the form of control, it is human nature, not spiritual nature, to fight against it. This is survival instinct.

When people remember they are spiritual beings in the physical form, they let go of this unsurpassed need to control. They realize everything is in divine order and allow what has happened, what is happening, to be.

Yes, pray and affirm that whatever happens is for the highest good of all concerned. All are experiencing life lessons at their finest. *We are One!*

September 10, 2009
Olim Moves On

My guides told me today that Olim will be leaving shortly. Colér left several days ago.

On the drive to visit our land down south, I saw three white doves fly in front of the truck. I pay particularly close attention to when and where I see wildlife and what sort of wildlife I'm seeing. I asked the guides what the dove represented, and their response was peace, love, and hope.

September 10, 2009
Breathe to Relax

The Akasie: Jackie, you have with you at this time three new guides assisting Olim. Quem is off doing something very important. We are here to assist you while on your journey on the Earth plane. That is what we are concerned with and what we do. We are here to meditate with you. We help you and assist you. We have advice for you concerning how you can relax easily during meditation.

Your yoga practice has been beneficial in many ways, one being how to focus on your breathing technique. We go over the breathing technique for the sake of the reader.

Take a slow, deep, steady breath in. Breathe down into your stomach and hold for a moment. Then exhale slowly, emptying all air from your lungs. Focus on the rise and fall of your stomach as you have been taught. Take a longer time exhaling than inhaling.

Go slow with your breathing, focusing on your relaxed state. With each breath, acknowledge that you are releasing all of your day's concerns; notice that you are becoming more relaxed. After the five deep inhalations, slow down all of the steps of the breath until you feel more relaxed and peaceful.

There is something else we wanted to say to you: Olim goes very soon. We have more people awakening, and these people need assistance. She must go.

Your father, Quem, doesn't think he can do for you any longer, Jackie. He says he has worked with you through several steps. You are to receive new guidance soon. He is looking for a teacher for you. He didn't expect you to go so far so soon. However, he is most pleased with your progress and he is most ready for his new assignment. We are not your new guides, Jackie, but tonight we are here to fill in. *We are One!*

September 11, 2009
Master Jesus

Nathanal: Miss, I will tell you a story about your beloved Jesus in a moment. First, I wish to let you know that I will be with you for a time.

My name is Nathanal. I am of the Comterous group. There are many of us here to assist you during your ascension process. Know this. Understand that you are to call upon us with what you desire. We are all masters who have agreed to teach you. What is it you wish to learn? What is it that you require in order for you to move forward? We ask you to ponder these questions we have set before you.

At this time, I wish to help you understand what happened to your beloved Jesus. His true name is Yeshua. There are many beliefs concerning this one that are incorrect. I openly set my intention here to not make any attempt to disprove those beliefs. Instead, I am to give you clear words that will gently guide you to fully understand Yeshua's gift to you and to all of the great peoples of this beautiful planet. In the day that Yeshua's soul walked the earth, he went by the name Yeshua. Understand that yes, Yeshua was a great teacher and healer. His spark is divine in nature just as your spark is divine. I tell you, each and every one of you is a spark of the Divine. Some sparks shine brighter than others for a time. We wait for all to become as brilliant as the noonday sun.

I wish to move on. It is a well-known fact that Yeshua was Master in that day. He continues to be Master and continues to receive much respect, love, and gratitude for all that he does for us. (I am speaking of the collective.) He continues to go forth and serve the Creator and all of creation. Some have the belief that when one passes from this Earth plane his or her work is finished. Not so! All continue to go forward, no matter who you are or where you are at. I speak of myself and all of the others who assist you at this time. We continue to learn, to go forward into the Light. My dear, know this now: by allowing us to assist you, you are assisting us in our own ascension. You help us and we help you. We work together. We always have.

Yeshua was a strong individual—is a strong individual. I will not refer to him in the past tense again. Yeshua lives on. His spark shines ever so brightly. He is but a beacon to those who walk the earth on the darkest of nights. He is always lighting your way.

Yeshua: I speak for myself at this time. I live on as Nathanal has said earlier. I have lived many lives in the physical body and in many planes. I journey about visiting my dear brothers and sisters who, like me, continue to evolve, going ever higher into the Light.

I have taken notice that many cultures make memorial of my life, my days that I served as Master and Healer on the Mother Earth. Many have created a holiday by the giving of gifts. Some take this time to go within. They fast and pray to the Holy One. Some set before them grand altars to attest to their spiritual and religious beliefs. I am here to share with you a great truth.

I set before you these words spoken long ago by the ancient one, Muhammad. "When I was a child, I thought like a child. My thoughts were one with God. I took to flight my desires knowing that all is given by our Lord in Heaven."

I have given careful examination to these words and conclude that we are one with our Lord, our God, who is just and kind. He gives to all our true desires. So I simply say unto you: Pay close attention to what desires you behold. Consider carefully the wishes that you create in your mind, as they will be given to you in abundance.

Quem: Miss, what you have received is a great gift—the words from our beloved Yeshua. Yes, Master Yeshua had and has great purpose here on this Earth plane for humanity. We tell you that Master Yeshua has a specific role to play, as we *all* do! Master Yeshua came to this great Earth to create a big stir amongst the peoples. That he did well, we tell you truth! Be grateful for all. Send love and gratitude for his life on Earth and his purpose.

September 12, 2009
The Human Body

The Akasie: We have spoken many times about the human body being a fine piece of art that is intricate and precise. Awesome! We encourage you to appreciate your body and all it entails.

It took thousands of years of evolutionary prowess to come to this stage in the human development. Always be grateful for the physical body. Go forward now and understand that you must talk to your body, affirming that it is healthy. Your physical body is an extension of you! Your body rejuvenates continuously and must have direction from you on how to proceed. You, the mind, are continually programming this beautiful piece of art, how it is to function.

Believe that the body is conditioned according to your beliefs. Know this, for it is truth! Your body has the capabilities to adapt and change the molecular structure according to how you view yourself. If you view yourself as fat, your body gets fat. If you think of yourself as sick, you become sick. If you believe yourself to be the instrument of fine health, you are healthy. This is art! The Creator did this for all. *We are One!*

September 13, 2009
Setting Boundaries

Quem: Before our meditation today, I'd like to say a couple of things.

For many days now you have been working to establish your boundaries. You have found that you must have time for yourself. I speak of your personal needs. You must rest. Yesterday was a fine day. You were able to stay quiet most of the time. Today you fell for Olim's lonely act. She worked you to engage you in conversation, but you were able to quickly disengage. This was expected because you have grown to know a bit about Olim, her personality, and her style of teaching.

I understand this was a teaching. You used this situation because I was sad that Olim was leaving. You were checking my resolve to see how strong I was concerning the boundaries that I have established for myself.

Quem: Do not linger in sadness. Rejoice at the new opportunities ahead! We tell you that you have new guides coming soon who will not communicate the way we do. They are Akasie also. They, however, are unique and like us have their own particular style of teaching. We do not attempt to know how they will work with you. This is all learning for you.

September 14, 2009
Olim Takes Leave

Olim: Jackie, I wish to tell you that we, the group, first the five of us—Quem, Colér, Jithury, Esse, and myself—all thought we would be with you much longer, but it wasn't meant to be. Jithury left, then Esse. You were sad for a short while. Quem, Colér, and I remained behind. Then Colér left. We miss them all, but at the same time, we know we will meet up with them again. Now it is time that I take leave. Jackie, I leave tomorrow. Be happy for me and for yourself! Don't cry. Celebrate! We both move on with our journeys, yes? I love you, Jackie. Farewell.

September 15, 2009
A Special Bond

Quem: Yes, Jackie, Olim leaves, but all is well. I must finalize the placement of your new teachers. I make new arrangements for you, as it is also my time to move on. This is a new beginning for me also! I am excited and very motivated! Even so, I will always hold fond memories in my heart of our stay here with you. I love you, Jackie.

Why do you arrange the placement of all of my teachers?

Quem: Jackie, there is much you do not understand at this time. Before, I told you that I am your Pleiadian father. I have watched over you always and am instrumental in your awakening process, which continues. Someone is always in charge of the ones on the Earth plane. There is hierarchy, dear daughter.

You feel it in your heart that I am the one; this is no secret. You are correct about us. We have much love that we share for each other, you and I. This love is special, I know. You feel it as we all do. There was another time for us. You remember that this is why you feel the way you do toward me. Jackie, you have always loved me much. We hold a special place in our hearts for one another.

What confuses you most is that you are comparing me with your Earth father. He put his time in until you were of age, and then he released you. The bond with the two of you is different. I am not like him in this respect. I continue to take care of you. Always, as long as you are in my charge, I will secure those who teach and watch over you.

Jackie, there is one more thing I must tell you. Our time, the music, the dance is sacred to me. I feel much emotion at this time. The time I spent with you cannot be duplicated in any other way. I cherish those memories, as I know you do. I will come back for you. Someway, Jackie, I will come for you. The other thing I say to you is don't get all crazy over the book. We will finish this project. Know it!

September 16, 2009
Minds Become One

Today I sat down to write and ... nothing. The words did not come. I am not hearing the guides for some reason. I was frustrated, but decided to work on something else. So I worked on some definitions of some words and pondered how emotions work for us. Then I decided to brainstorm and just write whatever came.

As I began to type, I felt this passion overtake me like never before. Quem—his words and actions—became very animated and passionate. The words came, but I couldn't type.

I was filled to overflowing by Spirit! I cried and cried. I asked Quem what I was to do. I asked for guidance. Quem said, "Go into prayer." I didn't understand his words. Now what? Quem continued to speak, "The words must be conveyed with passion and love."

Quem: The passion I speak of is an integral part of writing this book, of any book, but to get the emotion on paper is a tricky thing. The reader does not hear the tone of your voice or the pause in between your words. The reader just sees the words on the paper. The words must be descriptive and express the emotion that we feel. The words must convey the correct emotion to carry forth our intention. We desire the reader to feel what we feel as we write the words.

You, Jackie, must know my passion and feel my passion to know and understand what I am giving you telepathically. You must connect with me and become One. Jackie, to become One we must unite minds, become one thought. Listen carefully. I make my thoughts become your thoughts.

NO! You take my power away by doing this!

Quem: No, Jackie, I do not take your power away. I only give you my thoughts, but you say this is what we have been working on for months. What you say is true. Listen to what I say! I implore you! You must allow, and to allow you must trust; you must relax.

September 17, 2009
The Children: The Gift of Life

Quem: I wish to tell you several things at this time. We worked alone for a time; there were no others about. Today was a very good first day for us, don't you think?

Me too!

Quem: Jackie, your grandchildren are very important. They carry on—they continue life here on Mother Earth. We must have the children! Jackie, you know the importance of which I speak! It is of utmost importance for you to listen! The children have the gift of life. This is most precious. They are here for a reason, a purpose. Please listen to me. They are in your charge. You listen to me! They are here and you are here. It would be in your best advantage to take a vital interest in their welfare, their upbringing. Call them and spend time with them. They must know you. They must know *you!*

You are the grandmother—the matriarch—now. You have the wisdom. You are more centered and comfortable with what life has to offer because you know more about life. The kids, at this time, do not understand why they are here or what their purpose is. You are a role model for all of your children. Take time for them. They do not visit you every day, so relax while they are here. You require more practice at the art of relaxation. Just do it!

September 18, 2009
Moving On

Quem: Last night I wanted to speak on several other subjects, however, it was much too late to begin. The movie *The Knowing* brought on some points of interest in addition to what I'd like to speak on. We will begin with the movie.

The children were primary in the New Beginning, the New World. This is the way it is to be again. You, as a grandmother, will assist in giving knowledge to the children. The children are the New Beginning. The children continue the life on Mother Earth in the human form. You receive the words, the knowledge from us. You are to take this knowledge and give it to the children.

You are beginning to see another reason for your gift; this is to pass on the wisdom you have gleaned to the children. You are to pass on the love. You will soon experience the secret of knowing. You will soon "connect" to the Creator. It will happen naturally. I will not "teach" you this, but I will guide you in love always.

I tell you this to prepare you. When you allow, you will naturally connect and know. It is all about love. Allow. *We are One!*

Prayers and Closing Words

We send our love to the Creator. We are most grateful for all we receive. There are many life forms in the universe and we are grateful for all; the ones who have taken the human form, and the ones who have taken the animal form—the four legged, the two legged, the winged ones, the finned ones, and the many legged ones. The forms continue on with the trees, the grasses, all the plants, the seas, even the clouds. Although we can't see the winds, the winds also have form. They have energy just as the sun and the many planets have energy and form.

These are all different kinds of life. They are intelligent, you see. Each form is created from thought, by thought, with thought. Although each life form has a unique way of communicating, they communicate with each other and with all other life forms, all of creation, and with the Creator!

Does this make them any less than you? No! They are equal in the eyes of God our Creator. We thank God for these varieties of intelligence and thought.

~Quem Monteró Akasie~

There is something to be learned in every situation. Train yourself to look closely at the entire picture. It is easy to take a positive situation and see what you have gained from it. We tell you to take all situations, both positive and negative, and learn from them to better serve all of creation. *We are One!*

~The Akasie~

Conclusion

You have been gifted with the initial messages and teachings from the Akasie, a Pleiadian group of Light Beings who have remained steadfast in their role as teachers of Truth and Wisdom.

In this volume, *When Angels Speak: The Awakening, A Pleiadian Endeavor,* many topics have been touched on to give you pause; a reason to reflect upon your inner thoughts and feelings. Ultimately, the design is for your continued expansion of knowledge, allowing you to illumine more of the Divine Light on this planet. This is the way of our evolution. Through these writings—the Living Words of Light—the Masters nurture us.

Remember to follow the protocol given: To Ask, To Allow, and To Accept, as this is the course of action to receive what you require in your steps ahead.

Yes, you do have divine angels and guides who want to communicate with you—to teach you. *When Angels Speak* facilitates this expanded awareness to initiate a sure path to Oneness.

It is my prayer that by sharing my story, these teachings, that you, as well, will come to know and develop a relationship with the Masters of Light.

~Blessings, Nakala~

About the Author

 Kansas native, *Nakala Akasie*, contemporary Pleiadian Messenger, channel, and author of several metaphysical books currently resides in the spiritual mecca of Mt. Shasta, in northern California, with her husband, Ray El, to serve as a bridge for the Higher Realms of Light during the planetary and cosmic shifts taking place.

Nakala works with the angelic realm in assisting people in their creative process and healing different issues through her group and individual channeled readings as well as her presentations and workshops on "Communicating with your Spirit Guides."

Nakala, wife, mother, and grandmother, enjoys the disciplines of yoga and daily meditations. She teaches workshops on how to connect with your spirit guides using a pendulum. In her spare time she loves to garden, watch the sun rise and set, create different artistic projects, and go hiking on the sacred Mt. Shasta with her husband.

To comment or offer a book review or testimonial for advertising purposes, or to receive notifications of upcoming publications and events, email Nakala at:

WhenAngelsSpeak5@aol.com

To purchase other books by Nakala or to follow along in her continuing adventures, go to:

PleiadianPublishing.com
PleiadianTraveler.com
WhenAngelsSpeakToUs.wordpress.com

Be sure to like **Pleiadian Traveler** on Facebook

Also by Nakala Akasie

Awakening: The Gift
The Accounts of a Pleiadian Traveler
Book I

The Sacred Contract
The Accounts of a Pleiadian Traveler
Book II

In the Light of Day
The Accounts of a Pleiadian Traveler
Book III

Mirrors: Holding the Vision
The Accounts of a Pleiadian Traveler
Book IV

~ Soon to be released ~
Fifth Sphere: Attainment
The Accounts of a Pleiadian Traveler
Book V

A Point of Light
Pleiadian Publishing

Preview

Awakening: The Gift
The Accounts of a Pleiadian Traveler
Book I

In *The Awakening: The Gift,* Nakala's family is thrown into a desperate downward spiral when her fourteen-year-old son does the unthinkable: he commits suicide. Seeking answers to her endless questions surrounding his death she attends a series of spiritual events, leading her to a two-day workshop on advanced dowsing.

Soon after the workshop, without warning, Nakala begins to receive telepathic communications and to channel a group of Pleiadian Light Beings who call them-selves the Akasie, other masters, archangels and even departed loved ones, including her son.

The Celestial Beings comfort and teach Nakala by infusing her with waves of uplifting energy: Love, answering questions connected with her son's passing, and introducing her to the universal laws, all in preparation for the coming new age.

As Nakala becomes familiar with the communications, she is faced with another set of crucial challenges concerning her everyday life. Would people believe her if she revealed her newly acquired spiritual gifts?

Relationships with family and friends literally hang in the balance as Nakala learns to establish and maintain important boundaries and to reconnect with her heart's promptings. Is Nakala able to liberate herself from feelings of self-doubt and fear?

www.ingramcontent.com/pod-product-compliance
Lightning Source LLC
Chambersburg PA
CBHW071741190726
48292CB00003B/836